Outside the Lines

A Claudia Rose Novel

Sheila Lowe

Write
Choice
Ink
ESTABLISHED 2021

Write Choice Ink

ISBN-10-978-1-970181-11-1 (Paperback)
ISBN-13-978-1-970181-12-8 (Paperback)
ASIN-B01IPKPRNG (EPUB)

This book is a work of fiction. Names, characters, businesses, organizations, places, events, incidents are the product of the author's imagination or are used fictitiously. Any resemblance to actual events, locals, or persons, living or dead, is coincidental.

Cover Design: Jane Dixon Smith

Printed in the United States of America

PUBLISHING HISTORY

Write Choice Ink, Print and Digital Copy, 2021
Suspense Publishing, Print and Digital Copy, 2016
NAL/Penguin Group, Print and Digital Copy, September 2008

www.sheilalowebooks.com

Also By Sheila Lowe

FORENSIC HANDWRITING SERIES

POISON PEN

WRITTEN IN BLOOD

DEAD WRITE

LAST WRITES

INKSLINGERS BALL

OUTSIDE THE LINES

WRITTEN OFF

DEAD LETTERS

BEYOND THE VEIL SERIES

WHAT SHE SAW

PROOF OF LIFE

THE LAST DOOR

NONFICTION

GROWING FROM THE ASHES:

Learning from my daughter's murder about life after earth READING

BETWEEN THE LINES: Decoding Handwriting ADVANCED STUDIES

IN HANDWRITING

PSYCHOLOGY PERSONALITY & ANXIETY DISORDERS: How They

May Be Reflected in

Handwriting, and Other Important Topics

SUCCEEDING IN THE BUSINESS OF HANDWRITING ANALYSIS

IMPROVE YOUR LIFE WITH GRAPHOTHERAPY

THE COMPLETE IDIOT'S GUIDE TO HANDWRITING ANALYSIS

HANDWRITING OF THE FAMOUS & INFAMOUS

SHEILA LOWE'S HANDWRITING ANALYZER SOFTWARE

one

Sylvia Vasquez opened the back door and peeped out. The Señor would be angry if he knew she had not picked up the mail since Friday. He had warned her about mailbox thieves and instructed her to clear the box every day as soon as the mail carrier left, but Sylvia had been too busy enjoying the weekend with her new man to think about her employers' mail. They were out of town again and would be all week.

It was too early to worry about the neighbors seeing her in the ratty bathrobe and worn slippers, and the morning fog would provide cover for a quick run to the box. Unlocking the steel security gate that led to the alley, she opened the flap and started to reach for the daily stack of catalogs and magazines, letters on top. It took a second to comprehend that a mass of crumpled toilet tissue had been crammed into the box. That boy across the street, no doubt. *Tonto Adolecente!* With a sigh of vexation, Sylvia grabbed a handful of tissue.

A sudden flash erupted from the mailbox and a bright tongue of flame shot out. With a loud *crack-bang*, the box exploded, fragments of black metal and masonry flying into the alley in a cloud of blue-black smoke. The blast of searing heat sent Sylvia staggering backward, the acrid sting of gunpowder in her nostrils. She stared down at her right hand, confused to see blood pulsing from the stumps where her index and middle fingers used to be. Where was her *abuela's* ring? *Where were her fingers?*

The clamor of barking dogs came hollow and far away in her ringing ears. Unbearable pressure—the coils of a giant python squeezing her rib cage—robbed her of the breath to scream for help. Her eyes rolled back in her head. Her galloping heart had ceased beating.

Sylvia Vasquez dropped to the ground.

two

THE MARBLED COURTHOUSE HALLWAY was as silent as a held breath.

Claudia had been waiting on the cold, hard bench for ninety minutes to be called to testify, and her mind was as numb as her behind. She had reviewed her exhibit slides until she was sick of the sight of them. The handwritings on the tablet screen no longer registered in her brain.

The final witness from the morning session, a weapons expert, had been held over the lunch recess and was back on the hot seat. Endlessly, it seemed. A nearby courtroom door opened and two attorneys stepped into the hallway. They were not part of the Danny Ortiz trial in which Claudia was to testify; they were dueling over a hapless defendant's fate—negotiations that could mean the difference between bail or no bail, or a reduction in prison time. For someone facing a life sentence without possibility of parole, twenty years might sound palatable.

Claudia watched the minor drama unfold, her stomach clenched as it always was before she got on the witness stand. She was fully confident in her opinion, but what if she forgot something important while testifying? What if she flubbed it? The big question was, could she convince the jury of what she believed to be the truth?

A text popped up from Joel Jovanic, her fiancé. He had made dinner reservations at their favorite restaurant. After replying, Claudia slid the iPad into her briefcase and rose. She probably should have worn a different outfit for court, but Jovanic liked the way the pencil skirt showed off her long legs. Too late to change now. She strolled the long hallway, returned to the bench and waited some more.

It was 3:15 when the DA's investigator finally came out to say they were ready for her. Jesse Alvarez was a burly, dark-complexioned man from Belize who loved to make people laugh. The week before, when Claudia had met with him and his boss, Paul Feynman, he had cracked a couple of lawyer jokes that left Feynman shaking his head in mock despair. Today, though, the humor was gone from his eyes. There was nothing remotely funny in the trial of a cop killer.

Taking a deep breath, Claudia grabbed her briefcase and followed Alvarez through the heavy oak doors, aware of curious faces turning toward her. Looking straight ahead, she made her way through the gate that separated the gallery from the bench, and passed by the counsel table.

The District Attorney, always placed closest to the jury, was the one who has the burden of proof and was expected to be the ultimate champion of Truth, Justice, and the American Way. Seated behind him was the grieving family and supporters of the undercover cop Ortiz was accused of executing in cold blood.

The spectators were split into two sharply divided sides. The rows of seats behind the defendant, Danny Ortiz, and his public defender, Alison Smith, were occupied by young toughs sporting shaved heads and prison tattoos. Their *chola* girlfriends, clad in skintight Levis, wore penciled-in eyebrows that made commas over heavily rimmed blue-shadowed eyes.

Claudia had been brought into the case to authenticate the handwriting of a letter that took credit for the killing of Detective Hector Maldonado, whose cover had been blown at a drug buy. The detective had been forced to his knees and shot twice execution style; his body dumped in an East Los Angeles alley.

From his lofty perch on the bench, Judge George C. Abernathy glanced at Claudia. "Good afternoon, Ms. Rose."

"Good afternoon, Your Honor."

She had testified before Abernathy in more than one case and was aware of his reputation: a jaded, hardnosed hang 'em high jurist that made him the kind of judge the prosecution prayed for and the defense dreaded. Broad across the chest in his black robes, a ring of white hair on his mostly bald head. Add a long white beard to the bushy brows and he was Santa without the ho-ho-ho.

Claudia took the oath to tell the truth and mounted the witness stand. The unforgiving lens of a television camera stared at her from the back of the courtroom, reminding her not to swivel in her seat. Mindful that the slightest slip would be broadcast to the entire Southland, she carefully set aside a half-full cup of water left by the last witness.

"State and spell your name for the record." The clerk must have said those words at least a thousand times, and her bored tone proved it.

As Claudia recited her response, the defendant, who had been doodling on a legal pad, looked up and caught her eye. The loathing in that dead black stare chilled her to the bone. If Danny Ortiz could have shot poison darts at that moment, she would be one dead handwriting expert.

His public defender had supplied Ortiz with a conservative blue Oxford shirt that was intended to avoid the prejudice an orange jail jumpsuit might have raised. For the same reason, the defendant was neither cuffed nor shackled. A member of the 7th Street Crue, his gang moniker, "Li'l Dude," was ironic. There was nothing little about Ortiz, who stood five-ten and weighed in at two-twenty. The ink on his neck was mostly hidden under his shirt. The same could not be said of the crude prison-house tattoos on his face: devil's horns on his forehead, two blue teardrops below his left eye—the gangbanger's badge of honor awarded to a multiple murderer.

The high-profile nature of the case meant three deputies were stationed in the courtroom, rather than the standard two: a custody officer near the door to the holding area, a second at the back door leading to the judge's chambers. An elderly female deputy manned the desk where attorneys could quietly ask questions while court was in session.

Judge Abernathy surveyed his courtroom. His gimlet eyes came to rest on the attorneys. "Are we ready, Counselors?"

"The People are ready, Your Honor," said the district attorney.

"The Defense is ready," said Alison Smith, the public defender assigned to the case.

The judge nodded. "Mr. Feynman, please proceed."

The DA's doughy pink cheeks, sensuous lips and thick neck reminded Claudia of Alec Baldwin. He even wore the actor's hairstyle—salt-and-pepper, slicked straight back. In an election year this case would be a good win for Paul Feynman. He had already conducted a press conference on the courthouse steps, assuring the public that the cold-blooded execution of a police officer deserved nothing less than his personal attention. He rose, buttoning his hand-tailored, charcoal-grey pinstriped suit coat, and bid Claudia a good afternoon. "Thank you for coming today, Ms. Rose. Would you please tell the jury what your occupation is and what that means?"

Claudia turned in her seat to face the jury box, aware of the red eye of the TV camera blinking at her.

The jury did a fair job of reflecting the L.A. melting pot. In the back row, two young Hispanic women and a twenty-something Anglo in a UCLA sweatshirt all held steno notebooks at the ready—no electronics allowed in the courtroom. Three grandmotherly types were likely defense picks who might feel compassion for Danny, even in the face of the heinous crime with which he was charged. An African American woman in a business suit, two men in t-shirts—one African-American, one Hispanic. An elderly man, who Claudia guessed was Filipino, had already nodded off, chin on chest. In the front row a rail-thin Asian man in a cardigan wore the spaced-out gaze of a computer geek. At the other end sat his polar opposite: an obese, middle-aged white man in shirtsleeves and tie.

A jury of Danny Ortiz's peers? Gang members did not get picked for jury duty.

Claudia spoke into the microphone. "I am a forensic handwriting examiner. I compare disputed handwriting to known samples—exemplars—and offer an opinion about who wrote it."

"Thank you," said Feynman. "I know you've been practicing in this field for quite some time. Would you kindly tell the jury about your background and education?"

There was a fine line between reciting the many pages of her curriculum vitae that detailed what made her an expert in the field, and listing enough of her credentials so that the juror's eyes did not glaze over. Making sure to look at each member of the panel in turn as she spoke, Claudia kept the narrative moving. Along the way, the DA injected questions about papers she had published, conferences where she had spoken.

At the end, Alison Smith made a weak objection to her qualifications, but Claudia had testified in more than fifty cases. There was little chance the judge would not qualify her in this one.

"Overruled," said Judge Abernathy. "Ms. Rose may testify."

Feynman thanked him and turned back to Claudia, "Sometimes you are retained as a jury consultant, isn't that right?"

"Yes, in those cases I use handwriting analysis to help my client select jurors."

"And in such cases, you're analyzing *personality,* is that correct?"

"Yes."

"Did you use personality analysis in the case we are talking about here today?"

"No. My assignment in this case was to compare handwritten samples for the purposes of authentication."

"Please tell us more about your assignment in this matter."

"Certainly. Your office provided me a handwritten note that's known as a 'kite,' which is contraband communication passed between jail inmates. It's unsigned and I am told that the defendant denies having written it."

"Ms. Rose, do you see the Court's exhibit book on the table in front of you?"

She would have to be blind to miss the fat, black three-ring-binder whose contents had been entered into evidence before she took the stand. Over the course of the next thirty minutes, the DA walked her through the documents in the exhibit book. First, the pages that contained the questioned handwriting, followed by the exemplars that represented Ortiz's true, known handwriting. At last, he asked, "Have you formed an opinion as to whether the questioned writing is genuine or not?"

"Yes, I have."

"And what is your opinion, Ms. Rose?"

Claudia sat straighter in her chair and spoke clearly into the microphone. "It's my opinion, to a professional degree of certainty, that both the known and the questioned writing *were* written by the same hand."

Everyone knew it was coming—this was what she was here for. Still, her words brought a hush to the courtroom, as though it was she who had pronounced a death sentence.

After a brief pause to give the jury a chance to soak in what she had said, Feynman said, "I believe you have prepared some demonstrative exhibits for the jury?"

The judge gave permission for Claudia to step down from the witness stand. It was easier to get people to pay attention to visual cues than just talking at them, so she was not surprised by the subtle shift in the energy of the room. She took up a position before the jury in front of a large TV screen. Even the sleepy juror sat at attention when the first exhibit—the kite Danny Ortiz denied writing—came into focus. The damning words tumbled across the page from edge to edge without respect for margins, the rounded letters slanting strongly to the left.

Early in the investigation, Alvarez had run up against a brick wall in his search for exemplars—samples of the defendant's known handwriting that Claudia could use for comparison. Ortiz, citing the law against self-incrimination, had refused to provide additional samples of his handwriting, and the sole exemplar available was a form he had filled out in jail. The form, being hand-printed, was unsuitable for comparison, as the kite was written in cursive.

It was not until several months later—in what seemed an act of providence—that a packet of handwritten letters surfaced that Danny Ortiz had written to an ex-girlfriend on the outside. The girlfriend, who described Danny as "a piece of shit nastier than a cockroach," could not have been happier to turn them over to the prosecutor's office.

Examining the new evidence, Claudia found a few minor differences, but many significant similarities. Even if there had been no other commonalities, there was a rare distinguishing feature present in both handwritings: the bottoms and sides of letters contained a special type of gap, a result of the pen being lifted from the paper for a microsecond. The lift made it appear as if a tiny section of ink had been erased. There was no question in Claudia's mind that the girlfriend's letters could be used to identify Danny Ortiz as the writer of the kite.

She was not going to testify about his personality, but it was impossible to ignore what the handwriting told her about Danny Ortiz': immature, no more than average intelligence. He had a strong need for approval, unsatisfactory bonding with his mother, rebellion toward authority figures, an utter lack of morality. Add to that a short fuse and zero self-discipline and an explosion was just waiting to happen.

The jurors were alert and interested as Claudia explained the exhibits. The first sample was one of the letters from Danny to his girlfriend. He had written that he loved her and she'd "better never fucking forget it." He begged her to please start loving him the way she should, that his life was all about her.

From the corner of her eye, Claudia could see the defendant squirming in his chair. His attorney leaned over and whispered to him, her hand on his arm. Forcing herself to ignore the distraction, she asked Alvarez to show the second letter. "Fuck off and dye!!" it began. "You stupid lying fucking hoe."

As she pointed to the radical change in size and slant change in the document, Danny Ortiz pushed back his chair and started to rise. The two bailiffs immediately moved away from the wall, hands resting on their weapons. Alison Smith, who was half Ortiz's size, seized his arm and yanked him back down. Ortiz shook her off and slumped back in his chair, spewing a string of profanity directed at Claudia.

Judge Abernathy banged his gavel and jabbed an angry finger at the public defender. "Can you keep your client under control, Counselor, or do I need to have him restrained?"

Smith leaned down and whispered urgently in Danny's ear. He gave a sharp nod, but Claudia saw that his face had paled and he was breathing rapidly.

"My apologies, Your Honor. Uh, my client was embarrassed at, er, having words, which were written in anger—"

The judge's expression darkened to a thundercloud. "Do I look like I care *why*, Counselor? There will be *no* further outbursts. Do I make myself understood?" His gaze swept the defendant's supporters, who had begun chattering to each other. "*Quiet!*" Abernathy roared. "Or I'll have the place cleared." He turned back to the public defender, who was visibly trembling. "Ms. Smith?"

"Yes, Your Honor."

"Then sit down and let's get on with it." At the judge's nod, the bailiffs stepped away from the defendant and returned to their positions. Smith resumed her seat, her cheeks red. "Thank you, Your Honor."

The exchange left Claudia feeling sorry for the public defender, who was young enough to have passed the bar exam within the last couple of years. How had Alison Smith landed a trial opposing the high-profile district attorney himself? Had she pissed off the Chief Public Defender who knew this case was a no-win? Or was her boss showing confidence in her by giving her a big chance?

Gathering her wits, Claudia continued, glancing over at the jurors from time to time. She was pleased to see them nodding, their expressions rapt as they followed the red dot of her laser pointer. They did not appear to notice, as she did, that as she spoke about the similarities in the documents, Ortiz continued to glower at her.

At the end of her presentation she returned to the witness stand, preparing for the defense to take a run at her. It was the opposing attorney's job to make her look stupid. As Smith got to her feet for cross-examination, Claudia reminded herself not to help.

Alison Smith was medium height and thin, dressed in an ill-fitting, off-the-rack navy suit. Her wispy blonde hair, held back in a bun, needed a brush. Despite her harried appearance, though, she stood straight-backed and spoke in a firm voice. "Ms. Rose, did you at any time meet with my client?"

"No."

"You did not personally take a handwriting sample from him?"

"I was told he had refused—"

Smith broke in. "So your answer is no. Is that right?"

"That is correct."

"And all you have is an angry ex-girlfriend's word that the letters she submitted were written by my client. Isn't that right, Ms. Rose?"

"No."

"No?" Smith echoed, then made a rookie mistake that gave Claudia the opportunity to score an important point with the jury. "Then, how do you know those letters were written by Mr. Ortiz?"

"His inmate number is on the return address and his signature, which is consistent with other signatures on jail documents, is on the letters. The handwriting on the envelope is also consistent with the other handwriting."

Smith pressed on, ignoring the titter that rippled through the court-room. "But an ex-girlfriend could have had someone else—"

Feynman objected. "There's been no offer of proof anyone else wrote the letters."

"Sustained. Do you have anything else, Counselor?"

"No, Your Honor, thank you. Nothing further." Smith took her seat.

Claudia's testimony needed no rehabilitation; Paul Feynman passed on the opportunity for redirect. She had been on the stand for a little less than ninety minutes.

Judge Abernathy glanced at the clock, his lips twitching in an al-most-smile, no doubt pleased that the afternoon session was coming to a close a little early. He turned to Claudia. "Since there are no further questions, Ms. Rose, you are excused."

"Thank you, Your Honor." Sliding her paperwork back into her brief-case, Claudia's mind was already racing ahead to her dinner plans with Jovanic. She shot a glance at Feynman, wondering whether he wanted her to stick around. His head was bent towards Alison Smith, who was urgently whispering in his ear. Maybe the public defender was ready to cut a deal for her client.

Abernathy began thanking the jury for their day's service and instructing them not to discuss their opinions with anyone. Claudia stepped down from the witness stand.

At the same moment, one of the gangbangers in the gallery jumped up, his hands forming a gang sign. He pointed at Claudia, and shouted, "Better watch your back, *puta!*"

The judge rapped his gavel. "Bailiffs, get that person out of here. I'm holding him in contempt."

Claudia froze in place as the two deputies pushed through the gate to the gallery and dragged Ortiz's still-cursing homie past her to the lockup.

The door slammed shut behind them.

That's when Danny Ortiz leapt out of his seat.

three

JOVANIC

LAPD Homicide Detective Joel Jovanic had been working a gang killing in Mar Vista since early morning. By the time his team was free to respond to a second callout in Venice, the sun was struggling to burn through the thick marine layer haze.

The new crime scene was a wide alley behind a McMansion two blocks from the Grand Canal. Yellow crime scene tape restricted access at both ends of the alley where a clutch of frightened neighbors and their live-in help had gathered.

Built tall, rather than wide, to accommodate the relatively small lots in the little-known area on the Westside of Los Angeles, the expensive homes were occupied for the most part by high-priced lawyers, CEOs, and television producers.

Early in the twentieth century, Abbott Kinney, a developer and conservationist, had constructed sixteen miles of canals, intending to recreate the cultural vibe of Venice, Italy. Almost immediately, though, it became apparent that the public preferred the beach town's less highbrow amusements over art and speeches. Over the years, the waterways had been renovated and eventually reduced to six canals. The homicide had taken place behind one of the east-west ones.

The homicide team's sergeant, Marvin Williams, was standing outside the tape near his black-and-white, talking to a patrolman. He glanced over as the four detectives approached. "Took you guys long enough." His voice rumbled like a freight train. A defensive linebacker before joining the force, Williams made even Jovanic, who stood six-two in his socks, look like a runt.

"Hey, Sarge, what've we got?" Jovanic and his partner, Randy Coleman, added their names to the log. Every person coming and going at the scene was required to sign in and out.

"Female, late 40s. Mailbox exploded when the victim picked up the mail around seven AM. Nobody else in the house. Dispatch got calls on the blast from two blocks away."

"Witnesses?"

"You honestly thought it would be that easy?"

"One can always hope."

Williams explained what had taken place before his arrival. The EMTs had determined that there was nothing they could do for the victim. The home had been checked for any additional victims—under the exigent circumstances law there was tacit permission to enter and ensure that no one else was injured or dead inside. After that, no one was allowed to cross through the yellow tape until the lead detective had arrived.

While he listened, Jovanic observed the area, absorbing as much as he could before they entered the taped area. A sheet-covered form lay about twenty feet away, next to one of the three-car garages, of which there were three on each side of the alley. In a tony neighborhood like this one, there would be plenty of security. Glancing up, he spotted what he was looking for: a camera mounted in the garage eaves. Too bad it was pointed at the steel security gate, the wrong direction to be of much use, but with any luck, one of the neighbors' cameras would have caught something.

Jovanic, Coleman, and Williams crossed through the tape. Everything within a ten-foot radius of the blast point was coated with plaster dust and fragments of broken masonry. Torn Christmas catalogs and assorted mail pieces littered the ground.

There was a hole the size of a fist in the garage wall about four feet off the ground. All that was left of the mailbox was fragments of black metal strewn everywhere. Blood had spattered on the champagne-beige paint.

"Blew off a couple fingers," said Williams. "Right hand's a bloody mess. Kemp found the forefinger and the top section of the middle finger on the other side of the alley. One of the EMTs saw a dog sniffing around. Probably got what was left of the third finger."

Jovanic crouched to lift the sheet. "Glad I haven't had lunch yet."

The victim had been a small woman, five-four at most, and trim. Attractive, too, with a mane of thick, black hair. Her eyes were open wide and staring, hands drawn up to her chest. Blood had soaked into the terrycloth robe. A lot of blood.

"Her heart was pumping hard when she went down," Jovanic noted, mostly to himself, then added to his sergeant, "The coroner should be here in about thirty."

Williams said, "The folks next door said the vic was the housekeeper. They think the homeowners—name's Lockhart—are out of town, but nobody has their mobile numbers. We're calling the security company."

"Homeowner was lucky they had a housekeeper to pick up the mail," said Coleman. "Housekeeper, not so much."

Williams ignored him and went to greet the other team members—Detectives RJ (Rebecca) Scott and Huey Hardcastle, who had just arrived. They volunteered to canvass the neighborhood with the patrol officers and interview anyone who had seen or heard anything immediately preceding or following the blast.

Jovanic had already requested a search warrant to look for anything that would lead to the owner. The electronic warrant landed in his phone mid-morning. "Let's take a look inside."

The door to the security gate had been propped open by a brick, the back door to the house left standing ajar, as it had been when the victim left the residence. As they entered the house—upward of five thousand square feet of *über*-luxury decorator living—he was already think-ing about possible motives. Was it a prank gone horribly wrong? Or had someone set the device because they hated the homeowner? The cognac-hued, French Oak hardwood floors alone must have cost a fortune. It wasn't hard to imagine someone with this kind of buying power having enemies. Aside from the garage wall, the explosion had not caused any property damage. Was the blast intended as a warning?

The ground floor comprised the garage, a laundry room, the house-keeper's quarters and an enclosed patio that opened onto a terraz-zo-tiled courtyard rimmed with well-cared-for potted plants.

Leaving Coleman to work on the family living areas, Jovanic started his search in the housekeeper's room. The room was plainly furnished and her personal belongings relatively few. According to the driver's license he found in her purse, the victim had been Sylvia Vasquez, forty-eight years old. A dog-eared address book held faded names and phone numbers, but nothing to immediately indicate who should be notified of Vasquez's death.

The two detectives quickly recognized that the home was an adult domicile, with everything as pristine as a hotel waiting for its next guests. No rock star posters on the walls or other trappings of a teen's abode in any of the four third-floor bedrooms. A box of toys appro-priate for young children was in a guest room closet—most likely, grandchildren.

The second floor was a large, open-plan that appeared to serve as a family room or den. A mantelpiece over the fireplace held a collection of framed family photos. A handsome couple, aging through the years, along with two boys. Wedding photos, when the boys grew up, and the grandchildren whose toys were in the upstairs closet.

Jovanic rifled through a small stack of opened bills on a computer desk, most addressed to Evan Lockhart. He selected the mobile phone bill and called the number listed inside. A man answered.

"This is Detective Joel Jovanic, LAPD. Am I speaking to Evan Lockhart?"

"Yes, this is he." The voice sounded suspicious. "Who did you say is calling?"

"I'm sorry to call you with this news, sir, but there's been an incident at your house, an explosion." As he expected, there was a stunned moment of silence. Then, "*What*? Who did you say you are? Is this some kind of sick joke?"

Jovanic repeated his LAPD credential. "Unfortunately, sir, it's no joke. How soon can you get here?"

"Detective, my wife and I are out of the country. We're vacationing in the Maldives."

Jovanic was not sure where the Maldives was, but it sounded far. "When are you due back in town?"

"Not until next Sunday."

"Do you have any thoughts on why someone would do such a thing, Mr. Lockhart? Or who?"

"No, I don't. I just—I—how much damage is there?"

Jovanic noticed that he had not asked whether anyone was hurt or the cause of the blast. "There's very little structural damage, but I have some unfortunate news about your housekeeper..."

Lockhart listened in silence. "My God. We'll leave right away."

Jovanic could hear his muffled voice as he turned away and spoke to someone else. "There's been an explosion at the house. Yes, our house. I don't know—maybe a gas leak? Darling, Sylvia was *killed*." Jovanic heard a woman cry out. Lockhart said, "I know, it's hard to believe." There was a brief pause, then he returned to the line, "This is all a bit hard to take in, Detective. You're sure? Sylvia died?"

"Unfortunately, yes. Mr. Lockhart, are you aware of any family we can notify?"

"It's *Doctor* Lockhart. I believe Sylvia's from El Salvador. She doesn't have anyone here that I know of. Let me ask my wife." Jovanic heard him relay the question, then he returned to the phone again. "I'm sorry, Detective, my wife isn't aware of anyone, either." The call ended with a promise to contact Jovanic upon his return to L.A..

The deputy coroner arrived and examined the body. His preliminary opinion was that Sylvia Vasquez had suffered a massive heart attack and died instantly.

When there was nothing further to be done at the site, the team broke for lunch at the Firehouse on Rose, their informal conference room when they were out in the field. In between the lunch and dinner crowds, they had the place pretty much to themselves. No other diners in their section to complain about them ruining a meal with discussions of death and destruction.

The waitress showed up, joked with the group for a minute or two, then got serious and took their orders: meatball sandwich for Jovanic, tuna salad for Hardcastle. Scott wanted chili; Coleman, ever-health-conscious, ordered grilled chicken breast and broccoli.

As the lead, Jovanic started the conversation: "What do we know, or think we know?"

Hardcastle had a ready answer. "Kids setting off a cherry bomb. Who else is gonna blow up a damn mailbox?"

"They do it all the time," Coleman agreed. "They just love blowing shit up. Remember that case in Mar Vista? Idiots set off firecrackers in every mailbox on the street."

Scott was staring into her coffee, her expression contemplative as she dumped in a packet of sweetener. "It might just be a cherry bomb, but the vic is still dead."

"It wasn't the device that killed her," Coleman argued. "Coroner said it looked like a heart attack. Won't know for sure until they get her on the table."

"If you opened your mailbox and it blew off half your hand, I think you might have a heart attack, too."

"Seems like a lot of damage for a cherry bomb."

"That's why it's a felony," Hardcastle retorted. "The damn things can kill."

"There would have to be a way that opening the mailbox lit the fuse," Jovanic conjectured. "I doubt a kid is going to be watching at seven AM. for the housekeeper to come out, stick the cherry bomb in the mailbox and light the fuse, then duck around the corner to watch."

"Where would a kid get one, anyway?"

"Tijuana. Plus, there are plenty of YouTube videos on how to make them. We'll see what the fire investigator finds."

"Never gonna prove Murder One," Scott said. "Unless they stuck the bomb in her mouth, it's Man One at best."

"Was it random or targeted?" Jovanic mused aloud. "Was it a pro or, like Huey said, kids who made a big mistake?"

Scott nodded. "Or what if it was targeted and they hit the wrong house? Or right house, wrong person?"

"We need to talk to the neighbors again when people get home from work. Let's find out who's got issues with any of the homeowners, who's on parole that might have a beef with someone in the neighborhood—anyone who might have heard something. What do the owners do for a living? Any drug connections, etcetera."

Coleman plucked a paper napkin from the holder at the edge of the table and ran it around the lip of his water glass before taking a drink. "No witnesses, but there's gotta be plenty of security footage in that part of Venice. Those homes list in the multi-millions."

Jovanic said, "RJ and Huey, you can get started on that. Check with the neighbors on security cams on the alley and get their footage for the last forty-eight hours. The vic was picking up Saturday's mail. That means the device could have been left anytime between Saturday's mail drop and now. If we luck out, *all* the neighbors will give us access." He consulted his notebook, thinking ahead as he made assignments. "While you two check on the video, Randy and I will start looking into the vic's background, in case *she* was the target."

"You're thinking a drug thing?" Scott asked.

"Hey, guys," Hardcastle interrupted, pointing at the silenced TV above the bar, where the camera was focused on an ambulance in front of the Criminal Courts Building in downtown L.A. "Something's going down at CCB."

"I heard there was supposed be a green protest today out back of there," said Coleman.

Jovanic, whose back was to the TV, shrugged. Somebody was always protesting something around the courthouse. Then he remembered. "Claudia has a trial down there today."

"I hope she doesn't run into that mess," Scott said. "With that shitty downtown traffic, she won't get home till midnight."

Coleman laughed. "Where but L.A. would anyone talk about what time someone gets home from court?"

"Yeah, well you know how it is around here—traffic is like a monster. We all try to help each other avoid it."

"What's Claudia got going?" Hardcastle asked. "Anything interesting?"

"The Danny Ortiz trial."

"She's testifying on the kite he's lying about?" Hardcastle's opinion of Danny Ortiz was etched on his face. "Jury better crucify that motherfucker."

"They will," said Coleman, who was inexperienced enough not to be as jaded as his fellow detectives. "They have to."

"I saw Claudia's exhibits," Jovanic said. "Anyone with half an eyeball can see Ortiz wrote it."

Scott gave them all a knowing look. "You never can tell with juries."

"C'mon, RJ," said Jovanic. "Think positive."

Hardcastle snickered. "*Yeah*, Joel. Cause you're such a *positive* guy."

"Hey, I'm a realist. I—"

Before a discussion of Jovanic's philosophy of life and juries could get off the ground, he felt his phone vibrate in his pocket. He flicked a glance at the screen: Number Unavailable. Let it go to voicemail. His head was buzzing from lack of sleep—they had gotten to the earlier crime scene at three AM. His blood sugar was in the dumper, the result of the day's quota of sweetener-fueled coffee and Danish on the run. And his gut was lurching after dry-swallowing four Excedrin Migraine on an empty stomach.

Thirty seconds later the phone vibrated again. He let it go.

The third time, Jovanic started to get a bad feeling. Signaling the other detectives that he would be back, he slid out of the booth, answering as he strode toward the front of the restaurant. "Jovanic."

"Hey, Joel, Duane Roberts. Downtown?"

He recognized the name. The detectives were on friendly terms with the courthouse deputies, but none of them had ever called him before. Jovanic excused his way past a small knot of people in the lobby waiting to be seated. He pushed open the front door, squinting at the bright light after the dimness of the restaurant, and stepped out onto the sidewalk. In the background behind the deputy, Jovanic could hear the muffled whine of a siren. "Yeah, Duane, what's up?"

"Uh, listen, man, your girlfriend ran into some trouble over here. We're on our way to the hospital at USC."

four

DANNY ORTIZ ROCKETED ACROSS the defense table. File folders and paper flew into the air like gigantic pieces of confetti. Alison Smith's laptop hit the floor with a bang. People scrambled for cover. Somebody was screaming.

Two-hundred and twenty pounds of solid muscle slammed Claudia against the witness stand and her feet went out from under her. She went down, landing on her right arm, which was tangled in the strap of her briefcase. Her head hit the floor hard enough to jar her teeth.

The sharp crack of Judge Abernathy's gavel sounded like gunshots as he bellowed for order, but no one was listening.

Stunned, Claudia scrambled to get up, but Ortiz shoved back down. Teeth bared like a rabid dog, he straddled her, spraying her face with saliva. "*You're dead, bitch,*" he snarled.

His fist was aimed at her face. Hunching turtle-like, Claudia turned her head and tried to block the torrent of blows with her free arm. Two years of pumping iron behind bars had hardened Danny Ortiz' fists. Blood spurted hot and sticky as a punch glanced off her nose and landed on her cheek. His massive hands closed around her throat—sausage-sized thumbs squeezing her airway, cutting off her scream. She clawed at his hands, digging her nails into the flesh, but the glint in his murderous eyes promised no mercy. Danny Ortiz was going to kill her.

The grip tightened on her windpipe until her pulse roared in her ears, throbbing with her heartbeat. She could feel the oxygen draining from her body. Her grasp on his hand loosened and her eyes rolled back. The jumble of noise and motion in the gallery seemed dim and miles away. As consciousness began to fade, an image formed in Claudia's mind—Jovanic's anguished face, hearing the news of her death.

Later, she would not be able to say where the sudden jolt of power came from. Of its own volition, her left hand balled into a fist and smashed, engagement ring first, into Ortiz's eye. His head jerked back, the surprise loosening his hold. Her throat burned like fire but she could breathe again.

Finally, there were deputies dragging Ortiz off her. Louder than the bedlam around them they screamed commands at him, roughly yanking his arms behind his back and shoving him to the floor face down. Not ready to give up, Danny kicked out hard. The bolt of pain that shot through Claudia's ribs made her see stars, just like in cartoons. She rolled away, gasping, and vomited.

———⋈———

In the ambulance, Claudia lay back on the gurney feeling detached from her body. Everything and everyone seemed unreal and distant. Suspecting a concussion from her head hitting the floor, the paramedics were taking her and one of the deputies to the emergency room at St John's Medical Center. She strained to read the name printed on his badge, but the letters blurred together: DRoberts.

"It's Duane," the deputy said. "If it was up to me, the defendant would've been shackled the whole time, but the lawyers won't let us bring a prisoner to the courtroom in chains. They say it prejudices the jury." He shook his head in disgust. "Who could have known that spectator was going be such an asshole and the judge was gonna order Ratzel and me both to take him out? It was one of those 'perfect storms' they talk about. We should both have been on him every minute."

Roberts looked so crestfallen that Claudia was tempted to tell him it was okay. But it wasn't. *She* wasn't okay. Besides, it hurt too much to move her jaw and try to speak. She prayed it wasn't broken.

The deputy was explaining why it had taken as long as it had to get to her, but focusing was too much trouble. Something about Ortiz's supporters cheering him on and intentionally obstructing the path to her rescue. Her attention kept slipping away.

Claudia's eyes drifted closed on a fog of pain. Had she asked for someone to call Joel? She could not remember. She didn't even know whether her briefcase had made it into the ambulance with her. She knew she ought to be worried about it, and her car, which was parked in the Mark Taper Forum parking garage, but the pain in her ribs made simply taking a breath a chore. Her nose was swollen; her whole face throbbed. Her head felt like a block of concrete on her shoulders. And she could not bring herself to give a good goddamn about any of it.

—————— ✖ ——————

Arriving at the ER with a deputy got you special recognition and faster service, Claudia discovered. The doctor gave her something to dull the pain, but her brain still felt fuzzy and she drifted in and out.

She had no concept of how much time had passed when Jovanic's angry voice penetrated the fog. Claudia opened her left eye—the right one was swollen shut. A curtain had been drawn around the emergency room bed. The doctor was saying, "—concussion, contusions and lacerations. Ribs are bruised, not cracked. She's lucky it's not worse."

That appeared to further incense Jovanic. His voice rose. "Yeah, very *lucky*. Thanks, Doc."

"Joel." Had she said his name aloud? Or it had stayed in her head?

The curtain parted. Jovanic stepped inside and drew a sharp breath. "My God, Claudia—"

How bad did she look?

She could feel white-hot fury radiating from him as he appraised her split lip and bruised flesh. It showed in the compression of his lips and the paleness of his face. She knew he could not trust himself to speak. He stood there for an eternity, finally taking a deep breath and sitting on the edge of the bed. He reached out and lightly touched her face. "Oh, baby," he breathed, taking her hand in his.

Claudia struggled to marshal her thoughts and say something intelligent, but the words that came out didn't make sense in her own ears. Tears leaked from the corners of her eyes.

Jovanic leaned over and kissed her forehead. "It's okay, babe, you don't need to talk now. Just rest. I'll be right here."

Clinging to his hand as if it were a life preserver, she closed her eyes and let herself float away.

—————⋈—————

With a promise to send someone to retrieve her Jaguar, Jovanic drove Claudia home from the hospital, arriving in time to catch coverage of the attack on the eleven o'clock news. He argued against her watching, but Claudia, who was starting to feel more alert, stubbornly insisted on flipping to Channel 7, where she was the lead story.

She watched aghast, not just at witnessing the brutality of the attack. As she had squirmed under Danny Ortiz, the too-short skirt had ridden up around her hips. The lacy black thong she had worn for Jovanic's viewing pleasure exposed most of her derriere. It had had been blurred for TV, but the ignominy burned on her cheeks. Worse, as she flipped through the channels, it became apparent that the courtroom camera had not only captured her humiliation, but shared it with all the local stations.

Jovanic was kind enough and wise enough to leave anything he was thinking unsaid. He helped her upstairs and got her undressed, throwing her clothes to the back of the closet at her request. She would never again be able to touch that suit without the memory of Ortiz's hot breath in her face, his coarse hands on her. The offending skirt could go to the next charity that sent a truck to her neighborhood. The next time she got up the guts to return to court, Claudia promised herself, she would be wearing pants and steel-toed shoes.

The pain meds gave her a few hours of restless sleep. She awoke while it was still dark with an all-over ache that felt like she'd been stomped by a hippo. Even wrinkling her nose hurt. Her mouth was parched, but just the thought of rolling over and reaching for the water bottle on the nightstand made her wince. Lying silently on her back, careful not to disturb Jovanic, Claudia listened to the driving rain pelting the bedroom windows, thinking about her mortality. She had never been religious. Her views on life and death were pretty philosophical—you came here and learned lessons, then you went back to a spirit world and got recycled. Apparently, since she had survived Danny Ortiz, she had more lessons to learn.

On most days, Claudia was the first one up, making coffee while Jovanic dressed for work. He was groping to turn off the beep-beep-beeping when she started to push the covers off. Gently, he pressed her back on the pillow. "Are you kidding me? Stay in bed. *I'll* get the coffee. You've gotta take it easy today."

With her ribs taped up, lying flat was almost as uncomfortable as moving, and Claudia had a sinking feeling that taking it easy was not going to be all that simple. "Okay," she agreed meekly. "No acrobatic feats." She didn't tell him she had no intention of staying in bed, cataloguing her injuries and reliving the attack.

They kissed goodbye and she listened to the front door close and for the Jeep to start up in the driveway. Struggling out of bed, she screwed up her courage to hobble to the bathroom and look in the mirror.

The image that stared back at her reflected something from a slasher movie. Black eyes, swollen lip, a rainbow of bruises. And that was just her face. What was not visible were the bruises under her sweatshirt, or her taped ribs, which hurt like hell with every deep breath. Resisting the temptation to hang a towel over the mirror, Claudia went looking for her tablet. Deputy Roberts had taken her briefcase to the hospital with her.

Some of the courtroom spectators had posted the attack on social media. A TikTok video showed Ortiz punching her like a boxer hitting a heavy bag. The whole thing had lasted scarcely more than thirty seconds. It had felt more like thirty minutes.

Like a drug addict in need of a fix, Claudia watched it over and over again. The one moment of satisfaction was seeing herself punch Ortiz in the eye. She held out her left hand to admire her engagement ring. The diamond seemed to sparkle extra-bright, as if pleased to have played a part in defending her.

Dressing in baggy sweats that would not aggravate her injuries, she made her way slowly downstairs and zapped a bowl of instant oatmeal that she didn't eat; poured another cup of coffee and pretended to read a book. Despite the pain in her ribs, she washed the dishes and cleaned the kitchen sink, scrubbing as hard as she could manage, imagining Danny Ortiz's face under the Brillo pad.

She was looking for another distraction when a hammering at the front door scared her out of her wits.

five

Claudia looked through the peephole. Her friend, Kelly Brennan, was standing on the porch, the rain pouring down behind her. "Jesus Christ, Claudia," Kelly yelled, continuing to bang on the door. "Would you open the goddamned door?"

Claudia did.

Kelly's face crumpled and she burst into tears. "Ohmigod, look at your face. I saw it on the news this morning. I can't believe that asshole did this to you." She threw herself on Claudia with a hug that threatened to topple her.

Claudia pushed her away. "Ow, that hurts. And you're soaked. I'm going to get you a towel."

"You sound awful."

"Maybe because my throat feels like raw meat?"

"Dammit, Claudia, why couldn't somebody stop him? All those idiots taking video, nobody helping. What the hell is wrong with people?" She held up a Starbucks bag. "I brought comfort food. Now, tell me everything."

"Thanks. I can use some comfort. Throw your raincoat in the laundry room."

They went through to the kitchen. Kelly toweled off her short blonde hair and they settled into the breakfast nook. As a family law attorney, she was herself a veteran of the courtroom. She set out the two cardboard cups and pushed a chocolate croissant at Claudia, staring at the bluish-hued bruise where Danny Ortiz's thumbs had left an impression on her neck. "That looks like a giant hickey,"

Claudia shuddered. "He's in my nose. I keep smelling his foul sweat. I want to stand in the shower and scrub it off me."

"You poor thing." Kelly's eyes welled again. "Too bad Joel wasn't there. I'd pay good money to see that fight."

"He would've killed the bastard." Claudia repeated what the deputy had described as a perfect storm': two deputies absent from the court-room, the third busy at the other end of the courtroom, leaving a violent defendant without a guard.

"You should report it."

"To who? It was Judge Abernathy's fault. He never should have sent both of those deputies out of the courtroom and left just that one older lady deputy, who wasn't paying attention anyway."

"I'd like to know what happened to Ortiz after they dragged his sorry ass out of the courtroom."

"Duane Roberts called Joel last night and said they took care of him—he 'resisted arrest.'" Claudia took a careful sip of her latté, mus-ing on Ortiz's fate. "I have a feeling Danny is gonna be sucking through a straw for a while."

"I bet they rocked his world, and he deserved whatever he got."

"Joel was livid when he came to the hospital."

"Don't be surprised if Danny meets with an 'unfortunate accident' in jail."

"Don't be ridiculous. Joel isn't going to do anything illegal." Claudia wished it had not come out sounding defensive, but Kelly was not aware that not very long ago Jovanic had put his career on the line for her. That was one secret she had no intention of sharing. The incident, which involved her young friend Annabelle Giordano, had nearly ended their relationship. She loved Annabelle deeply, but at the end of last summer, returning the girl to her father, who had been in Europe making a movie, had been a relief.

She reached up and touched a fingertip to her swollen right eye, where a scattering of tiny red dots—a result of being strangled—speckled the white. "Guess I won't be entering any beauty contests."

"Yeah, I recommend you stay away from mirrors for a week or two. It looks like you finger-painted half your face."

Claudia turned the stink eye on her. "Uh, remind me again why we're friends?"

"Because friends tell the truth, even when it hurts. And honey, that has got to hurt like hell."

"It does," Claudia admitted.

Kelly gave her a long, considering look. "Want me to hang out with you until Joel gets home?"

"No way; you have work to do. Go. I'm fine."

The pat answer was out before she could censor her words, but Claudia knew she was miles from being fine. She had faced frightening situations before as a result of her work—had been threatened, even physically harmed—but with yesterday's assault, something had snapped in her. She felt fragile and agitated, afraid she would never be the same again.

The truth was, she badly wanted Kelly to stay. But something stopped her from admitting what she considered weakness, even to her closest friend. Not that Kelly was fooled. Claudia could see the understanding in her keen gaze.

"Honey, there's no shame in being scared," Kelly said. "You *just* got the shit knocked out of you. If I were you, I'd be scared to death."

"Fine, I'm scared. I admit it. But I can't let myself be ruled by fear. I've done that before, and I don't want to go through it again."

"Maybe it's time you started practicing with that gun Joel got for you."

"I hate those things. I'd end up shooting myself." That the gun was no longer in Claudia's possession was another secret she had kept from her friend.

"Yeah, but—"

"Danny Ortiz isn't going to send his crew after me. He doesn't know where I live."

Kelly rolled her eyes. "You don't think bangers use the Internet? Nobody's information is truly private."

"Gee, thanks for the boost; I feel much better now." Claudia got up from the table and took an ice pack from the freezer. She wrapped it in a dishtowel and held it against her face. "The Vicodin is making my head fuzzy. I think I need to lie down."

"An excellent idea." Kelly cleared their empty cups and trash from the table and dumped everything in the bin under the sink. "You call me if you need *anything*. Promise?"

"Promise." The ER doc had said that lightheadedness was a symptom of the concussion that could last for weeks.

At the door, Kelly leaned in with an air kiss. "When *will* Joel be home?"

"Hard to say. They're working that bomb case in Venice. Did you see it on the news?"

"Yeah, but I thought the bomb squad—"

"Somebody died, so Homicide gets it."

"Did you hear there was a whole string of small bombings? It was on the news this morning."

"In *Venice*?"

"No, no. Other countries—France, Italy and, um, England, I think. But the police seem to think they're all connected. Nobody died, anyway."

"That's amazing. These terrorists usually want to kill as many people as possible."

"Apparently, these are not your garden variety terrorists. They're protesting some chemical company."

"Well, I'm glad Joel's case is 'just' a cherry bomb, which is bad enough since somebody did die."

"Most of the time those things are set by stupid kids who need a good spanking, or at least parental supervision." Taking care not to squeeze hard this time, Kelly gave Claudia a last hug. "Go get some rest. I'll call you later."

Claudia closed the door behind her and locked it, then checked and rechecked the locks, ruminating on Kelly's comment about Danny meeting with an 'unfortunate accident' in jail. She thought again of the harrowing experience she and Jovanic had gone through that resulted in his breaking the law for her sake. No one had found out. She would not want him to risk his career for her a second time.

Once again, she checked the back door to make sure it was locked and dead bolted, although it had not been opened that morning. Halfway back to the living room, she turned around and went to check it again. Jovanic had been right, she admitted to herself. Watching those videos had been a mistake. Now, along with the pain and the memory of the abject terror she had experienced, she had visuals to keep it alive. She tried to convince herself that she was lucky Ortiz hadn't broken any bones or teeth, but with every muscle screaming at her it was a hard sell.

She checked her emails and found one from a colleague in the UK. They had become friends long ago at a conference hosted by the British Institute of Graphologists, and stayed in touch ever since. Daphne Spencer was chairing this year's conference and had been trying for months to persuade Claudia to come to London as the keynote speaker.

To be invited was a high honor, an opportunity for increased prestige, plus the organization would pay for the travel. Claudia, caught up in work and keeping an eye on Annabelle, had regretfully declined. Now Daphne was emailing to say that she still had a slot to fill and she still wanted Claudia to fill it. She also issued an open invitation to stay at her house for as long as she liked.

Leaning back in her chair, Claudia thought about the offer. She and Jovanic had made plans to visit family over the upcoming Christmas holidays. The conference was in January. . .

Suddenly, her heart was racing. What was that noise?

There's someone in the house.

Sounds of someone crossing the living room. But how—?

"Claudia?" a voice called from downstairs. "Are you home?"

Annabelle.

Annabelle had a key.

Faint with relief, Claudia clutched the arms of her chair with shaking hands. "Up here," she croaked, sounding, thanks to Danny Ortiz, as though she had laryngitis.

Sneaker-clad feet pounded up the stairs and hurried along the landing. "Guess what—my dad's taking me to Paris and—" Annabelle bounded into the room, skidding to a shocked halt. "Holy *shit*, Claudia, what happened to your face? Did you wreck your car? *What happened*?"

Claudia struggled to push down the tears that suddenly threatened to overwhelm her. The wobble in her voice gave her away. "It's not as bad as it looks. Nothing to worry about."

She should have known better. Annabelle was a street-wise almost-sixteen-year-old whose hands were currently squeezed into fists. She was small for her age, but she looked as fierce as a mother tiger. "Who did that to you? I'll fuck them up."

"You aren't going to do *anything*. The guy's in jail already. And watch your mouth." Claudia rose slowly from her desk feeling like a creaky old woman. She went to sit on the comfortable old sofa where they had spent many hours together, talking about the ups and downs of twenty-first century teen angst, and patted the cushion. "Come and tell me about Paris."

"No way." Annabelle said, like a parent talking to a wayward child. "You're not getting out of telling me what happened."

Seeing her standing there in her knee-high boots and long fisherman-knit sweater, fists on her slim hips, Claudia suddenly realized how grown-up Annabelle had become. The realization slapped her in the face: no longer was this the prickly fourteen-year-old she had met and grown to love. It was as though she was really seeing her for the first time in a long time.

She knew the girl would not give her any peace until she gave in. Besides, the moment she checked her phone she would find the whole story for herself—*and see that humiliating video.* Claudia sighed in surrender. "Calm down and have a seat."

Listening to her bare bones account of her courtroom misadventure, Annabelle's expression darkened to the old scowl that she had not displayed in some time. "That asshole needs to die," she said through clenched teeth.

Panic rose again. The last time the girl had acted on her own was when Jovanic had stepped in and the affair had gone badly for everyone involved. "*Please*, Annabelle—"

Annabelle threw her arms around Claudia's neck. "I can't stand that he hurt you."

The uncharacteristic show of affection almost moved Claudia to tears, too. Annabelle was the closest she would ever come to having a daughter. She held her close, afraid to say anything that might break the fragile bond. When the moment passed, Annabelle got up and went in search of a tissue.

"It's okay to be mad, kiddo," Claudia said when she came back blowing her nose. "But please listen to me—you *can't* take matters into your own hands this time."

Annabelle ducked her head, a little sheepish. "Don't worry, I learned my lesson. I promise I won't do anything like that again."

Claudia smiled. "Thank God. Now, let's change the subject. I want to know all about this trip to Paris. That is way cool."

After Annabelle had heated a can of soup for their lunch—Claudia couldn't handle chewing a sandwich, she left with further promises not to wreak her own vengeance on Danny Ortiz.

———⋈———

Jovanic phoned between witness interviews, checking on her, and several media outlets called, wanting an interview, which she refused.

Turning to work—her standard distractor—Claudia started work on a forgery case involving a celebrity who was fighting to quash a former employee's upcoming "tell-all" book. Supposedly, the employee had signed a nondisclosure agreement. The employee denied that the signature was hers. The questioned signature was indisputably genuine. However, the original document had been lost, or perhaps had never existed, leaving Claudia to work from an old photocopy. There was a possibility that the celebrity's minions had digitized a genuine signature and placed it on a fake document. Without an original, it would be impossible to prove otherwise.

Claudia wrote her report, but she found herself gasping for air. She knew it was an anxiety reaction, this feeling that her lungs had forgotten how to take in a full breath. But knowing did not help. Eventually, she took a pain pill and stretched out on the sofa, falling asleep almost immediately, and waking with a start from a nightmare. Fuzzy-headed, she reached for the remote and flipped to the Food Network. *Cutthroat Kitchen* kept her distracted until nearly midnight, when Jovanic arrived home, exhausted, but wanting to hold her in his arms.

She loved him for wanting to protect her, but she couldn't help tensing and he sensed it. "Are you okay, babe? Am I hurting you?"

"It's just that I keep feeling him on me. It's like I'm in a straitjacket, I can't move."

Jovanic released her. "It'll be better tomorrow. It'll start fading."

They climbed into bed together, Claudia taking comfort in spooning against him. But then he rolled over and circled his arms around her and she felt trapped again. She wanted to slide out of bed and lock herself in the bathroom.

Am I going crazy?

Jovanic's breath warmed her neck. "Won't be long until Christmas. We'll be on our way up north. It'll be good to get away."

"M'hm." Claudia hoped he was too tired to pick up on her lack of enthusiasm, but it was too much to expect from a seasoned detective who was accustomed to listening for the nuances in conversation.

"We could take the train up. That might be fun." His voice was beginning to slur as sleep started to overtake him.

The thought of a train filled with strangers made her nauseous. A relentless dread had started up that Ortiz might send his gangbanger homies after her. She told herself that post-traumatic stress was a normal, natural response to the violence that had been inflicted on her. *Yada, yada.* "I'm thinking about going to London in January," Claudia said, surprising herself.

"London?" Jovanic said sleepily. "London, *England*?"

"Daphne still wants me to speak at that conference I told you about."

There was such a long silence that she thought he might have dozed off. But he grunted and she realized he was mulling over the idea. "I think you *should* go," he said at length.

"Seriously?"

"Seriously. You should accept. You need this."

"As busy as you are, you wouldn't even miss me," Claudia said. She meant it as a joke, but it sounded pitiful.

Jovanic pulled her closer, bending his head to press his lips against hers; a perfect fit. "Now, that, GraphoLady, is where you're wrong."

six

JOVANIC

Every scrap of crime scene tape had been removed from the alley, all signs of the explosion cleared away. No speck of debris dotted the ground; the blood that had stained the concrete scrubbed clean. Apart from the barely noticeable lighter paint color on the garage wall, where a new mailbox had already been installed, no indication of the homicide remained.

Evan Lockhart, the homeowner, had insisted that his neighbors should not be made anxious by the presence of a police car in front of his house, even if it was unmarked. He preferred that the detectives enter through the alley. Coleman pulled in behind a cranberry-colored Hyundai Crossover parked in front of the garage and switched off the engine.

Pulling up their collars against the steady drizzle, the two detectives left the warmth of the department Crown Vic and hurried to the locked gate, where they rang the bell. Lockhart immediately answered the intercom, which Jovanic took to mean they were being monitored via security surveillance. He identified himself and Coleman and the latch released.

He recognized Evan Lockhart from the family photos in the den. Tall and thin, silver-haired, Lockhart was clad in an elegant lamb's wool cardigan and pleated trousers. The pipe in his hand completed the cliché.

Colonel Mustard in the library with a candlestick, Jovanic thought with secret amusement as they exchanged handshakes and introductions.

"Come in, detectives." Lockhart led them through the service porch to the front entry. "My wife is interviewing an applicant the agency sent over. She's showing her the housekeeper's quarters. You can imagine how stressful all this has been for her, for both of us."

The detectives acknowledged that it must be very stressful, although neither of them was ever likely to be in a position to afford a live-in housekeeper.

"Will your wife be available to speak with us?" Jovanic asked.

"She may join us, although I doubt there's anything she can tell you that I can't. Naturally, we'll offer whatever assistance we can." Lockhart gestured to the curved staircase behind them. "Let's go up to the great room."

The two detectives exchanged a glance and followed him to the second floor. The great room was the wide, open-floor plan Jovanic had mentally tagged as "the den." From this elevation, the tall windows looked beyond the Grand Canal to the ocean, where uninviting slate-gray waves lapped the shore. Aside from a few diehard surfers astride their boards in the water, hoping to catch a ride, the beach was deserted.

Offering the detectives one of the two facing sofas, Lockhart sat on the other. Jovanic sank into the buttery leather cushions, wishing he could take a nap on them. He had slept fitfully the night before, on alert in case Claudia was in pain and needed his help. "I hope under the circumstances that you had a good trip home," he said.

"We had the company Gulfstream. Considering we had to cut our vacation short, it was as comfortable as it could be. This has been a real tragedy, with Sylvia's death."

"Yes. We've got all available resources on it."

"I'd hoped you were here because you'd arrested the young devils behind the bombing."

"No arrests have been made, sir. Do you have some idea of who the offender might be?"

"Who else but juvenile delinquents would do such a harebrained, stupid thing?"

"Other than that, have you thought of anyone who might wish you, or maybe Ms. Vasquez, harm?"

Lockhart gave a snort of disbelief. "You think this was directed at *Sylvia*?"

"We're looking at all the possibilities."

"How long did Ms. Vasquez work for you?" Coleman asked.

"At a rough estimate, I'd say six or seven years. If you need an exact date, my wife keeps those records." He cleared this throat. "Naturally, Sylvia produced all the proper documentation to prove her immigration status. I would never have allowed my wife to hire her otherwise."

"At this point I'm less interested in the victim's immigration status than the person who killed her," said Jovanic. "According to the coroner it was a heart attack, not the explosion. But whoever set the explosive is still responsible for her death."

"Yes, of course."

"Do you know of anyone in her life that might have been a problem?"

"I am aware of an ex-husband who's been incarcerated. He came around here once. We made it clear at the time that he wasn't welcome. Sylvia knew that if she wanted to see him, she had to meet him elsewhere. We don't need his kind around our home."

"What kind is that, sir?"

"A criminal, Detective. A drug addict. A gangster from south of the border. That kind."

"Do you remember when it was that her ex was here?"

"Too long ago to be behind this. Besides, I don't think a mailbox bomb would be his style."

"What would be his style?"

"He was more of a knife-you-in-the-back type."

"Is that just an impression you got, or do you have a particular reason to think so?"

"He killed someone in a bar fight—one of many such fights, no doubt. As I recall, he slashed the other man with a broken bottle. That's why he went to prison. Sylvia was very upset, wanted to borrow money for his bail. Naturally, we refused."

"Naturally," Jovanic echoed dryly. "Do you remember what the charges were in that case, Mr. Lockhart?"

"As I recall, it was voluntary manslaughter. He got an eleven-year sentence, but was released after five. We never saw him again. I got the impression that he slunk back to El Salvador or wherever it was he'd come from, and good riddance."

"What about anyone else in her life? Children? A current boyfriend?"

"Not that I ever heard about. I believe any family is in Central America. But that's a question for my wife. Sylvia certainly never confided anything of a personal nature in me. In fact, I can say we never had much contact at all." The expensively clad shoulders lifted in a slight shrug. "I spend a great deal of time at the office. Lisa—my wife—handles the household help."

"Then let's talk more about you. Any problems with neighbors?"

"Neighbors?"

"No complaints, no bad blood with any of them?"

"No. We—" Lockhart broke off, his eyes narrowing. "That damn Stone kid. He's got to be the one."

"One of your neighbors' kids?" Coleman asked.

"The Stones—Sam and Rina—they live on the next street over. Our garages face each other. Jason is a piece of Goth garbage. Wears those outlandish clothes; always in black. Sullen, hair and nails always filthy."

"And you have reason to believe he might have been involved in the bombing?"

"He ran over our dog a few months ago."

Coleman's eyebrows rose at what sounded like a non sequitur. "You're saying he deliberately ran over your dog?"

"You better believe it was deliberate. And this bomb could be retaliation because I called the police on him. He could be a little serial killer in the making. You know how they start with torturing animals. He could be working his way up to something like a Sandy Hook or Virginia Tech."

Jovanic refrained from telling him that Sandy Hook and Virginia Tech were mass murders, not serial killings, which were different types of crimes. "Most teenagers aren't likely to delay gratification for 'a few months.'" Jovanic kept the skepticism out of his voice. "What makes you think Jason was involved?"

"Lisa and I were getting ready to leave for a weekend in Palm Springs. Our son was bringing the grandkids to our condo for a family party. We don't get to see them nearly enough since they moved to Scottsdale. We were really looking forward to going." Lockhart, whose expression had brightened while he spoke about his grandchildren, paused, switching gears. "Sam and Rina had gone off somewhere and left the boy at home alone, which is the dumbest decision they could have ever made. He's all of sixteen and, of course, he had to throw a party. Rowdy teenagers skateboarding up and down the alley, beer bottles, loud punk rock music blaring. The entire neighborhood *reeked* of marijuana. You could smell it up here with the windows closed."

"You called the police?" Coleman prompted.

"Naturally. They came out right away and shut it down; sent those entitled brats packing. I spoke to Sam about it when they got home. A complete dead end. He has no idea how to discipline the boy. Lazy brat hangs around watching TV all day and partying all night. I doubt he makes it to school half the time."

"You know a lot about Jason's activities," Jovanic said, thinking that Lockhart seemed to know more about the neighbor's kid than his own housekeeper of several years. "Has Jason ever been in any serious trouble that you know of, Mr. Lockhart, aside from when you called the police on him and his friends?"

"You'd have to ask the Stones. I wouldn't have heard unless it was something egregious. If that happened, there are a couple of old biddies in the neighborhood who would have made sure it got around."

Jovanic made a mental note to have Scott and Hardcastle interview the biddies. "I'd like to get their names and addresses," he said. "You're not aware of him getting into fights at school or making threats against other students, or violence of any other kind?"

"As I said, he ran over my dog shortly after the police incident. Isn't that enough?"

"Ran over your dog, driving what?"

"His mother's Lexus, Detective. I'm telling you, this boy runs wild."

"Are you close friends with the family, Mr. Lockhart?"

"Not at all. We see Sam and Rina occasionally for drinks because they're our neighbors, just like we see our other neighbors, but that's all there is to it." He pointed a long, thin finger at the detectives, speaking with more than a touch of asperity. "You should definitely be looking at that boy."

"You can count on it, sir. We will." It was doubtful the lead would go anywhere. Still, you never knew when a tip might be worth pursuing, and when you had nothing else to go on, you followed what you had. He wrote "Jason Stone" in his notebook and jotted the address Lockhart gave him. "What about anyone else? Have there been any kind of threats, or are you aware of anyone that might have a grudge against you?"

"No, no personal threats—" Lockhart broke off. The sudden bunching of his jaw told Jovanic that he was withholding something. Before he could ask about it, female voices echoed from below and Lockhart turned expectantly toward the sound. They heard a door close, then the tap-tap of light footsteps on the staircase and a woman glided into the room.

The men rose when Evan Lockhart introduced his wife. In her early fifties, Lisa Lockhart was a striking woman by any standard. She wore a navy-blue sheath under a white cashmere sweater with a lustrous strand of pearls. Frosted blonde hair swept into an up-do. The fingertips she extended to each of the detectives were cool, her handshake delicate. She turned golden eyes on Jovanic, reminding him of a tiger, flashing a warning: *Watch out. I'm dangerous.*

"Good morning, detectives," she said, with a warm smile that evaporated the fierce feline image. "Please sit down. I hope my husband has offered you something to drink?"

"We're fine, thank you."

"I would be more than happy to get you a cup of coffee or tea, a glass of water?" Lisa's musical voice carried a slight southern twang. "I'm assuming you can't drink anything stronger on the job?"

"Please don't trouble yourself; we won't be much longer."

Lisa Lockhart sat beside her husband and crossed one slim ankle over the other. "Have you learned anything new? Poor Sylvia." She shuddered. "Can you imagine anything more awful? What she must have gone through? It makes me sick to think about it."

"The coroner has established Ms. Vasquez's death was the result of a heart attack. Were you aware that she had heart problems?"

"No, I can't say I was. But Sylvia has always kept pretty much to herself. She did a fine job for us, Detective, but we never discussed things of a personal nature."

Confirming what her husband had said.

"I understand she worked for you for six or seven years?" Jovanic asked.

"Is that what Evan told you? She was actually with us for almost nine years. The thing was, she didn't speak much English—just enough to get by—and I've never learned much Spanish, though I know I should. All I know is, *buenos dias, por favor, gracias.* Just the basics. It's never been a big problem because we have another woman who comes in twice a week to help out; this house is too much for just one person to keep up. Maria is fluent in English and Spanish; she always translates anything important." Lisa Lockhart's fashionably tattooed brows knit in a perplexed frown. "I can't understand someone living in a country all those years and never learning the language, can you?"

"I think she understood plenty," her husband chimed in. "It was just easier for her to let us think she didn't. That way, she didn't have to bother."

Lisa pointed an indulgent smile at him. "I know you think that, darling, but who's to say? Besides, I can't imagine her grasp of the language had anything to do with what happened here."

Considering Evan Lockhart's lack of knowledge about the housekeeper, Jovanic found it interesting that he had an opinion about her grasp of English. "Mr. Lockhart, before your wife came in, we were talking about possible enemies. You specified that you had no *personal* enemies, but what about in your business? Anything you can think of there that might be an issue?"

Lockhart looked uncomfortable. "Any company like ours is the target of protests from time to time. But this was an attack on my home, not my office."

Jovanic's research had turned up the fact that Evan Lockhart, MBA, was chairman of the board of Agrichem, one of the world's largest pesticide corporations, a fact that raised interesting possibilities. Sidestepping Lockhart's last comment, he asked, "Protests about—?"

"Oh, you know the kind of thing. People claiming we're killing the bees, or that our products are harming babies. Those claims are entirely without merit."

"What happens when these protests take place? How are they handled?"

"We prefer to avoid unfavorable publicity. We handle it privately whenever we can."

"What does that mean?" Coleman probed. "*How* is it handled?"

For the second time, Lockhart shifted in his chair, re-crossing his legs. The crease in his trousers was sharp enough to cut paper, but he fiddled with it anyway, his fingers plucking the fabric into a peak. "Sometimes people are misguided in their grieving. Maybe a loved one has been sick, perhaps died. The family is devastated; they're looking for someone to blame. From time to time someone claims one or another of our products has caused them harm. Occasionally a lawsuit is threatened. In those cases, our attorneys have a tendency to advise settling in order to avoid getting into the news cycle."

"What happens if the person agrees to a settlement?"

"The complainant is required to sign a document releasing the company from liability and the agreement is sealed. They are not permitted to discuss the terms of the agreement with anyone."

A little frisson of instinct told Jovanic there was more to be discovered in this line of questioning. "And what if the person doesn't agree?" he asked.

"Oh, they always agree, Detective. It's all about money."

"Other than those instances that have been settled, sir, have any personal threats been made to you or anyone else at the company?"

Almost before he had finished speaking, Lockhart was shaking his head. "No, nothing personal. The last event was a break-in about three months ago at our laboratory up in the Antelope Valley in Lancaster. Vandals broke in and did some damage to the lab, spray-painted the walls, that kind of thing. Nothing major, and nothing was taken."

"Was this over animal experimentation?"

"No, no, nothing like that. Just computers, paperwork."

"What did they paint on the walls? A message?"

"I'd have to check with the lab director, Detective."

"Was a report filed with the police?"

"I wouldn't expect so. As I said, the damage wasn't all that great, a few thousand at most. Since we're trying to keep a low profile, it seemed best to keep it internal."

Jovanic rose. "Mr. and Mrs. Lockhart, thank you for your time. We'll be speaking with you again soon."

"He's not telling us everything," Coleman said. "What's he hiding?"

"Could be corporate nonsense, trying to hide behind the legal crap. We might get more out of him if we corner him in his office; or better yet, ours." Jovanic checked his watch. Close to noon. School was closed for winter recess. "Let's hop over to the Stones' house. Maybe Jason the dog killer is home."

seven

Rina Stone could not have been more unlike her neighbor, Lisa Lockhart, if she had spent a month working on it. Short, heading toward pudgy—Jovanic's Jewish grandmother would have called her *zaftig*—she wore a black T-shirt dusted with something that looked like flour over loose-fitting mom jeans. When she opened the door, the aroma of baking cookies wafted onto the porch, momentarily diverting Jovanic's attention from the hard-pounding sounds of a video game that echoed from the second floor. It curled into his nostrils, making his mouth water. Breakfast seemed a very long time ago.

He showed Rina Stone his ID and introduced himself and Coleman. Her eyes widened in alarm. "Oh, dear God, what happened? Is it Sam? Did something happen to Sam?"

Jovanic put up a calming hand. "We're not here about your husband, Mrs. Stone. Is Jason home? We'd like to speak with him."

Rina frowned. "Jason? Why? What's he being accused of now?"

"Nothing that we know of. We've been talking to some of the neighbors about what happened at the Lockharts' home the other day—the explosion? Jason's name came up in connection with something else, a disturbance a few weeks ago."

"That darned Evan Lockhart. I know that's who said something." From the way her expression hardened, Jovanic had a feeling there would be no more sharing of drinks between the neighbors.

Stone said, "He's got it in for my Jason. He'd find any excuse to give our boy grief."

"May we come in, Mrs. Stone? We'll just take a few minutes of your time."

"You said this was about the explosion. We already talked to the police on the day that poor woman died."

"I understand, but we still need to speak to your son." Jovanic moved a half-step toward the door, guessing that her automatic reflex would be to give way. He guessed right.

Rina Stone stepped back, opening the door wider. "Well—I guess—" The two detectives moved past her into the entry hall, but she stopped short of inviting them any further inside. "Why are you here?"

Jovanic could see over her shoulder into the living room. This home reflected its mistress: lived in, a newspaper spread out on the couch, a coffee cup on the cocktail table. On a wall-mounted wide screen TV, Drew Carey worked up the audience on *The Price is Right*.

"We'd like to speak with your son, please."

Rina Stone bustled over to the cocktail table and snatched up the remote, muting the sound. "What is it you want from Jason?" she asked again, returning to face the detectives. She might not be as well put together as her neighbors, but when it came to her son, she was ready to defend him against attack.

Jovanic ignored her question. "You indicated that Mr. Lockhart has something against your son?"

Stone hesitated. "There was an accident." She gave a defensive sniff. "It was *Evan's* fault. He'd left his stupid dog running around the alley. It's illegal to let a dog run loose around here, isn't it? They're supposed to be on a leash, right?"

When the detectives said nothing, she went on. "Barton—can you imagine naming a dog *Barton*? It was some yappy little breed. A Jack Russell, I think. You know how they jump up and get in your face, bark constantly?

Anyhow, Jason was practicing for his driving test and that darn dog ran right out in front of the car. You can just imagine how traumatic it was for a sixteen-year-old boy."

Pretty traumatic for the dog, too, Jovanic thought. "The dog died?"

"Oh yes. It was horrible. A real mess. I can't stand to think about it." She winced as if to emphasize her aversion to the memory.

Jovanic calculated how fast the boy might have been driving in the alley between the homes. Had he been aiming for the dog, as Evan Lockhart had accused, or was it truly an accident? If not, would that extrapolate to setting a cherry bomb? "Was anyone in the car with Jason? An adult?"

"Well, no." The woman's face flushed. "Look, I *know* he's supposed to have a licensed adult driver with him, but he was just driving around the block, practicing. Didn't you do that when you were learning to drive?" When neither detective responded, she raised her chin in defiance. "If the Lockharts had obeyed the law, the accident never would have happened and their dog would be just fine. Then they'd just have to find something else to gripe about."

And if you had obeyed the law and not allowed your unlicensed son to drive, the dog would be alive and well.

He wanted to tell her to go fuck herself, but that would not be productive. "Is Jason home, Mrs. Stone?" He asked the question again, though the video game sounds streaming from upstairs had already supplied the answer. "We won't take long."

Rina Stone glared at him, but she shouted up the staircase, "Jase! *Jason!*"

As loud as the soundtrack was booming, Jovanic did not expect a response, and there was none. Jason's mother raised her voice, calling his name louder.

A sullen voice yelled back. "*What?*"

"The police are here. They want to talk to you."

"The fuck, Mom?"

"Language Jason. Would you please come down here, honey?"

Jovanic put his foot on the bottom riser of the staircase. "If it's all right with you, Mrs. Stone, we'll just talk to him in his room."

"Well, I'm not sure. I guess it's okay. But I'm going to call my husband. He's on the road today. Maybe I should call our lawyer if I can't reach him."

"That's up to you. We just have some questions for him."

Rina Stone answered with a grunt that implied she had long ago given up on getting what she wanted. "Jason's room is at the top of the stairs, first on the right. Just follow the noise."

Jason Stone, a brown knit beanie drooping off the back of his head, slouched in a red vinyl beanbag chair that faced a widescreen TV bigger than the one in Claudia's living room. He was swaying from side to side, the game controller clutched tight enough to whiten his knuckles in an attempt to prevent a helicopter from landing on the roof of a yellow Ferrari. Jovanic recognized the game as *Grand Theft Auto*.

Before coming to the house, the detectives had decided that Randy Coleman would take the lead. In his early thirties, he was young enough for the teen to identify with him more than Jovanic, but old enough to carry some weight. It left Jovanic feeling ancient.

Coleman gave him the 'I'm a cop, you'd better listen up' tone. "Jason. We're here to talk to you."

The boy ignored him and continued to tap buttons and jerk the joystick. Coleman strode over to the TV and switched it off. Jason slammed the controller to the floor and erupted from the beanbag chair. "The fuck you do that for?"

"Do I have your attention now?"

"You totally fucked me over, dude. I was almost done with that level."

Jovanic took in the bloodshot eyes and pasty skin. Coleman must have too. He sniffed the air. "You smoking weed in here, Jason?"

Jason whined, "What do you want?" His eyes went toward the door, as if willing his mother to come and rescue him.

"Hey, *look* at me when I talk to you," Coleman said.

Grudgingly, the boy brought his eyes up. "What the *fuck*?"

"You got no room for attitude, dude. We heard about you driving your mom's car without a license. Killed your neighbor's dog. You do it on purpose?"

Jason was unimpressed. "That was like, a long time ago. Moms lets me practice in her car if I stuck to the 'hood.'"

"Did she say it was okay to smoke dope in the house, too? I could smell that shit a block away."

More sulk. "No."

Jovanic decided it was time to cut in. "What else you been up to, Jason? Why don't you tell me about planting that bomb in your neighbor's mailbox? Was it a prank, or were you *trying* to kill that woman, like you did the dog?" He knew he had hit a soft spot when a fine sheen of sweat broke out on the teen's forehead.

"Hey, what are you talking about? I didn't have nothing to do with what happened to that lady. I swear to God, you guys. That Lockhart dude, he hates me, but I didn't *touch* his mailbox, but—" he broke off, his lip curled in a sneer. "Whoever did it was pretty badass."

Jovanic took a threatening step towards him. "You think it was badass that their housekeeper was killed, you little punk?"

Tall and gangly as the boy was, he backed up and tripped over the beanbag, landing in an ungainly sprawl. Flushed a deep beet color, he leapt back to his feet and tried to gather his dignity.

"Well, uh, no, that part wasn't cool, but I didn't know her. What do I care? Blowing up that ole fucktard's mailbox, though—wish I *had* thought of it."

"Oh really? You want to go to jail for two or three years?"

Jason's eyes widened. "You're shitting me. Just for setting off a cherry bomb?"

"How'd you know it was a cherry bomb?"

"That's what everyone at school said."

"Is everyone at school talking about who did it?"

"No, dude. They just thought it was pretty funny. I would hear about it if a kid at my school did it."

"Well, somebody died. Either way, it's a felony. Think about it, asshole."

"Hey, I'm totally sorry, dudes, er, I mean...detectives." Apparently sensing an opportunity to get himself out of a jam, Jason spread his hands in a gesture of entreaty. "Honest, sirs, I didn't mean anything by what I said. I'm serious; I didn't have *anything* to do with that cherry—thing that blew up."

The way he was falling over himself to be polite reminded Jovanic of a character in the *Leave it to Beaver* TV show of his youth. Eddie Haskell had adopted that same shit-eating smile when he knew he was in trouble. He poked the boy hard in the chest, meaning to cause pain.

"You'd better adjust your attitude, *dude*. You're nowhere near as tough as you think you are." He pulled a business card out of his coat pocket. "If you hear *anything* about how that device got into the mailbox, or why it was put there, I expect you to call me. Got it?"

"Yeah, sure, sir. I will, for sure."

From the doorway behind them, the boy's mother loudly cleared her throat. "Uh, excuse me, Officers, I just spoke to my husband and he said you have to leave *now*. He's on his way home."

"We were just leaving," Jovanic said. They stepped past her on the way out. "Thank you for your time."

Rina Stone followed them downstairs and shut the door hard behind them. They heard the lock engage.

"That kid's gonna end up killing someone one day," Coleman said as they trudged back to the Crown Vic. The rain had dwindled to a fine mist, though the sky was still the color of an arctic seal.

"Yeah, but his daddy will cough up the bucks for a big mucky-muck attorney to get him off." Jovanic climbed into the passenger side, glad to let Coleman drive. Too bad the lead on the Stone kid hadn't panned out better. But it was a lead he was not giving up on yet.

He got out his phone and checked a text message that had arrived while they were in Jason Stone's bedroom, relaxing when he saw it was from RJ Scott calling them back to the station.

Since the assault on Claudia, every call or text that landed in his phone made him jumpy. She tried to hide it from him, but her brittle emotional state was never far from his mind. How could he not notice the jittery way she kept peering through the drapes of her upstairs office, standing off to the side so that someone standing on the street looking up would be unable to see her? Whenever they left the house together, she was hyper-vigilant, constantly on the alert, scanning for danger. He had asked for a patrol unit to keep watch, but the department's budget would not allow more than two days.

Scott and Hardcastle were at their desks. Jovanic plopped into his chair. "What's up?"

Scott waved a pink slip of paper. "Front desk took a call, sounds promising. Some geocachers found—"

"Wait," Jovanic interjected. "Geo-whats?"

"Geocachers. You don't know what geocaching is?"

"Pretend I don't. Enlighten me."

"It's sort of like a modern treasure hunt. People register on a website. Either they hide something in a container—the geocache—and list it on the site for other members to find, or they search for a geocache someone else has listed there. The GPS coordinates are posted. They give the general area to look."

"You mean, it's like a search for buried treasure?"

"No, it can't be buried. That's in the rules—the container has to be above ground. When someone finds the cache, they'll find a logbook inside for them to sign. Sometimes the finder might take something from the container, but if they do, they're supposed to leave something in its place."

"Why have I never heard of this?" Jovanic asked.

"Because you're older than dirt," Coleman cracked. "I have friends who've been geocaching for years. They love it."

"I know a bunch of people who do it, too," said Scott. "The website says there's over a million geocaches worldwide."

"A *million*?"

"Gamers have to follow the rules or they can't play," Hardcastle added.

"Wait. You knew about this, too?"

"Sure, JJ. I'm kinda surprised you didn't."

"What are the rules, besides not burying the container?"

"Like, don't leave food in the cache so it doesn't rot, or so animals can't get to it and get the container open and mess everything up."

"And this relates to our case how?" Coleman asked. "Yogi Bear was the bomber?"

"Very funny, Randy, I'm getting there." Scott's rejoinder was tinged with annoyance at Coleman's silliness. "The person who called in located a container in Venice and found—wait, let me show you." She fished her phone out of her pocket and tapped a few commands. "I told him to email me photos."

Displayed on the screen was a plastic baggie that contained a wrapped candy bar and a folded piece of paper. "Somebody broke the 'no food' rule," said Jovanic.

"Big Cherry," said Hardcastle. "I didn't think they still made them. Used to eat 'em all the time when I was a kid."

"Yeah, and that makes *you* older than dirt squared," said Coleman. "But what's the connection, RJ? Cherry—cherry bomb?"

"What's this piece of paper, RJ?" Jovanic broke in. "Something that made the finder think they ought to call it in?"

"Ding, ding, ding, you win the prize." RJ Scott flipped to the next screen, a photo of the paper, now unfolded. On its face were a few hand-printed words:

More bombs than cherries soon. It's personal.

Randy Coleman frowned. "Another bombing?"

Scott flipped to the next screen, which showed what appeared to be a page from a small notebook. The paper was unlined and contained a row of signatures and handwritten notations with dates. The logbook she had told them about.

The last entry on the page contained the words "People for Safe Food."

"People for Safe Food?" Coleman echoed as Jovanic passed the phone to him. "Who the heck are they?"

"Huey checked it out," said Scott. "It's an organized group that protests pesticides being used around food sources."

"Our homeowner, Lockhart, is the chairman of the board of Agrichem," Jovanic said, feeling a thrum of interest. "They make pesticides. Maybe their products harm cherry trees? Could the use of a cherry bomb be ironic? And now they've gotten personal by targeting the CEO of the company?"

"In that case, they screwed up royally," Hardcastle said. "Killing the housekeeper was probably not on the agenda."

"And it shoots our theory to hell. This wasn't done by kids."

eight

"Yes, Aunty C, I know who Jason Stone is."

Claudia's niece, Monica, was a sweet girl who had a habit of giving the benefit of the doubt to everyone, even when they did not deserve it. The disdain in her voice spoke volumes.

"It sounds like you don't think too much of him."

"Jason Stone thinks he's God's gift to everything. He's always bragging how his parents don't know what's up and how he can get away with whatever he wants. I know, because my friend was going out with him and he dumped her."

"He's not in your grade, is he?"

"He's not supposed to be, but he got held back. He's always cutting school and he never studies."

"Sounds like a real prince."

"Why are you asking about Jason?"

"Just something that came up."

"Is he in trouble or something? He probably deserves it if he is." The scorn again. "He's such a creep. I heard he killed his neighbor's dog and thought it was funny. What a sicko creep. Annabelle wanted to kick his butt, but I talked her out of it."

"I'm glad you stopped her. I don't suppose you've heard anything about Jason and a cherry bomb?"

"You mean that bomb in Venice? Did Jason do that?"

"Not that I know of. Anyway, you're smart enough to stay away from someone like that."

"That's for sure," Monica agreed. "Do you need me for anything else, Aunty C? Annabelle just got here. We're doing our algebra homework."

"No, kiddo, that's about it. Have fun and say hi to Annabelle for me."

Claudia ended the call, nostalgic for the "old days." She remembered her school years as a time when all she had to worry about was whether a guy she liked felt the same way, not whether her classmates were setting off bombs and killing neighborhood pets.

Sweeping aside the memories, she checked her email. Jovanic had sent photos of two sets of handwriting along with a note that he would call to explain. There was a new development in the Venice bombing case and he was interested in learning what the handwriting might say about the personality of the writer or writers. One photo was labeled "logbook.jpg" and the other was "note.jpg."

Unlike in Danny Ortiz's case, where her task had been to authenticate certain handwriting, today she was being asked to determine the potential for pathological behavior.

After enlarging the pictures on screen for better viewing, Claudia printed the photos on glossy paper and placed them side-by-side on her desk. Having a sheet of paper to hold and examine provided a different perspective from the monitor. Still, having just a few words to examine made the task more difficult. The more handwriting, the more comfortable she could feel in the accuracy of her assessment. She was working largely in the dark.

Studying the image from the logbook, first on paper, then the enlargement on the monitor, she could make a few educated guesses and report to Jovanic what she had found. Not knowing the gender or the age of the writer further limited the conclusions she could reach. He understood the restrictions in doing an analysis this way.

If she'd had the writer's chronological age, she could have formed an opinion about the depth of his or her emotional maturity. However, age could not reliably be determined from handwriting alone. There were plenty of samples in Claudia's collection that looked as though they had been written by a teen, but had actually been produced by an adult in their thirties or older. Since many schools no longer taught children penmanship it had become even more true.

Furthermore, handwriting revealed traits that might be considered traditionally "masculine" or "feminine," but could not conclusively identify gender. Some women wrote in a more linear style, which pointed to more interest in intellectual pursuits than people and emotions. The converse was true, too. Some men's handwriting displayed what used to be considered feminine traits of empathy and compassion. In the twenty-first century, those lines were becoming blurred, making gender even harder to define.

The handwriting Jovanic had sent was linear and small, with wide spaces between the words. This put it in the category of more intellectually than emotionally oriented. The left slant, Claudia thought of as being like a slingshot drawn back as taut as it could be. It signified one who tended to filter all his experiences through his intellect, was uncomfortable expressing feelings, and who restrained them until the pent-up emotions built to a point where they had to be released—or, in Claudia's mental image, letting go of the sling.

What kind of stimulus would it take to release the "sling?" she wondered. It was a question she could not answer. But one thing was for sure: when the writer let go, she would not want to be there to bear the brunt of the explosion. In this case, perhaps literally.

Was she looking at the handwriting of the person responsible for booby-trapping the mailbox with the cherry bomb—the cause of that poor housekeeper's death?

Claudia released a big sigh. In addition to the lack of information about gender or age, without the original document it was impossible to determine the absolute pressure of the pen against the paper. From what she could tell from the photos, the pressure appeared to be exceptionally light. Assuming that was the case, it affirmed her earlier opinion and added to a strong potential for the writer to be a hell-raiser.

She tapped a few keys to enlarge the writing on the screen even further. Spotting a tiny bend in the *ductus*—literally, the "channel" that carried the ink on the paper—she zoomed in closer. The bend appeared at the tops of some letters that had upper extenders, such as "l," "h," and "b."

In similar instances, where she had observed the same phenomenon, the writer's thought processes had been affected by a blow to the head, which was reflected in their handwriting. Even a supposed minor closed head injury, depending on where it occurred, had the potential to change the victim's worldview.

Paranoid ideation. The words came to her automatically. Was this writer the suspicious type who believed others were out to harm him, despite evidence to the contrary? That's what the diagnostic term meant. If he had left the cherry bomb at the residence in Venice, would he have acted alone, or was he part of an organized group?

Judging from the handwriting, he lacked true emotional connection to others. He might well be amenable to participating in a group, yet keep his distance on a deeper level. He would allow very few others to get close.

He would question authority and was suspicious of anyone who might try to put one over on him. Yet, he did not look like someone who would take the lead in a group. These were questions the police investigation would need to address.

By the time Jovanic phoned, Claudia was prepared to give him her opinion on the handwriting samples. It turned out that he wanted more than that. "I need you to meet me near the Lagoon." He was referring to a park not far from Claudia's house where families came to feed the ducks and play in the sand.

Her heart rate quickened at the thought of leaving the house, though the Lagoon was scarcely more than a mile away. Her ribs were healing and her face no longer looked like she'd been stung by a thousand bees, but every time she looked in the mirror the faint bruises that remained reminded her that 'outside' was just not safe.

"Why?" she asked him. "What's going on?"

"I have to pick up some evidence—the items in the photos I emailed you. I want you to see them before I book them into evidence."

"But I've already done my analysis."

"Understood. But if this case ever goes to court, you'll be able to testify that you saw the originals. You've always told me that was best."

She could hardly argue with the logic since it *was* her own. And, as she had just told herself, without the original documents she would not be able to determine the pressure. Without the added dimension of viewing the originals she would have to qualify her opinion.

"One other thing," Jovanic added. "I'd like you to take handwriting specimens from the couple who found the container—"

"To rule them out as the writers," Claudia finished for him. Research showed that often, the person who received an anonymous note, or in this case *found* a note, was the one who had written it. Some did it out of a need to draw attention to themselves. Receiving an anonymous note was one way of getting into the spotlight. Others had vengeance in mind. More than once Claudia had identified a spurned wife as both the recipient and the writer of a note that outed her husband as a cheater. By taking a sample of the finder's handwriting she could determine whether they were dealing with someone who was on the up-and-up, or someone who had planted evidence.

"Just bring them to my office. It would be more comfortable and I have all the proper equipment here."

"I can ask them to come to the police station, but you can't stay holed up in the house forever, Claudia." His exasperation came through loud and clear.

Her instincts told her to refuse, to make an excuse and beg off. But she knew he was right. She had to fight the urge to hide. Besides, she reminded herself, Danny Ortiz had come close to killing her and she had survived. She was damned if she would let him interfere with her work, her life. She pulled in a deep breath. "Where should I meet you?"

"Park near the bridge at the sea wall end. I'll find you."

nine

THE CROWN VIC WAS in the small parking lot at Pacific and 62nd, but he was nowhere to be seen. Claudia parked in the space next to the vehicle and texted Jovanic to let him know she had arrived. She switched off the Jag's engine and the windshield wipers abruptly stopped flapping back and forth, leaving behind a gray silence.

In a matter of moments a steady drizzle had accumulated, obscuring her view of the long rock jetty that separated the Pacific Ocean from Ballona Creek. The bicycle riders and joggers who frequented the path across the footbridge were absent in the miserable afternoon. She was alone.

She checked to make sure the doors were still locked, then leaned back against the headrest and let her eyelids drift closed. The last few nights had been far too short, though it was not the beating she had taken from Danny Ortiz in the courtroom that invaded her dreams and kept her staring at the ceiling. It was the memories of kidnapping, torture, and murder that coalesced into a single nightmare that had returned to haunt her every night—places her work had taken her in the past few years that she would be happy to forget. Staying awake was the one sure way to deflect them, but she was so tired ...

A light knock on the passenger window nearly sent her through the roof.

Jovanic's worried face peered in at her from the passenger side. Claudia fumbled the electric door lock, angry with herself for overreacting.

He opened the door and leaned inside. "Sorry, babe. I didn't mean to scare you." He slid into the seat, brushing mist off his suit coat, and shut the door.

She couldn't help lashing out. "Where the hell were you?"

"In Coleman's ride on the next street, talking to the witnesses."

Reminding herself that Jovanic was not the enemy, sleep was, she modulated her tone. "I was dozing. I didn't hear you."

He reached over and squeezed her hand. His skin was cold, but not as cold as her own. "Maybe you should consider taking something to help you sleep at night."

"Thanks for the advice, but I'd rather not walk around like a zombie the next day."

Jovanic's lips flattened as if he would have liked to say something more. Instead, he said, "These kids found a geocache container under the bridge—" He broke off to make sure Claudia knew what a geocache was, then continued, "When they read the notation in the logbook—which is what I emailed you—they called in to report it. They'd seen the news about the mailbox bomb the other day and made the connection."

"Where are these people now?"

He jerked his head in the direction of the footbridge. "Waiting in Randy's car. I know it's not an ideal place for you to take their exemplars, but it's best to do it while everything's still fresh."

"Before they have time to think up ways to disguise their handwriting if they have any involvement with the bombing," Claudia added.

"Precisely." Jovanic gave her a rare wink. "You sure you don't want to become a cop?"

She grinned back at him. "Because I'm *so* good at following orders?"

"Oh, that. Maybe not." He handed her a bulky manila envelope he'd been protecting inside his coat. "This is the original logbook and note. Did you bring gloves?"

Claudia reached over for her field case on the floor next to his feet. "This ain't my first rodeo, Columbo."

She fished out a pair of nitrile examination gloves and two plastic sleeves the size of a sheet of copy paper. Since the witnesses had already handled the evidence, there was little point in wearing the gloves, but at least she would not further contaminate the documents. The gloves warmed her hands, but made her fingers a little clumsy as she opened the envelope and withdrew the contents.

The small sheet of paper—the note—and the bound logbook, were already familiar from the photos she had viewed in her office. After placing the original note inside one plastic sleeve and the logbook in the other, Claudia asked Jovanic to hold them while she got out her cell phone and a miniature magnifying lens. She fit the lens over the camera's built-in one to increase the magnifying power and held it over the note, viewing it little by little until she was satisfied. She took a series of photographs, then repeated the process with the logbook.

"Is there that big a difference when you see the original?" Jovanic asked, sounding genuinely curious.

"It's like the difference between seeing someone in the flesh and looking at a painting. The original documents bring the writing to life."

"What do you think?"

"Don't rush me, I need a minute."

The logbook was a small leather-bound journal, its pages filled with the signatures and notations of gamers who had found the geocache and logged their find. Running a practiced eye over them, Claudia saw nothing of interest for the purposes of her examination until she came to the last entry, the one they were concerned with.

The words "People for Safe Food" had been written in place of a signature.

"Is Amy Reed the witness?" she asked, pointing to the signature below the questioned writing.

"Amy Reed and the one above hers, Chad Walton. They're a young couple. Twenties. Their story is, they signed the log, but after reading the note that was left in the geocache, then hearing about the mailbox bomb on the news later, they started getting suspicious and decided to report it."

"Sounds pretty responsible."

"Yes, and I bet they're just peachy. But we can't assume anything, which is why you're here."

"If you're hoping these kids might have written the note, I can tell you right now that neither of them did."

"Good to know. I still need you to take exemplars from them, for the record."

"Of course, but there's some other things you need to know. The document—the logbook—has been altered. Whoever wrote 'People for Safe Food' was attempting to cover up some other writing by writing over the top of it."

"How can you tell?"

Claudia directed him to the entry. "See here, the ink looks heavier at the beginning of the word 'People.' That word was written right over the top of something else. I could see that much in the image you emailed, but when I enlarged it with the computer, it wasn't possible to tell what was written underneath. I need to get the original under an alternate light source."

"Go for it."

"I'd like to use UV, but it's not dark enough out here."

Jovanic shook his head. "Chain of custody. Just in case a miracle happens, we get lucky and arrest someone, file a case with the DA. The whole geocache container and everything in it has to be booked into evidence before any part of it goes anywhere else, including your office."

"You're telling me you always play it strictly by the book?"

"Are you sure you want to go there, Claudia?"

She started to make a snarky crack, but looking back into the face she loved—now set in disapproving lines—she decided to back off. Jovanic had sacrificed plenty for her, and this was not important enough to make an issue.

"You're right. We don't need to go there. You're just lucky I brought along my handy-dandy portable infrared viewer, which is the next best thing. I do need some room to work, though."

"No problem." Jovanic climbed out, then leaned back to haul out her field case. "Care to join me in the backseat?"

"Oh yes, but we're working."

They grinned at each other like teenagers.

The temperature had dropped several degrees in the short time since Claudia had driven down the hill. The few moments it took to move from the front seat to the back left her face icy. She pulled the door shut behind her, her breath clouding in the warmer air inside the car. "There's not much more room back here," she grumbled, shifting her booted feet in the small area. "Your knees are under your chin."

"I'm fine, just do your hocus pocus."

As she plugged her portable digital microscope into a USB port on her laptop and booted it up, Claudia explained that she had rigged it to take photographs in the infrared spectrum. "This should show up what's written underneath that word. I need you to hold the IR flashlight. Just aim it at the altered writing." She showed him how.

Under the infrared light, the ink fluoresced and brought four letters into view that had been concealed. Claudia clicked an icon on the laptop and the software captured the image. She squinted at the screen. "Looks like a capital D, lowercase a, and a lowercase x. D-a-x. That's a man's name, isn't it?"

"Yeah, I've heard it before. I think there's an actor with that name."

"We've got the start of another capital, too. I'm not sure, but I think it could be a C or possibly an O. First name, and a segment of a stroke that goes nowhere."

"I'll run it through the databases when I get back to the office, see if anything comes up."

"Can I take a stab at what happened?"

"Go for it."

"This Dax person started to sign his own name, then realized that was a bad idea—too incriminating if he'd just left a bomb and was writing a note that connected him to it. He stopped what he was writing and wrote 'People for Safe Food' over the top to cover it up."

"Good guess. I'll see what I can dig up on that group, too."

"That's all I can do here." Claudia repacked her field case. "Let's go and take the exemplars before your witnesses start getting antsy."

Randy Coleman's bright red Prius stood out against the drab afternoon, like a robin on a winter postcard.

Coleman climbed out of the vehicle and greeted them. He opened the front passenger door for Claudia, then he and Jovanic moved a few feet along the sidewalk to give her some space with the young couple huddled together in the backseat. Their eyes were bright with the feverish thrill of having discovered something potentially important.

"Hi, I'm Claudia," she said, slipping into the front seat. "I'm the handwriting examiner."

"I'm Chad," the young man said. "And this is Amy."

Both had the Hollywood look common to many West L.A. residents. Chad's spiky blond hair and wispy moustache pegged him as a wannabe actor. Claudia imagined him waiting tables between auditions, the standard occupation for entertainment industry hopefuls. Amy's winged black brows and wet-look crimson lips seemed incongruent in the casual setting. Glossy black hair flowed from under a knit cap that framed a pretty face. She, too, was ready for her close-up.

Claudia apologized for keeping them waiting.

"No prob," said Chad. "It's actually been kind of interesting, seeing how the cops work."

"How long have you been geocaching?"

"We started a few months ago. It's really cool, you find all kinds of things." He grinned. "Obviously."

"That guy in charge." Amy glanced longingly at the cell phone in her hand. "What's his name, Chad? Detective—?"

"Yo something, something. It sounded like Russian maybe."

"Detective Jovanic," Claudia filled in for them. "It's spelled with a 'J' but pronounced 'Yo-*Vah*-nitch.'" She refrained from telling them the name was Croatian, not Russian.

"Yeah, that guy. He told us we can't text or call anyone about what we found. We had to promise."

Claudia gave a sympathetic smile. "It wouldn't be good to have it all over the Internet before the police get to do an investigation."

Amy wrinkled the pert nose, which made her look like a twelve-year-old. "That bites. You know it's gonna get out anyway. Stuff like this always does."

"Just think, you'll be able to tell your friends later; maybe get interviewed on the news, who knows?"

"That'd be cool."

Chad said, "That Detective Yo-jo told us we have to give you some handwriting, but like I told him, I never handwrite. I always text or IM."

Claudia guessed he was talking about Snapchat or something equally 'today.'

"Why do they need *our* handwriting?" Amy asked.

"We'll use it to eliminate each of you as being the person who wrote the note you found."

"Well, that's easy, we didn't write it."

"I know, but this is to protect you. It won't take long and it's super easy."

Chad gave Amy a gentle nudge. "You know, Ame, this could be all kinds of exciting. Hey, maybe it'll be like on TV, when someone who reports a crime gets accused of being the suspect. I could use that in my next audition."

Claudia had to grin at his enthusiasm. "Down, Chad. Nobody thinks you planted the note." Then, noticing that Amy was peering at her with frank curiosity, she asked, "What? Do I have dirt on my nose?"

"No, no, sorry, I didn't mean to stare. I just have this feeling like we've met before. I'm trying to figure out where."

"Maybe you've been to a lecture I gave. I speak about handwriting to all kinds of groups."

"Mmm, no, I'm pretty sure that wasn't—hmmm."

Claudia saw it the moment the memory kicked into place. Amy's mouth dropped open. "I remember now. Some guy attacked you at the court-house the other day. You were trending."

Trending? Oh my God. Suddenly, Claudia had a splitting headache.

"Is that why your face is all bruised?" Chad said. "I noticed your makeup is kinda heavy."

Amy dug a sharp elbow in his ribs. "Shut up, Chad, that's rude."

"Hey, sorry. I noticed it because they do makeup when I get TV jobs and—"

"Let's get on with your handwriting samples," Claudia interrupted. The twenty minutes she had spent staring into the bathroom mirror, convincing herself that the makeup did a good job of masking the yellowed bruises, had obviously been a waste. She should have refused Jovanic's request and stayed home. Covering her embarrassment, she reached into her field case and took out some papers.

She passed some papers over the seat to them. "This is called 'taking a request writing.' You'll each fill out and sign a form with your contact information and permission for me to take the exemplars." She held up a second printed form. "On this form you'll write the alphabet in all capitals, then all small letters, then write a series of words. After that, I'll dictate the words written on the paper you found in the geocache. First you write it with your natural writing hand and then with the other hand. You'll sign and date everything as you complete it, and we're done."

"Sounds pretty easy," said Amy.

Claudia gave each of them a sturdy clipboard to provide a solid writing surface, and two matching pens. "Just write the way you always do. Don't try to be extra neat."

"My handwriting sucks anyway," said Chad.

Watching the two bent heads as they labored over their task, giggling and elbowing each other like two high schoolers, Claudia envied their ingenuousness. It seemed like eons since she had enjoyed that kind of freedom.

"I can confirm right now that neither of them wrote any of the questioned writing," said Claudia later when Jovanic walked her back to her car. "They signed their names in the logbook, that's all. Amy's handwriting is what I call 'Valley Girl' writing. The forms are generally round, the letters are highly connected, and it's right-slanted—very different from the note. Chad's printing is much more creative than the writing in the note. You can rule them both out."

Jovanic gave a grunt of dissatisfaction. "It would be easier if it were them. But we knew it wasn't. Back to square one."

"Not quite. You've got that name, 'Dax O' or C. Or maybe Q. Or I guess it could be a G or even an A. Gives you a few letters to work with."

"I'm just lucky it doesn't say *John Smith*." He leveled his piercing gaze at her. "Do you want me to follow you home and see you inside?"

How long would she be afraid to drive down the street, enter her own home by herself? Danny Ortiz was still in the hospital ward at the jail. What could he do to her? Send someone after her? The probability was small. Claudia forced a smile. "I'll be fine."

"Go in through the garage. You know what to do."

"Keep one eye on the rearview mirror," Claudia recited. "Don't exit the car until the garage door is down. Yes, I know. *And* I know I'm boxing at shadows."

"It wasn't a shadow that put those bruises on you, babe. It's smart to be cautious; just don't be paranoid."

"Hey, remember the saying: just because you're paranoid doesn't mean they're not out to get you."

His wry grin let her know he understood that making light of the situation was her defense. Claudia wanted to move into his arms, but that was out of the question. She climbed into the driver seat and faked a smile. "Don't worry, Columbo, I'll be fine."

ten

JOVANIC

Someone had erected a bedraggled-looking Christmas tree in the lobby of the police station. Half-hearted decorations pointed to Hanukkah and Kwanzaa, too. The meager pile of wrapped gifts at its base intended for poor kids made Jovanic a little sad, and he resolved to stop at Target as soon as he had some spare time to pick up a few toys.

He had not felt good about leaving Claudia to go home from the Lagoon alone, but she was fierce in asserting her independence and it would not have gone well if he had insisted on following her. She might think he didn't know what she was going through, but he had a pretty good sense of it. He just knew better than to let her know.

He sat at his desk and pulled up Google on the computer. In the search bar he entered, "How common is the name Dax?" The name, which was considered rare, had started showing up in the 1970s. Dax was number 604 in popularity.

That narrows it down. Yeah, right.

He entered the name and each of the initials Claudia had suggested, one at a time. He would need to have some kind of information to enter when accessing the law enforcement databases.

The first names that came up were Griff, Garner, and Germaine. He searched on each one in turn. Dax Griff was an actor in New York, Dax Garner, a teacher in Detroit, Dax Germaine, a chef in New Orleans. He would get Randy Coleman to check on their whereabouts, but they sounded dubious. Dax O'Callaghan was a soldier currently posted in the Middle East. That let him out.

He sat back, thinking about what other leads were worth pursuing. But there were no other leads. Under Claudia's infrared light the letters had looked like Dax, but what if they weren't? Frustrated, Jovanic wanted a smoke, but he'd given it up years ago when the department went smoke-free. He jammed a toothpick between his teeth. Claudia said it helped satisfy the oral need in lieu of a cancer stick.

Maybe Dax was a dead end after all. He returned to the list of names and kept searching. Twenty minutes later he was congratulating himself that he had not given in to the temptation to drop the search.

The name that caught his notice was *Dax Odell*.

An agitator and leader of protests worldwide, Dax Odell had drawn the attention of law enforcement in several countries, but to date, had managed to avoid arrest. In his younger days, Odell had joined in political unrest in Russia, student rallies in France, a police brutality march in the US.

Allowing himself to get a little bit fired up over his find, Jovanic paged through dozens of references. Over the past two years, Dax Odell had shown his face in demonstrations related to green science and saving the earth. Of late, his efforts had focused on eco-protests dealing with the use of pesticides and herbicides.

The most recent article, dated six months earlier, placed Odell in Argentina—a leader in a demonstration against the chemical giant, Monsanto. He was thought to be part of a movement in New Zealand, where suspected eco-terrorists had threatened to poison baby food. There was, however, no proof of his involvement in that effort.

The photographs that accompanied the articles portrayed a man in his mid-forties. His left brow sat a tad higher than the right, conferring character on an otherwise extraordinarily handsome face. Odell favored a scruffy moustache and soul patch with a goatee, dark hair trimmed close to his head. In one of the photos, Jovanic sensed a flare of fanatical zeal in the indigo eyes. In others, they seemed to reflect a deep pool of sadness.

"You think this is our boy?" Randy Coleman asked, reading over Jovanic's shoulder.

"Could be. Dude gets around."

Coleman dug into his pocket and pulled out a container of Tic Tacs, offered them to Jovanic and popped a few into his mouth. He pointed at the monitor. "The lad's an Irishman."

Jovanic ignored his partner's poor attempt at an Irish brogue. "According to this article, his parents were killed by British soldiers in a riot when he was eight and he was raised by militant Irish grandparents. The grandfather was IRA, arrested in a bomb plot in '88, spent the next ten years in lockup."

"So, Odell comes by it honestly."

"And now he's in L.A. Or was a few days ago, if he's the one who wrote his name in that logbook, which would make sense. If we can get some of Odell's handwriting, Claudia can compare it to what we've got."

Jovanic picked up his desk phone and punched in the number for ICE, the US Immigration and Customs Enforcement agency. He asked the agent who answered for information on whether Dax Odell of Northern Ireland had been allowed into the country.

"We have a flag on his passport," came the reply. "It's UK issue." There was a pause, during which Jovanic heard the agent tapping on her keyboard. "That's all I've got for you."

"Do you know whether he's currently in the US?"

"The last information we have is that he came into LAX last week."

Bingo.

"Is there a way for you to keep me in the loop as to when he's leaving and where he's headed next?"

"Sorry, Detective. That information won't become available until he's departed the US."

eleven

AND THEN IT WAS Christmas.

As low man on the totem pole and the one single member of the team, Randy Coleman volunteered to cover the homicide table during the last week of the year. Claudia and Jovanic flew to the San Francisco Bay Area to spend the holiday with his mother and his sister's family, then on to Seattle, where Claudia's parents lived. Her mother, who held strict fundamentalist religious views on cohabitation without the benefit of marriage, had extended an invitation to host them, but in separate bedrooms.

Jovanic, amused by the offer, was willing to go along with the program, but Claudia seized on the excuse that her brother Pete and his daughter Monica would be staying there and the house would be too crowded. She booked them instead into a hotel a few miles away.

For the first time since Danny Ortiz attacked her, Claudia found herself breathing freely. Her injuries were healed, rendering the need for awkward explanations unnecessary. Her mother would have wanted to know all the details and then criticized her for getting beaten up. Her father, an inveterate pacifist, avoided confrontation whenever the sparks flew between his wife and daughter, which was often. For as long as she could remember, Claudia yearned for him to take her side once in a while, but he was too invested in trying to keep the peace. Too bad most of the time his efforts failed.

After making a determined effort to enjoy the time away, the exchange of gifts and sharing of holiday meals passed in relative peace. Returning home to Southern California to start the New Year was bittersweet. Now it was time for Claudia to throw herself into preparing her lecture for the BIG conference in England. Concentrating on working on an outline and selecting the handwritings she planned to present provided some respite from the nightmares, which had resumed immediately upon their return.

Kelly phoned, wanting to catch up. She picked up Claudia and drove her down the hill to Cowboys, the neighborhood bar and grill. After exchanging holiday news, Kelly turned the conversation to Claudia's upcoming travel plans.

"Are you sure it's a good idea? Are you sure you want to travel that far alone? I mean, *England*—"

"That's exactly what I want—to get far, far away. I felt fine while we were on vacation."

"You felt fine because Joel was with you. What if you have a panic attack and you're all alone over there and you need help?"

"A panic attack? Thanks for the vote of confidence. Anyway, I won't be alone, I'll be with Daphne."

"Hey, don't kill the messenger, I'm just trying to look out for you." Kelly stuck out her lip in a childish pout. "Or maybe I'm just jealous. You know I'd love to be going."

Claudia brightened. "Why don't you come with me? We could check out London and—"

Kelly stopped her. "I'm in trial next week. Much as I'd love to go, my client might not appreciate me not showing up because I'd buggered off to London on vacation." She broke off, narrowing her eyes in suspicion. "I'm sensing something else going on here. What aren't you telling me?"

"Nothing. You're dreaming."

"C'mon, Claudia, give it up."

Claudia hesitated, not wanting to voice a thought she had been struggling to suppress. But Kelly was unrelenting and stared her down until she sighed in surrender. "The truth is, I've been asking myself whether getting engaged was the right thing."

"Hell, Claudia, I knew that was coming."

No surprise. That was why they had been best friends since kindergarten. Claudia glanced down at her ring. She loved the simple elegance of the design Jovanic had chosen for her. She loved him. "I'm just scared to death that once we're married everything is going to change and fall apart."

Kelly gave a rude snort. "I might buy that if it was me saying it. But you and Joel—you're like, joined at the hip. Or more salacious body parts. Why the hell would it fall apart?"

"You know what they say is the biggest cause of divorce?"

"No, what do 'they' say is the biggest cause of divorce?"

"Marriage."

Kelly gave a dramatic eye roll. "You've been more or less living together for the last couple of years. How is signing a piece of paper supposed to change anything?"

"I'm just afraid it will."

"You're afraid of *everything* right now. It's the PTSD talking, and it's time you got some help."

Claudia had resisted the idea of therapy. She had good self-awareness and insight, she told herself. But she also knew that self-therapy in a situation like this was akin to performing self-brain surgery. If she was ever to have true peace of mind, she had to find a way to address her fears head-on and deal with them. She had to admit that despite the many attempts she had made on her own, her failure to make any real progress meant she needed help.

"I was wondering how long it would take you to call me." Dr. Zebediah Gold ushered her into the guesthouse where he lived in Venice and wrapped her in a bear hug.

His office was just a few stepping stones away, through the Zen garden behind the main house, but he had asked her to meet him in his living quarters. As her longtime friend, long-ago lover, and a semi-retired psychologist, Zebediah had refused to see Claudia formally as a paying client.

He brewed jasmine tea and set the teapot on a hand-painted trivet after pouring for them both. "After everything you've been through over the past couple of years, I'm surprised you haven't gone to pieces before now."

Aside from Jovanic, Zebediah was one other person in the world Claudia trusted with her innermost secrets. "I've been on the edge for a while now," she admitted, leaning into the fragrant steam, breathing in its sweet scent. "That situation with Annabelle and the tattoo—everything else I've never fully processed. Ortiz attacking me in court was the last straw. It all caught up with me."

Claudia put down her mug and held out her hands. "Look at this, Zeb. I can't stop trembling. I was fine while we were out of town, but now that we're home I'm back to feeling like I can't catch a breath."

Zebediah leaned toward her and took her hands in his big paws. His amber eyes were brimming with compassion. "You don't have to live with it, sweetie. If you're ready, we can get to work. It's up to you." The warmth of his touch and his soothing tone seeped into her, infusing her with courage.

"I *am* ready," she said with conviction.

"Good. I'd like to try EMDR with you. It's proven very effective for Post-Traumatic Stress, as you know."

Having referred a client to Zebediah for treatment, Claudia did know something about EMDR—Eye Movement Desensitization Reprocessing. The therapeutic process would work on the experiences from the past that had left her fearful all the time, as well as the current situations where emotions were triggered that created a panic response.

Zebediah had been there to comfort her in the wake of each of the traumatic events that continued to dog her. He did not need to take her history before they began, as he normally would have with a patient.

Claudia sat back in her chair. "I'm ready."

"Darling," Zebediah said with a gentle smile. "Can you put your hands in your lap?"

Following his glance, Claudia realized she was clenching the arms of the chair. "Oh." She let go and put her hands in her lap, fighting a strong urge to clasp them together. What if the treatment didn't work? *What if it did?*

Zebediah gave her some stress reduction techniques to use during the treatment session, and later. Then he asked her to choose a single memory from those that were causing her the most distress.

Claudia closed her eyes and breathed deep. At once, an image of Danny Ortiz's face came to her. Feeling her breathing get shallow, her respirations faster, she did what Zebediah had instructed: she banished the image and replaced it with one from a time where she had felt strong and in charge.

The memory she settled on came from several years ago. She had been one of the first women invited to lecture in the hallowed halls of a prestigious 'old boys' club in San Francisco. Standing before the movers and shakers of the Bay Area had been a powerful moment for her, made even more gratifying by the accolades and invitations to return.

Claudia opened her eyes and, staying with the good memory, fastened her gaze on Zebediah's right hand. As he had told her to do, she followed his fingers as they moved back and forth a few inches from her face, shifting her eyes rapidly from side to side. She allowed thoughts about Danny Ortiz's attack to flow freely.

Two hours later Claudia left Zebediah's home feeling light enough to fly. She knew in her heart that the straitjacket that had imprisoned her had been unlocked. The crippling anxiety was already weaker. She was on her way back.

twelve

JOVANIC

Jovanic had never had a talent for relaxing. Even on his days off, the homicide victims whose cases he investigated were rarely far from his mind. Having no voice of their own, they visited him in his dreams, preyed upon him until either he had identified their killers or there was nothing left to be done. The spirit of Sylvia Vasquez, the housekeeper who had died in the mailbox bombing, was telling him that he had not yet done enough for her.

With a sigh of regret that the holidays were already receding in the rearview mirror of his mind, he opened the Vasquez murder book.

The season had brought a fresh crop of homicides to investigate, stretching the unit to the limit, leaving Randy Coleman no time to work on a case that was now weeks old. Sometime during Jovanic's absence a note had been placed in the murder book: call Wayne Wyatt at the bomb squad. He picked up the phone and dialed. He was in luck.

"That was a no-brainer," Wyatt answered when he learned the reason for Jovanic's call. "Took all of five minutes to figure out."

"For an experienced investigator, maybe. Care to enlighten me?"

"Sure. Here's how it worked: the suspect superglues a group of wooden matches together and sticks them onto the mailbox door right at the edge. You with me?"

"Got it."

"Next, he glues some sandpaper to the inside wall of the box. Now, this part is conjecture, but most of the time, what they do in cases like this is stuff a bunch of toilet paper in the box..."

"Toilet paper?" Jovanic echoed.

"Yeah, you oughta try it out, have some fun. Take a metal bucket outside, make sure you're away from the house and trees. Tear off a yard or two of TP and put it in the bucket with a little toluene, toss in a lit match and stand back. It'll go up with a big whoof. It's a blast." He laughed at his own poor joke.

Jovanic did not even pretend to be amused. "When the victim opens the mailbox door, the matches scrape the sandpaper causing a spark, which then makes the TP flare up, which ignites the cherry bomb?"

"You got it, Detective. Now all you've gotta do is go around to all the stores in your victim's neighborhood that sell sandpaper and wooden matches, and see if the suspect was dumb enough to use a credit card, right? Good luck with that. And that's assuming he was dumb enough to buy them in his own neighborhood. These guys tend to use stuff that's been lying around the garage for fifty years. They're too stupid to try to cover it up, too. You just have to find the right garage."

Jovanic knew that Wyatt was dead serious. The prospect gave him a headache. "What about the device itself?" he asked. "Anything out of the ordinary I should be looking for? Something they'd have to order online; anything like that?"

"Nah, this is all homemade shit. They use a ping-pong ball and twine. These assholes don't bother searching for hazardous materials or anything like that."

"A ping-pong ball? How's that work?"

"Okay, here's what you do. You poke a hole on one side of the ball with a nail, just big enough to stick the twine in."

"The twine is the fuse?"

"Yeah. You insert the fuse through the nail hole and put some glue around the hole to make a smooth seal. Then, on the other side of the ball, you cut a bigger hole with a razor and fill it with black powder. You have to patch it so the powder doesn't fall back out. When you're done, just dip it in plaster of Paris and let it set. Keeps the air out once it's dry."

"Where are they going to find black powder?"

"Hell, Joel, you can buy it online, or go down to your local Bass Pro Shop."

"That's it?"

"Pretty much. Now, you want this thing to go off fast once the TP flares up. That means cutting the fuse pretty short. Dip it in toluene to make it extra hot, and the explosion will be louder—which is what they want."

Ending the call, Jovanic contemplated what he had just heard. He needed to start contacting the local hardware stores. A monumental waste of time, he was sure, but it had to be done. Coleman was out interviewing witnesses to a gang shooting and not available to help. Scott and Hardcastle were handling a domestic.

As a delaying tactic, he phoned Claudia. They had sworn off discussing work during their vacation, but now he updated her with what he had learned about the bombing suspect, Dax Odell.

"I'm searching Google Images as we speak. If you can find some of this Dax guy's handwriting, I could compare it to the logbook and the note and—here's a photo—ooh, he's *hot.*"

"He's an asshole who killed an innocent woman."

"Fine. But he's still hot. What are the chances of locating any handwriting samples?"

"Dunno yet. I'll check some official channels first."

"More productive than combing the hardware stores for sandpaper and ping-pong balls," Claudia said. "Especially if he used his brains and paid cash. Plus, he might not have bought it around here."

Jovanic conceded the point. "Agreed. If you can authenticate the writing in the logbook, it'll help develop probable cause toward getting an arrest warrant. Assuming I can find him."

After their conversation, he logged into Palantir, a shared resource for federal and local law enforcement agencies. The database was a repository for a wide-ranging array of information, from arrest records to warrants to traffic tickets. He entered his search parameters and was surprised when he got a hit almost at once.

While leading an unpermitted demonstration on December 19th near the Criminal Courts Building, downtown Los Angeles, Dax Odell, a citizen of the United Kingdom of Great Britain and Northern Ireland, had been placed under arrest on a charge of obstructing traffic on North Broadway. Additional charges included resisting arrest.

The date of the arrest jogged Jovanic's memory. He checked last year's calendar. December 19th, a Friday, was the day Claudia had been attacked at CCB. The same day as the mailbox bomb homicide. The attack on Claudia was coincidental, but the date told him that Dax Odell had been in the L.A. area on the same day Evan Lockhart's mailbox exploded. Downtown L.A. was less than twenty miles from the crime scene.

Odell must have shit a brick when he was arrested. Probably expected to be charged with the homicide. Or had he even known his actions were responsible for Sylvia Vasquez's death? With a stirring of excitement that came from knowing he was on the right track, Jovanic snagged his suit coat from the back of his chair and headed for the door.

The Los Angeles County District Attorney's office occupied a suite on the seventh floor of the Clara Foltz Criminal Courts Building. There was nothing fancy about the county law offices, which had the look of the more than forty years they had occupied CCB. The offices were small and cramped, loaded with stacks of case files on every surface, including the floor.

Jovanic hit the intercom on the entry door and asked for Anna Yu, the deputy district attorney assigned to the Dax Odell case. He had phoned on his way over and asked her to pull the file. He could have read on his computer any reports that had been submitted electronically into the system, but he was old-fashioned enough to prefer taking the paper in his own two hands and paging through it himself.

He got buzzed in and someone pointed him to Yu's office. In her thirties, she was a good-looking Chinese-American woman in a crisp white blouse, narrow dark skirt and high heels. Her thick black hair was arranged in a youthful pageboy style, but the faint lines around her mouth betrayed her age. She was having a conversation on an old-fashioned desk phone as Jovanic appeared at her door, and motioned him to sit while she finished up her call.

"He was arrested on a 2686," said Yu after putting the phone down and greeting Jovanic. "Refusal to Disperse, Unlawful Assembly."

He interpreted her words: a peace officer had ordered the defendant to leave and Dax Odell had refused. "There was also a PC 148?" he asked, remembering the additional charge.

"Yes, he resisted arrest. That's how it was filed."

Jovanic was well aware the cop could have filed the charges that way if Odell had pissed him off, whether or not he had indeed been resisting. He considered asking Yu whether it was a righteous charge, but what could she say?

Yu added that Odell had been fomenting disorder, stirring up a large group of protesters in the grassy area behind CCB when he was arrested. The protest had spilled into the street, and when Odell was directed to break it up, the arresting officer reported that the protestor had gotten in his face, screaming at him and refusing to follow orders.

"What were they protesting?" Jovanic asked.

"Who knows? You could Google it and find out."

Hoping he would find the Irishman still in lockup awaiting trial, he asked about the disposition of the case. Yu, after flipping through a few pages, dashed his hopes.

"He was arrested on a Friday, which means he was arraigned the next Monday. He made bail the same day. Let's see, his next court date is—" She checked the file and looked up at Jovanic. "It was calendared for yesterday, but he didn't show."

"Was a bench warrant issued?"

"Of course. And he'll be caught. They all are eventually. And when he's hauled into court and is in custody, his bail will be forfeited. Then we'll add new charges for his failure to appear."

"Who was his public defender?"

Once again, Anna Yu consulted the file. "He had private counsel. Jeffrey House. He's a pretty pricey lawyer. Odell must have some means, or maybe the group he's protesting for hired House. His bail was reduced from twenty thousand to ten. All he had to put up was a thousand."

"How would he get connected to House? He's here on a visitor's visa from Ireland."

"No idea, but his flight shows consciousness of guilt. I just love these guys who make my life a whole lot easier."

Her smug tone irked Jovanic. "Dax Odell is a person of interest in a homicide," he said curtly.

Anna Yu's face fell. "A homicide?"

"Yeah. And, oh, by the way, he's a flight risk."

He summarized the bombing at the Lockhart home in Venice while Anna Yu scribbled furious notes in the file. She was all business now, and promised to put a flag on Odell's file. "Good luck tracking him down. I hope he's still in town."

After struggling through a major traffic snarl on the 10 West, Jovanic found a Carl's Jr. drive-through and wolfed down a burger on his way back to his desk at Pacific Division. He would need to remember to dump the paper sack with its incriminating logo before he went home. Since being hospitalized last year after getting gut shot, and a second time when the wound got infected, Claudia was vigilant in trying to get him to watch his diet. With the crazy hours he worked it wasn't always possible to avoid fast food, but she would have something to say about it if she saw the evidence.

Back at his desk, Jovanic checked the NCIC database—the National Crime Information Center. Finding nothing further on Odell, he phoned the local FBI field office and asked for the SAC—Special Agent in Charge. He had met Roland Sparks on a recent case and they trusted each other.

"Yeah, we have a flag on Odell," Sparks said. "He's been on our watch list for a while."

"He had no priors that I could find until this December arrest. What's the flag for? Is he referenced as a target or a witness?"

"Both. We've been listening to his calls and—"

"Hold on," Jovanic broke in. "There's already a warrant?"

"No, we don't need one. Odell isn't a US citizen; we're good on that."

An advantage of being the Feds. "What can you tell me about him?"

"He travels a lot and leads protests where there's been a lot of civil unrest. We believe he bears watching."

"Are you picking up anything of consequence?"

"As it happens, there's been money exchanged between him and someone in the US. Not a huge amount, but we believe it's used to fund protest efforts; we aren't sure yet what those efforts might be. The amounts are always a few thousand at a time and not on any regular schedule. He's been in contact with a scientist in the high desert. Their code words aren't all that sophisticated, but they're pretty cagey."

Jovanic remembered with a small jolt that Evan Lockhart had mentioned Agrichem had a lab facility in Lancaster, which was in the high desert, and that the lab had been the target of a recent protester attack. "Where in the high desert?" he asked.

"Lancaster."

Another *bingo*. Jovanic explained the situation to Sparks. "There's some evidence linking Odell to a mailbox bombing that resulted in a homicide. I'd like to talk to him."

"Good luck on that. He left the country on January 2nd."

Fuck. The Immigration officer he'd spoken to had neglected to let him know. "Do you know where he went?"

"Argentina. He's got something of a support system there. We've lost track of him for the moment, but we'll find him again."

"What about the scientist you mentioned? What have you got on him?"

There was a pause while Sparks checked. "Doctor Garret Lashburn. Chief chemist at the Agrichem labs."

"You gotta be shittin' me."

Sparks' tone sharpened. "What've you got?"

"The mailbox bombing was at the home of Agrichem's CEO."

"That's a pretty big coincidence."

"Tell me about it. What do you have on Lashburn?"

"Except for his association with Odell, we don't have anything much on him. Guy's sixty-two, been working at Agrichem since the late 80s. No wants or warrants, never been in any trouble; not even a speeding ticket."

Jovanic rang off and fished out his mobile phone. He thumbed through the contact list and selected a number. After a long pause, he heard a ring, then a voice he knew.

"Hey, buddy, long time no talk," said Special Agent Mike Chapman.

"Hey, Mike, how's it hangin' at the Feeb?"

"The Company never changes. Did you hear I'm not in L.A. anymore? I transferred across the pond a few months ago."

"That explains the funny accent."

"Right you are, mate," Chapman said in a lackluster Cockney accent. "London's rubbing off on me."

"Even I know that's more Aussie then Cockney," Jovanic jeered. "I'm calling you because I heard you're a big, fancy—what is it—ALAT?"

"Yeah, yeah, FBI Assistant Legal Attaché at the embassy," Sparks recited. "Not so fancy. We get daily intelligence briefings with the Ambassador, who's a charmer in public and kind of an SOB behind the office door. Other than that, I'm just sitting at my desk, waiting to hear from the likes of you."

"Uh huh, sure."

"What can I do for you, old chum?"

"The local SAC said the feds are watching a person of interest from Ireland." Jovanic gave him a rundown on the mailbox bomb homicide and told him who he was interested in. He could hear Chapman tapping on a keyboard.

"Looks like Odell's been on our radar for a while."

"That's what everyone's saying. Then, why is he still out there?"

Chapman asked Jovanic to wait while he pulled up the file. "We're aware of him," he said after a pause. "He's pretty small potatoes, mostly rabblerousing at protests. Homicide jacks it up a notch."

Jovanic had called his friend, not really expecting results. Now, he felt a zing of optimism. "Can you get me his phone records for the past thirty days, the most recent data? The local SAC, Sparks, told me Odell's been in contact with a chemist in my area, Garrett Lashburn. Lashburn's been sending him money."

"I'll have to get the go-ahead from New Scotland Yard here, but that shouldn't be a problem. I have a contact there—DCI Ash Hanley. Don't worry, Joel, I'll hook you up. Sounds like you can provide some info to support a phone tap; we can look at similar activity in the UK. They'll be as thrilled as these Brits get."

"Thanks, dude, appreciate it."

"No problem. That it?"

"There is one other thing. Claudia's going to be in London later this week for a conference. If you could find some of this guy's handwriting, it might help tie him to the homicide."

"Handwriting, huh? No prints on the logbook?"

"Nothing clear; too many people handling the book before these two kids got it and figured it was worth turning in. Besides, he could've worn gloves. It was a cold day."

"What was it, 65 degrees? You California mofos don't know what cold is."

Jovanic snorted. "Didn't take you long to switch sides."

"When in Rome—or London. Anyway, tell Claudia to call me when she gets here and we'll get together for a beer. I mean, a cup of tea."

"Jeez, Mike, I've never seen you without a cup of *coffee* in your hand."

"Just yanking your chain. Don't worry about your girlfriend. I'll take real good care of her."

"She's my fiancée. Keep your paws off."

"No friggin' way. *You,* the most confirmed bachelor I ever knew. You—taking on the old ball and chain? Never saw that one coming."

"Yeah, well..." All at once, Jovanic felt uncomfortable. "Give me a heads-up if you come up with anything on Odell. I want to get this guy. The lady he killed didn't deserve to die."

"You got it, pal." Then Mike Chapman got serious. "Hey, this is a break for us, JJ. We just got a note in a geocache, too."

thirteen

JANUARY IN LONDON MEANT bundling up in a heavy coat and gloves against a freezing rain. Claudia pushed through the door of the St. George Hotel, thankful for the rush of warm air. Following close behind, Daphne Spencer said, "Did I remember to tell you a TV reporter's coming to interview you?"

"What? No, you didn't tell me." Considering all that Daphne had on her mind with her duties as conference chair—and a slight tendency to be scatterbrained at the best of times—Claudia was not surprised by the omission. She peeled off her gloves and unwound the hand-knit scarf from around her throat. The scarf was a late Christmas gift from her neighbor as she'd left town. Stuffing it into her suitcase at the last minute, she'd had no idea how much she would rely on its warmth.

"We sent a press release about the conference to all the local media outlets with photos of the headliners and all," said Daphne. "It's rather impressive you know, having the keynote speaker come all the way from America. *Good Afternoon London* got in touch straight away and said they'd send someone to do a remote interview. They're coming here in—" Daphne checked her watch. "Well, they ought to be here any minute. You know how these things go—a few sound bites, finished in no time at all. You don't mind, do you?"

"It would have been nice to have a bit of time to prepare."

Daphne shot her a cheeky grin. "Prepare for what, my love? If you aren't ready after all these years, it's a bit late to start worrying about it now, isn't

it? Don't worry, you're always bloody brilliant and I hate you for it."
She hooked her arm through Claudia's. "Come on, then. Let's see if the
staff's got the meeting room open for us yet."

"That's why you hurried me through lunch," Claudia grumbled. "You
should have told me. I might have worn something a bit more interviewy."

"Codswallop. You look perfectly interviewy. Now let's get a move on."

Claudia, insisting on doing a quick inspection before meeting the
reporter, ducked into the Ladies. She had caught a few hours of sleep
on the plane the day before, but since Daphne had picked her up
at Heathrow, they'd been running nonstop and she was beginning to
droop. With a critical eye on the mirror, she ran a quick brush through
her hair and touched up her makeup. Thank heavens she no longer had
to worry about covering up bruises on her face.

"This had better go well," Claudia said in mock annoyance when she
rejoined Daphne. "Or you won't hear the end of it."

Daphne rolled her eyes. "Listen to yourself. Doesn't take you long to
get into the accent, does it, ducks?"

"Blame it on the two years I lived with my British grandmother in my
misspent youth."

Together they cut through the small lobby of what had once been the
middle of a group of Victorian town homes set in the heart of London.
An enterprising builder from Dubai had converted them into a charming
boutique hotel with meeting rooms to let on the ground floor. The
annual conference of the British Institute of Graphologists, which had
opened that morning, was being held in the Victoria and Albert Room.

They were not the first ones there. An impossibly slender blonde
woman in a smart carnelian-colored suit was already waiting for them,
along with a cameraman and a sound technician.

"Poppy Adair." The woman extended a hand. "And you're Claudia. I
recognize you from the publicity photo. *Lovely* to meet you."

The two men were moving things around on the stage at the front of the room. The podium had been pushed to one side; two chairs had been taken from the front row and placed opposite each other. Tall LED light stands pointed at them from behind.

Adair introduced the men. "This is Dan, my cameraman, and Ahmad, my soundman."

Claudia gave a hand to each of them in turn and introduced Daphne, who looked slightly star-struck. "I understand you're covering the conference?"

"Actually, we're covering *you*." Poppy Adair put her hand on Claudia's arm. "I'm absolutely fascinated by what you do and I'm *dying* to talk to you about it."

Claudia smiled. "I was just told you were coming. Will we be covering any particular topic?"

"Don't worry, it'll take no time at all," the interviewer said, expertly sidestepping the question. "Give your coat to your friend and let's go over here, shall we? Ahmad will mic you up."

The soundman was waiting for her on the stage. As a veteran of numerous television interviews, Claudia knew what was expected. She took the lavalier microphone Ahmad handed her and tucked it under her shirt, deftly threading it up through the neck. He took it from there and attached the tiny mic to her jacket collar. The battery pack clipped to the waist of her skirt around the back, where it wouldn't be visible to the camera. He then did a sound check, having her count to ten, while Dan confirmed the lighting was set correctly.

The conference attendees were beginning to filter in—a small group by some conference standards, but they comprised the elite in the handwriting world. Poppy spoke to them with a warmth that looked almost genuine.

"Ladies and gentlemen, we're going to be doing a very short interview. You've got to be very quiet, please. Would somebody stand outside the door and not let anyone else in until we've finished? Shan't be long, promise."

She mounted the stage and took the chair opposite Claudia, fussing with her microphone until it was set the way she wanted it. "We can get some B-roll later," she said to the cameraman.

Claudia knew what that meant: after the interview, Dan would video-tape her looking at handwriting samples or from a distance, maybe talking to someone—filler that would be edited into the piece while Poppy did the voiceover.

Dan fiddled with his camera, which was on a tall tripod set back from the two chairs. "Ready, then?" he asked Claudia.

"Ready as I'll ever be." Claudia glanced over at Daphne, who had taken a seat in the front row next to a heavyset older gentleman. She had never met Hewett Pflueger, but knew him by reputation and had noticed his name in the program. In his tweed jacket and dark gray flannel trousers, he could have passed for a university professor. His face reminded Claudia of a baby bird—not a cute, fluffy hatchling, but one that had broken out of the egg too soon and wasn't quite finished. Then it came to her: peevish. That's what his expression said. He looked cranky and dissatisfied.

She saw Pflueger lean over to whisper in Daphne's ear and wondered whether he was complaining about something.

Dan trained his camera on Poppy, who had applied fresh red lipstick and was dabbing powder on her nose and forehead. He asked if she was ready.

"Ready." Poppy slipped her compact into the handbag under her chair and turned an approving eye on Claudia. "Your makeup doesn't need anything at all."

Dan held up three fingers, two, one, and pointed at the interviewer. Go.

Beaming into the camera, Poppy Adair began her spiel: "*Good After-noon London. Today, we're out of the studio and on location at the St. George Hotel near Bloomsbury, where the distinguished British Institute of Graphologists is holding its annual conference. What are graphologists* you might well ask? They study handwriting and what it tells about personality. Our very special guest today is Claudia Rose, a leading expert in the field who's here from America. She's the keynote speaker tomorrow. The title of her talk is—" With a dramatic pause, Poppy consulted an index card in her lap, and read, "*The Narcissistic Personality Disorder and How it Can Be Seen in Handwriting.* That's quite a mouthful, isn't it? Let's start with something a bit more basic. Why do we even need handwriting anymore, Claudia? With computers, smart phones, tablets, what's the point?"

It was a question Claudia had been asked many times before and she was ready with her answer. "That's an excellent and timely question. First, let me be clear that we handwriting analysts love our technology every bit as much as the next person. We're not interested in minimizing its importance.

"The big issue is that current research in brain development shows that children who learn to write in cursive—joined up letters—tend to do better at remembering written and oral instructions, and are better at spelling and reading. The research also shows college students who take handwritten notes remember the material better than those who only use the keyboard."

"Oh dear, I think I'd better start practicing my handwriting."

"Brain scans show more areas of the brain 'light up' when a child is writing in cursive than when they're using a keyboard or printing. They think in a more adult manner, too. Their fine motor skills develop faster, and even their self-discipline is better developed. Teachers like that."

Poppy gave a laugh. "*My* teachers always complained they couldn't read my handwriting. I wouldn't want you to see it; it's horrible."

Claudia smiled. "Don't worry, that's what everyone thinks. But the fact is, handwriting tells the truth about who you are, and I'm sure you're not a horrible person, are you?"

Poppy made a rueful moue at the camera. "I hope not, but my producer might disagree." As she spoke, she slid a sheet of paper from under her index cards and unfolded it. A cold prickle of intuition went up Claudia's neck.

"I understand you arrived in England yesterday," Poppy continued, "so you might not have heard about an incident in our news last week. Someone blew up a sundial in a garden in Sussex. The police have said this note plays a significant part in the crime. It was found a few miles away in a geocache container." She looked into the camera, and explained, "For those who don't know, geocaching is like a modern-day treasure hunt. Players hide things in a container and other players use navigation coordinates to find them."

Poppy returned her attention to Claudia. "We've shown this note to a handwriting expert we've used before and asked to have it compared to a similar note that was found in another geocache in America—perhaps you've seen that one?"

"Yes, I have seen it." The note had been published in the American media, but Claudia wasn't sure Jovanic would want her discussing it on live TV.

"We thought you might have a look at this one and see if you agree with our expert."

Her mind racing, Claudia took the paper Poppy handed to her and glanced at the handwriting before handing it back. Mike Chapman, Jovanic's FBI friend in London, had emailed her the second note after it had been discovered. "I've already seen both notes," she said.

"What's your opinion, then? Were they written by the same person?"

Claudia replied with care. Her antenna was twanging with the distinct feeling that she was being set up. "It's my opinion that there are two different writers."

Poppy's eyebrows went up. *"Oh, really?* Our expert told us that both notes match, and furthermore, they also match the handwriting of an Irish protester named Dax Odell."

"I don't know who your expert is, but I disagree. And that's why it's called an opinion."

As if there had been a collective gasp, Claudia felt the room go still. A couple at the rear of the room started whispering to each other, glancing in her direction. Had she just made a terrible *faux pas?* Her opinion regarding the two sets of writing was firm, but it was possible something else was involved, perhaps information to which she had not been privy. She added quickly, "As for Dax Odell, I've not seen any exemplars of his known writing. My opinion is limited to one of common authorship. I can't address the question of whether any of the handwriting is his."

Poppy Adair, having unmasked her hidden agenda for the interview, flashed a big white smile, casting a glance at the front row. Dan followed her gaze with the camera.

"We'll leave you and our expert, Mr. Hewett Pflueger, to thrash it out between you. Thank you *so* much for sharing your fascinating work, Claudia. I do hope you'll enjoy the rest of your stay in the UK."

The TV crew did an efficient job of packing up their equipment and vacating the room, allowing conference attendees to file in and reclaim their seats. Daphne was rushing around, taking care of last-minute details before opening the afternoon session a few minutes hence.

Squelching the urge to ask why he thought a Donald Trump comb-over was a good look to imitate, Claudia took the empty seat next to Hewett Pflueger. "We haven't met."

The heavy-lidded eyes Pflueger turned on her were reptilian, the thin lips unsmiling. "Your diplomacy was charming, Ms. Rose. Pity our disagreement had to be public, wouldn't you say?"

"More's the pity that I got sandbagged by Poppy Adair, Mr. Pflueger. I'd be interested in hearing the basis for your opinion. Maybe I can learn something that will change mine."

He looked at her as if she were something he had picked up on the bottom of his shoe. "I very much doubt it. We both examined the same evidence and produced our own conclusions. Giving you a lesson on my methodology isn't going to change what you said on television, is it?"

"No, I don't suppose it is," Claudia said mildly, ignoring the insult and his 'too-too' posh accent complete with a condescending air. "Would you agree, though, that the styles of printing in the notes were quite different from each other?"

"They were. And there's an utterly reasonable explanation. The writing in the note was deliberately disguised."

"I didn't notice any signs of an attempt to disguise, but I'll take a closer look. Were you able to examine any of the original handwriting?"

"Not necessary; the truth of the matter was instantly clear to me."

Ah, he's a magician.

"But it sounded like you gave an unqualified opinion."

"That's right, I did. Any first-year pupil ought to see that the same person wrote both notes."

That sent her chin up, but before she could accuse him of arrogance, Claudia bit her tongue. She was tempted to counter that even a first-year pupil would know better than to give an unqualified opinion based on copies, but there was something she wanted from him. Eviscerating him would have to wait.

"Would you consider showing me the samples of Dax Odell's writing that you compared to the notes—the ones Poppy Adair referred to? I'd love to see them."

His eyebrows rose in skepticism. "What do you know of Odell?"

"I've read some articles about him. He seems to be quite a passionate activist in several areas."

"Phhht." Pflueger dismissed the Irishman with a wave of his hand. "Odell is nothing more than a common criminal. A bomber, no less. Fancy blowing up a sundial."

"That may be so, but I'm still interested in seeing his handwriting. I'm hoping you can share it, even if you just show it to me without giving me a copy."

Claudia watched the conflicting emotions play out in his eyes, guessing that he would rather keep it for himself. On the other hand, there was the brag factor—he wanted her to know he was in possession of an important sample to which she'd had no access.

"I suppose it will be all right," he said grudgingly at last. "I shall email the samples to you. They aren't particularly recent or of good quality, mind you."

Then how did you form an unqualified opinion? Claudia thought, thanking him.

"I'll send them over this evening. I suppose your email address is in the program book?"

"Yes, it is. Thank you again, I appreciate it."

Pflueger brushed his trousers with his hands and rose. "If you'll excuse me, I have a paper to present." He started to leave, then turned back. "I do hope my presentation meets with your approval, Ms. Rose."

Claudia gave him a smile as insincere as his own. "I look forward to hearing it."

fourteen

"Thinks he's the dog's bollocks, doesn't he?" Daphne's mouth twisted in disgust. "He goes around giving all these public talks and he's
got himself quite a following among the too-stupid-to-know-any-better
crowd. I'll tell you one thing: if I'd been on the programming committee,
he would never have been allowed to speak."

"You can give a good talk without being a good person. His lecture today
was pretty superficial, but he's entertaining. Some people like him. He's a
rotten document examiner, though. What he said to me was completely
off-base."

"Not surprising, that. The man's a windbag."

Claudia grinned "Don't hold back, Daph. Let's know how you really
feel."

They were at Daphne's home in Kent, having taken the Tube from
London Bridge, then the railway to Sidcup station, where they had parked
her Fiat.

Since her husband had left her the previous year for a woman half her
age, Daphne had been living alone in the house. Determined as she was to
put a brave face on it, the betrayal had been a tremendous blow. Claudia
had no illusions about it. She knew that her friend was still suffering
mightily.

She had confided to Claudia that her election to the British Institute
of Graphologists' management committee had offered a personal outlet.
Throwing herself into the heavy responsibility of chairing this year's con-

ference had saved her from sinking into a deep depression. With those duties nearing completion, she was grateful to have company for a few more days.

With a welcome cup of tea in hand, Claudia watched Daphne cook dinner. All offers of help had been politely but firmly refused. She stood in the kitchen doorway, salivating over the aroma of bangers and onions frying on the stove. Potatoes were boiling in one pot, peas simmering in another. Daphne was stirring the Bisto gravy.

"There's one good thing I can say," said Claudia. "At least he followed through and emailed the samples."

"He's still a right prat. He was abominably rude to you."

"It was a little excessive. I don't know why he hates me. We've never even met."

"Professional jealousy, my darling. Pure jealousy."

"Of what? Oh hell, never mind. Let's not waste our energy on Professor Dickweed." Claudia put her cup down. "I'm in the mood for a glass of wine. Can I pour you one?"

"Gawd, I thought you'd never ask."

"What did you think of the handwriting Pflueger sent?" Claudia asked once they each had a glass in hand.

Daphne set the spoon on the Aga cooker and turned off the gas under the gravy. She dried her hands on a tea towel, plucked a pair of reading glasses from a pocket in her apron, perched them on her nose and turned to the counter behind her.

"Not much to go on, is there?" Daphne peered at the first of the two sheets Pflueger had emailed. She had printed them out for Claudia. "Odell was still a schoolboy when he wrote this one. I'm a graphologist, not a document examiner, but how can an essay written by a fourteen-year-old boy be compared to adult writing?"

"Exactly. It's not suitable material to compare to something written thirty years later. Pflueger is either stupid or simply drowning in arrogance to give an opinion on something like this. He was right about one thing, though, the second sample is a lousy copy."

Daphne switched pages and shook her head. "It's a nastygram Odell apparently wrote to an old girlfriend. Why on earth would she give it to the television people?"

"Some people just want their five minutes of fame."

With a sound that clearly stated what she thought of publicity-seekers, Daphne handed the papers over and turned back to the stove.

The handwriting on the first page was as childish and undeveloped as one would expect from a teenage boy. The topic of the essay was, *British Opresion of the IRA*. Apparently, Odell's activism had started young, before he'd learned to spell "Oppression" correctly.

Claudia had to strain to read the second sample, a few scribbled words on what appeared to have been a small scrap of paper: *You're suffocating me, Tanya. Leave me the hell alone.* With no signature and no date, there was no telling when it was written, but the handwriting was far more adult than the other one.

"I'd be embarrassed to share that if someone wrote it to me," Claudia said. "The pressure looks very light. I could adjust the contrast on the computer, but as it stands, I would consider it too faint to use for a comparison. I think it was written in pencil. Anyway, it's just a handful of words. You'd have to be a crystal ball gazer to get much out of that."

"Well, if Pflueger had *any* balls, he wouldn't have gone on the telly with *that* opinion. It's a crying shame, but at least you cast doubt on what he said."

"Joel won't be too thrilled about having his case discussed on TV, but once word gets out, there's no way to put the genie back in the bottle."

"Will he be annoyed with you for talking about it?"

"I didn't give anything away that hasn't been discussed in the American media. I'm sure he'll understand I was in a difficult position." Claudia turned the stink eye on her friend. "Which is why I don't like off-the-cuff interviews."

"Sorry, love," Daphne said, sounding not the least bit contrite. "I should have given you a bit of notice."

"Oh well, it's not the worst thing that's ever happened to me."

As she set the table for dinner, Claudia continued pondering the penciled note and the man who supposedly had written it. Though the lightness of the copy made the text hard to decipher, the wide spaces between the words was plain enough. "He's a loner who needs plenty of elbow room," she mused aloud. "It's consistent with the geocache note in California, but *not* the one found after the sundial explosion. It's hard to believe Pflueger thinks they were written by the same person."

Daphne carried the pot of potatoes to the sink, steam rising up and enveloping her face as she drained the boiling water. "Give me the bottle of milk from the fridge, would you, luv? I've already got the butter out." Claudia handed her the bottle; Daphne poured some into the pot and began to work the masher. "What did the sundial note look like?"

"It was an altogether different style. Gender can't reliably be determined from handwriting, but it was a more feminine hand—rounded, not linear, like the one in California. The spacing was more compact, too, and the words had a stronger degree of connectedness. They were nothing alike."

"Thank God no one was hurt when that second bomb went off."

"Joel's FBI friend told him that the two devices were different in construction, but both carried about the same explosive force."

"Scared all the neighbors out of bed. The bomb was on a timer set for half-past two in the morning."

"That would get me out of bed, too."

Daphne shook her head and made a sound of disgust. "That poor old sundial was over a hundred years old. It sat in the garden all those years until this bloke comes along and blows it to smithereens. I saw it all on the news. Bits of stone blasted all around the garden—a lovely garden it was, too. Glass from the French doors on the terrace shattered everywhere. And the gnomon—"

"Wait, what's a gnome got to do with a sundial?" Claudia broke in.

"Not a gnome, a *gnomon*. It's the marker piece—I know this because I happen to have a sundial in my garden. Anyway, it turns out they come in different shapes, and the one in that garden was bronze, cast in the form of an arrow. They found it embedded in the trunk of a walnut tree near the back fence. If anyone had been in the way when it hit, they would have been killed."

Curious to learn more about the story, Claudia looked it up on her tablet. The fine hairs rose on her neck as she read that the Victorian garden in which the sundial had once stood was the residence of the local director of a subsidiary of the American company, Agrichem.

Certainly, no coincidence.

Reading on, she saw, as Poppy Adair had said, that it was several days later that the note was discovered in a geocache not far from the house and reported to the authorities. In the same way Chad and Amy, the American geocachers, had made the connection, the Englishman who found the container had put two and two together and telephoned police.

The article quoted the note inside the container: 'Agrichem must be stopped from killing off the wildlife.' It was accompanied by a photograph of a small stuffed hedgehog whose cloth belly was slit open, the stuffing bulging out in a gross unspoken threat.

Late that night, having coordinated the eight-hour time difference to catch him when he would be getting ready for work, Claudia spoke with Jovanic on FaceTime. When she mentioned the Agrichem connection, it came as no surprise to him. She guessed he and Mike Chapman had been in touch. He told her there was nothing new on the mailbox bombing and there had been no sightings of Dax Odell since his departure from LAX.

Downplaying Poppy Adair's ambush, Claudia let him know about the TV interview, but he was distracted, in a hurry. His team was investigating a new drive-by shooting and had been forced to relegate the Vasquez homicide to the back burner. They knew who the trigger man was in the drive-by. He figured it would make for a quick wrap-up. They exchanged 'I love you's' and clicked off, promising to talk more the next day.

Claudia and Daphne arrived at the St. George early for the final day of the conference. After her keynote presentation, Claudia returned to her seat to the sound of enthusiastic applause, noting that Hewett Pflueger had already taken his leave. No doubt a deliberate snub.

She gathered her notes and placed them in their folder, her mind returning to the two bombings. If Dax Odell had not written the second note, then who had? And that was assuming Odell had written the first one. The short note to the ex-girlfriend was the only handwriting available for comparison, and that was not enough to reach a strong conclusion regarding authorship.

She was pondering this problem when her silenced cell phone buzzed in her pocket. A text from Jovanic's FBI friend, Mike Chapman: "Got some Odell writing. Meet to discuss?"

Slipping out of the meeting room and into the lobby, Claudia tapped in Chapman's number. "Should I pretend not to be excited that you found some of his handwriting?" she asked when he answered the call.

"Why would you do that?"

"I know how buttoned-down you feds are. It might look unseemly if I jumped up and down, squealing in delight."

Chapman chuckled. "Oh yeah, we couldn't use your help if you were unseemly."

"I'll contain myself. What have you got?"

"Can you come to my office? I'll show it to you then."

"I'm at a conference near Bloomsbury for the rest of the day. Can we meet after that?"

"Sure, that'll work. I—wait, hold on ..."

She could hear muffled voices as Chapman covered the phone to speak to someone. Then he came back on the line; his tone had changed. "I'll get back to you."

The line went dead.

After the final speaker had wrapped up and the BIG Chairman had closed the event, Daphne and the organization's treasurer went off to settle their account. Waiting in the lobby, Claudia wondered what had taken Mike Chapman away so abruptly. She had heard nothing further from him in the four hours since their call.

Daphne was already buttoning her coat and pulling on gloves. "Come on then; I'm knackered."

"You must be. Let's stop at that pub on the corner. I'll buy you dinner and a glass of wine."

"Sorry, luv. I've got a foul headache coming on, can't bear the thought of food."

They pushed through the hotel's front door to a blast of cold air. Claudia coiled her scarf around her face, pulling it up to cover her nose and mouth. "Good lord, it's freezing."

"Never mind, we'll be home soon. I'm going to toddle off to bed straight away, if you don't mind fetching your own dinner."

"Not at all."

It was not yet five o'clock as they descended the front steps of the hotel, but already the street was cloaked in darkness. Grateful the rain had slowed to a light drizzle, they hurried around the corner to St. Pancras International where they would catch the Tube back to Sidcup.

Inside the warm terminal, Claudia stuffed her scarf and gloves into her pocket. This part of the journey meant ten minutes on the Tube before switching to the overground railway. She dreaded the claustrophobic feeling that going down the steep staircases gave her, borne along on the wave of passengers into the depths and through the maze of subterranean corridors.

Londoners had used the Tube tunnels as shelter during World War II. Scenes from a documentary of the Blitz had haunted her for weeks. For fifty-seven consecutive nights, air raids had sent thousands of families into the makeshift bomb shelters. Mothers, children, old people, carrying what they could—blankets and packets of biscuits, a teddy bear or doll, crowding into these very tunnels.

She could almost feel their terror; it seemed to linger in the walls. How they must have prayed to escape the missiles raining down on them by Hitler's *Luftwaffe*. The miles of Underground platforms were their refuge. But had they feared being trapped by the explosions rocking the city above? The documentary showed Balham Station, where a bomb had penetrated thirty-two feet underground, killing sixty-eight people sheltering there...hoping they again would get to see the light of day.

"Please mind the gap."

The prim, recorded voice jolted Claudia back to the moment. Looking like an enormous caterpillar, the red face of their Tube's driving car appeared at the mouth of the tunnel. The train slid into the station and came to a stop with a hiss of the pneumatic doors opening.

She followed Daphne through the surge of commuters onto the train, where her friend collapsed, pale and clammy, into the nearest open seat.

"Are you okay, Daph?" Claudia asked with concern.

"I feel rotten."

"Is there anything I can do?"

"Don't worry, luv." Daphne closed her eyes. "I'll be all right once I get some paracetamol in me."

Claudia's eyes flicked past two young men across the aisle who were chatting in low voices, to the wide windows behind their heads. The curved station wall outside was close enough to touch if she could have reached through the window. She could hardly wait to switch to British Rail Overground where she could watch the towns fly past without the stifling feeling of the Tube.

To distract herself, she engaged in a game of guessing what her fellow passengers' handwriting might look like: a woman in a sari, her face half-covered by a veil, staring down at her hands. Her writing would look tired and droop downwards, perhaps in depression. The businessman in his expensive suit, gaze buried in a newspaper, briefcase guarded between his feet. Hmm...with those lips pinched tight, she decided, he wrote with tense, angular forms and sharp edges.

At the far end of the compartment, a couple lost in each other's eyes. Hard to come up with anything on them. Two teenage girls, their voices loud enough for everyone to hear every word of their conversation. Claudia wanted to knock their heads together and suggest they learn some manners. They would have 'all about me' bubble writing. She moved onto the tough-looking dude in a leather jacket and a tall purple Mohawk—were those still in fashion? Mohawk Boy would use a writing style like his hair; spiky, running all over the place, aggressively demonstrating his independence.

Claudia glanced back at the two men across the aisle, heads close together. They were talking in low voices, but the conversation seemed to have the intensity of an argument. One of them punctuated his comments with sharp, stabbing gestures. That could mean heavy pen pressure, signifying someone who would never forget an insult or a compliment. The event would be re-experienced in living color, even years later.

The train slowed to a stop at Leicester Square. The two men rose and headed to the exit still bickering. The doors closed, and as they pulled away from the station, Claudia lost interest.

A middle-aged woman plopped into the seat vacated by the men. "Oww," she muttered, shifting sideways. She reached behind her. "Eh, what's this, then?"

Daphne opened her eyes and sat up with a groan. "What's the matter?"

The woman was holding a phone, which she had just sat on. "Must have fallen out of a pocket."

"There were two men sitting there," said Claudia. "I expect it's theirs."

"You're an American, are you?" the woman said.

"Yes, just visiting."

"My sister lives in America. San Diego."

"That's about ninety miles south of where I live. What are you going to do with the phone?"

The woman looked at it, a brand-new Android. "I'm going to leave it right where I found it. Silly buggers ought to be more careful; these things cost hundreds of pounds."

Daphne squeezed Claudia's arm. "I've *got* to get some paracetamol. Let's get off at Charing Cross. There's a Boots Chemist in the terminus."

"Fine with me," said Claudia, glad for any excuse to leave the Tube.

Three minutes later, they were first out the door and heading up the tunnel that led to street level. "Can you make it up the stairs all right?" she asked.

"How feeble do you think I am, you silly cow?"

Claudia grinned. "Keeping a British stiff upper lip, are you?"

Daphne landed a light punch on her arm. "Do shut up and get on with it."

They climbed the three flights of stairs that would take them where shops and take-away stands lined the terminal: Burger King, Funky Pigeon, The Pasty Shop.

Claudia spotted the Boots in the corner. "Look, there's a bench outside the store. Why don't you sit down, I'll get the Paracetamol."

"Thanks, luv. There'll be another Tube along in a few minutes."

Claudia hurried to the drugstore and grabbed a bottle of water and a small packet of paracetamol, the British equivalent of acetaminophen.

"That'll be one pound sixty-four," said the shop assistant at the checkout. It sounded like a lot for the two items, but not knowing whether the price was reasonable or not, Claudia dumped several coins on the counter and sorted through the unaccustomed currency for the right amount while the assistant shoved her purchases into a bag.

She pushed through the shop door and spotted Daphne through the bustle of passengers, fingers pressed to her temples. As Claudia started toward her, a tremendous boom sounded from somewhere far below. The building shook like an earthquake.

But London didn't have earthquakes.

For about five seconds there was silence. Then the screaming started.

fifteen

THE LIGHTS IN THE terminal flickered and went out, leaving behind the sounds of panic. Moments later they were back on, revealing frightened commuters rushing toward the "Way Out" signs.

Claudia's ears were ringing as she hurried over and helped Daphne up from the bench.

"Just a problem with an electrical panel," a railway worker in an orange vest was telling a group of passengers. "Nothing to worry about, the trouble is farther down the line."

"Do we really have to go back down there?"

"It's the fastest way home. Let's get down there before it gets too crowded."

They were down the first flight of stairs to the tunnels when a second blast from below rocked the building.

"Let's get out of here," Claudia urged.

As if coming out of a trance, Daphne swung around. "Come on, follow me."

Back in the terminus crowds of people were streaming through every exit. Claudia and Daphne went out through the Boots, where there was an exit to The Strand. Outside, they saw a dozen or more uniformed police officers running into the station through the main entrance.

To their left, two hundred feet away, was Trafalgar Square. Daphne turned right. "We'll catch a black cab up to London Bridge. We can take the train from there."

Claudia followed wordlessly, thinking of the recent bombings in Paris, Turkey, Israel, and closer to home—the terrorist shooters in San Bernardino. Was this another such attack? Her heart was in her mouth as they joined the throng leaving Charing Cross to hurry past the shops and eateries, the classy Savoy Hotel, and a theater advertising a performance of *Kinky Boots*.

Traffic on the always-crowded Strand had come to a standstill. Horns blared; frustrated drivers shouted. Tourists and business people clogged the sidewalk as word of the explosions spread. Daphne took a moment to down the painkillers, as Claudia wondered how they were going to get through the jam.

They started walking again. From time-to-time Daphne stepped into the road to hail a taxi, but the black cabs were already crammed with passengers trying to leave the area. Sirens sounded in the distance.

"We should be able to get the 321 bus to Sidcup," Daphne said, giving up. "It'll stop a dozen times, but at least we'll get home. It's about a two mile walk from here."

They sped along the crowded sidewalk, Claudia's thoughts racing at warp speed. Common sense told her this was why Mike Chapman had abruptly ended their conversation. Maybe there had been a warning that a bomb was about to explode. It had happened before in London, back in 2005, when fifty-six people were killed, and hundreds more injured.

The images flashing through her brain skidded to a halt at the cell phone their fellow passenger had found on the seat. Could those two bickering men have left the phone on purpose as a detonator? Or was that just paranoid thinking? She did not think so. At least two blasts had occurred. The tubes came through the stations briskly, disgorging one group of passengers, taking on another and leaving within moments.

Claudia thought of the people who had shared the compartment with them, and their imaginary handwritings, and felt a wave of nausea. She prayed they had all made it safely off the train, but from the intensity of the explosion, that hope seemed overly optimistic.

White emergency vans raced past, lights flashing, klaxons wailing. Claudia pulled out her phone and tried Jovanic's number, but there was no cellular service. She would have to wait until they got back to Daphne's house and hope the landline phone or the computer would work.

They entered a Cross Rail tunnel erected during roadwork at one of the nearby Tube stations. A busker in a red hoodie sat on the floor, oblivious to what was going on a few dozen feet below, playing his guitar and singing off-key. Emerging at the far side they found traffic still set at a crawl.

Upon reaching the bus stop at Tower Bridge, they learned that every Underground station had been closed. The word 'bomb' was on the lips of many they passed by.

"It's going to be quite a long wait, I'm afraid," Daphne said as they joined the long line. "Everyone who doesn't live in the City is trying to get home."

More than an hour later they boarded one of the big, red double-deckers en route to Sidcup, standing room only. Holding onto a seat back for balance, Claudia could not help comparing the stunned silence of the passengers to reactions to disasters back home. Everyone on the American bus would have been exchanging stories: "Where were you when the bomb went off?" As a people, the British were more reserved. And this sort of thing had happened too many times in their metropolis.

By the time they were sitting at Daphne's dining table with glasses of wine, it had passed nine o'clock and they were both exhausted. Neither had an appetite for food, and Daphne was still nursing the remnants of her headache. The television was on in the lounge and they could hear the continuing litany of horrifying details as they came to light: definitely a bomb, at least twenty dead, scores injured.

"I can't believe it," Daphne kept repeating. "If we'd stayed on that train we might have been killed."

"Your headache saved our lives," Claudia agreed. She kept asking herself why she was not more shaken by the experience. Why she was calm and composed. Maybe it was shock. As she had done every hour, she got out her phone and checked the bars. Still no service.

"I need to get hold of Mike Chapman. I hope he checks his email—good thing your computer wasn't affected. I have to tell him about those two men who left their phone, if it was a phone. Do you remember what they looked like?"

Daphne made a face. "The way I was feeling, I wouldn't have noticed if Hugh Grant had sat on my lap and planted a wet one on my lips. Thank God for paracetamol." Her eyes filled with sudden tears. "Oh, those poor people. That could have been us. That lady who found the phone..." her voice trailed off on a sob.

They had watched the coverage—the twisted tangle of train carriages, people being helped from the tunnels by emergency responders. Some were covered in blood, some with multiple gashes or bits of glass marring their faces and arms. They were called the lucky ones, the ones who had not lost limbs, or their lives.

The news media was out in force, shoving microphones in the victims' dazed faces. The survivors wore the same stunned expression as Claudia had after being assaulted by Danny Ortiz—as if they could not fathom what had happened to them. She wanted to yell at the interviewers to leave these people alone. But some of those people seemed to have a need to talk about it. At least if their loved ones were watching the broadcast, they would know they were alive.

She drifted back into the lounge and dropped into one of the armchairs facing the television.

"Law enforcement officials received a non-specific warning of a bomb that was about to be detonated in what appears to be an act of terrorism," the news anchor said. "The information did not include a time or location, and police had no time to check out the merits of the claim and close the Underground. At the moment, no terrorist organization has taken responsibility for the attack."

The camera cut to a reporter outside the station, talking to a young man who looked to be in his twenties, his eyes wide and round, as if he was seeing something no one else could see.

"I understand you were on the train just before the bomb went off," said the reporter.

"I was with my mum. I'd just said, 'Bye mum, see you tonight,' and I got off..." As if he had just realized that his mother was dead, the lad's mouth opened in a wail that raised the hair on Claudia's arms. She snatched up the remote control, unable to endure his grief, and switched stations.

A group of talking heads in suits sat around the large, circular newsroom desk, hashing and rehashing the bombing. "It's quite possible Dax Odell, the Irish activist, could be responsible," said the sole female contributor, perking up Claudia's ears. "He's suspected in at least two recent bombings."

"That's quite a stretch," said Claudia, as Daphne entered. Carrying her wine glass, she dropped into the other chair. "To go from blowing up a mailbox or a sundial—assuming he did—to killing dozens of people on a train, doesn't sound like the same kind of person."

"Still, a bombing is a bombing."

"Maybe. But it seems like a different M.O. If a note turns up in a geocache, it might convince me."

Daphne's reply was interrupted by the ringing of the landline phone. She glanced at the clock on the mantelpiece. "It's gone ten. Maybe your Mike Chapman?" Leaving her glass on the side table, she bustled into the kitchen, returning a few moments later. "It's Joel calling for you."

It was two AM in L.A. Jovanic, who had been working late, had heard the news of the bombings and had been trying to get through to Claudia's mobile phone for hours. Eventually, he had searched out Daphne's contact information.

"We're fine," Claudia assured him. "We were on one of the trains that was bombed, but we got off a stop early. We were quite far away, on street level, when the explosion happened." She realized that although she was exaggerating the distance for his comfort, her voice was steady, quite matter of fact. Again, she wondered why she wasn't more shaken.

"Thank God you're safe," Jovanic said. "That's all that matters." He hesitated. "Are you *sure* you're okay?"

His tone told her he was worried she would relapse and lose the ground she had gained from the EMDR session with Zebediah Gold.

"I swear to you, Joel, I'm good. If you need to worry about something, think about all those families whose loved ones won't be coming home tonight."

"No one has taken responsibility yet."

"Some people here are trying to hang it on your suspect, Dax Odell. Has there been any word about him?"

"Not that I'm aware of. As far as I know, he's still out of the country. Did you connect with Mike?"

"We were supposed to get together this afternoon. He'd got hold of Odell's handwriting. But then the bombing happened. Joel, I think Daphne and I may have seen the bombers."

"*What?*"

Claudia explained about the two men who had left the cell phone just minutes before the bomb detonated.

"I'll see if I can reach him. You and Daphne need to make a record of everything you can about what they looked like—height, weight, ethnicity. Write it all down. You know what to do, you've been there before."

Claudia figured he was thinking something along the lines of: *There she goes again, getting involved in another dangerous situation.* More than once their relationship had been threatened by what he viewed as her reckless behavior. It wasn't that she intended to piss him off, but sometimes things just seemed to happen. She had not followed those two men onto the Tube and sat down across from them. She had just been trying to get Daphne home. It was sheer coincidence they had taken that seat.

They had no more than ended the call when the phone rang again. Thinking Jovanic had forgotten something, she picked up the receiver. "Did you forget to tell me you love me?"

"Er—could I speak to Claudia Rose, please?"

Not recognizing the male voice, Claudia felt warmth creep into her cheeks. "Who's calling?"

"My name is Elliott Field. I'm a reporter with the *London Morning Daily*. I wondered whether—"

"How did you get this number?"

"Um, I saw you on *Good Afternoon London.* The television station had this as your local contact number. I apologize for calling at this late hour, but with the chaos this afternoon—"

"Yes, it is late," Claudia interrupted. "What is it you want?"

"Ah, yes, er…in the interview, you were commenting on Dax Odell's handwriting. Now that he's being looked at in this latest bombing, I'd love to get a quote for the morning edition."

"I didn't comment on Dax Odell's handwriting. I hadn't seen any authenticated writing of his. What I said was, the two notes that were found didn't match each other."

"I see." He paused. "When you say you 'hadn't' seen it, does that mean you've seen it since?"

The guy had a good ear. She would have to watch what she said. "I've seen something that's purported to be his," she admitted with reluctance. "But it wasn't very good quality."

"Was it good enough for you to decide whether Odell wrote either of the notes?"

Knowing from bitter experience that reporters had a habit of taking things out of context and twisting them, creating new so-called "quotes" out of whole cloth, Claudia answered the question with caution. "It was not consistent with the note found after the sundial bombing. It wasn't good enough for me to compare to the one found in the US."

"Here's the thing, Ms. Rose. Our newspaper received a note this afternoon that seemed to warn of an imminent attack. We turned it over to the authorities, but I've got a copy. Might I email it to you and get your opinion?"

"You want to know if Dax Odell wrote it?"

"That would be brilliant. If you could tell me something about the personality of the person who wrote it, too, all the better. I've got your email address from your website. I'm sending the photo of the note to your email now. Could I hang on while you have a look?"

"No. I'll need some time to look at it. If I have anything to say, I'll email you back." She hung up the phone before the reporter could protest.

With the mobile networks still inaccessible, Daphne was happy to let Claudia check her email on her computer. She logged on to her email account and found Elliott Field's message already waiting in her in-box.

She downloaded it and enlarged the photograph of the note on the screen, then printed it out. It did not take a second thought to see this was not the same hand that had written either of the notes found in the geocaches. Her quick first impression before reading the words was that the author was foreign born.

The note, which had been photographed through a plastic evidence bag, was written in all capital letters, a style known as block printing. The primitive letter formations reasserted Claudia's belief that the writer was not at ease writing in the English language.

The words she now read chilled her:

WE CANNOT BE STOPPED.

WE ARE ALL AROUND YOU.

YOU SHOULD BE AFRAID. TODAY.

BOOM!!!

GOD ISGREAT

The note was unsigned.

Claudia hit Reply and composed a brief email to the reporter. First she wrote her opinion that no correlation could be found between the three questioned letters. Then she added that this new letter had probably been written by someone educated in a non-English speaking country.

She continued: "The extreme space between words represents more than just difficulty with the language. Along with the printed style, it suggests someone with no empathy; one who feels isolated and disconnected from others." As she keyed in those words, Claudia reminded herself that she had thought something similar of Dax Odell. But there were important differences. In Odell's case, his writing showed emotional detachment, but not the lack of empathy she saw here, which was an important distinction.

From the small amount of writing she had analyzed in the logbook, Claudia believed that the roots of the writer's emotional detachment were to be found in a painful childhood. From Jovanic's research, she was aware that Odell's parents had been killed during an IRA protest against the British government when he was a young child. As his grandfather was also an activist who had done some serious prison time, chances were pretty good Dax had been raised in an angry home.

She keyed in her thoughts about the most recent bomb threat: "The handwriting in the threat letter you received indicates the writer never bonded with a loving caregiver. He has little to no capacity for caring about his fellow humans. Handwriting cannot predict actions, but this person has the *potential* for violent acting out in the name of a cause." And that very lack of empathy made him far more dangerous than Odell. She hit Send and waited for the phone to ring.

When it did ten minutes later, Claudia snatched up the receiver before it could ring a second time and disturb Daphne, who had turned off the television and gone up to bed.

"Thank you very much, Ms. Rose," Elliott Field said. "You've confirmed my feeling about this. I'll give you credit in the article, of course."

"I don't care about that. But I have one question."

"Yes?"

"What other handwriting analysts have you asked for an opinion?"

"I'm sorry, but we don't give out that kind of information before the article is in print."

"You called me at ten o'clock at night after a very stressful day," Claudia flared. "I did what you asked..." She left the rest of what she was thinking unspoken.

The line went quiet as Field hesitated. "You're right; we did contact one other expert."

"I'd like to know who I'm being quoted with."

"It was..." Claudia heard the tapping of fingers on a keyboard, then Field said, "Uh, the other expert was Mr. Hewett Pflueger. I believe you're aware he'd given an opinion earlier that the two notes found in geocaches were written by Dax Odell."

"So I hear. And what did Mr. Pflueger say about the authorship of the bomb note?"

"It was his opinion that the third letter was also written by Odell."

sixteen

"PFLUEGER HAS GOT TO be the biggest hired gun in the world," Daphne said at breakfast the next morning.

"Some people are willing to pay for the answer they want, and people like Pflueger have zero scruples."

"But how can he take three handwritings that have nothing in common and say they came from the same hand? Even that reporter knew better."

Claudia dipped a corner of toast into her soft-boiled egg. "If Pflueger believes that, it's a case of confirmation bias."

"What's that mean?"

"Knowing they expected the handwriting to be done by this Dax Odell person, he found a way to justify an opinion that it was Odell's."

"He'd say anything that got him a bit of notoriety."

"I'm afraid so; it makes the whole field look bad." Claudia poured cream into her coffee and stirred, her eyes on her tablet next to her plate, where Elliott Field's article filled the screen. To her relief, the reporter had done a creditable job of presenting her analysis of the two sets of handwriting.

She had insisted on emailing her comments to him, rather than making them verbal, because that would make it harder to misquote her. Field had given Pflueger a small quote near the end of the article, merely stating that the other handwriting examiner had offered a differing opinion. Below the article, dozens of readers had left comments, several of them hateful. Some were trolls who decried handwriting analysis as voodoo. Claudia was used to it, but it always raised her ire. It was all she could do to restrain herself from rushing off a scathing reply, but that would lead to a useless escalation of the insults.

Her phone sounded the tone that a text message had come in. At last, cell service was back up.

"It's from Joel," she said, reading the short missive. "Mike's going to call me later. Oh, get this—he's liaising with New Scotland Yard. We'll both have to be interviewed."

Daphne frowned. "I've got nothing to say about it. I know those men were on the train because you said so, but I couldn't possibly describe them."

"That's all you can—" Claudia's phone rang. The screen showed "Unknown Caller."

"Go on. It might be Mike. I don't mind." Without another word, Daphne got up from the table and headed for the kitchen, leaving Claudia to answer the call with some privacy.

"Can I speak to Miss Claudia Rose?" The voice was male, deep, but with a slight lilt.

"Who's calling?"

"You're the handwriting expert, right? The one on television yesterday, and quoted in the paper this morning?"

"I am. Who is this?" She was beginning to get the feeling that she knew who was on the other end of the line. Still, at his next words, her heart beat faster.

"My name is Dax Odell."

Even though she had half-expected it, she swallowed hard. "What can I do for you, Mr. Odell?"

"What you said about me in the paper—that I didn't write those notes—the sundial one and the one yesterday about the Tube bombing?"

"Yes?"

"I wanted to tell you that you're right, I didn't."

"Well, thank you, it's good to be validated. What about the one in the US, the one about the bomb in the mailbox?"

He hesitated. "It's not what you think."

"What I think, is a woman is dead because of the bomb you set. I guess you know the police there would like a chat with you."

"Yeah, I know it. It's a terrible tragedy that was never meant to happen."

"But it did happen. And if you planted that bomb, you're responsible for her death." She withheld the information that Sylvia Vasquez died from a heart attack, not as a direct outcome of the cherry bomb. That fact had been kept from the media, and as far as she was concerned, Dax Odell did not deserve to be absolved in any way.

"There's a bigger picture here, Claudia—d'you mind if I call you Claudia?"

The more Odell spoke, Claudia noticed, the stronger his Irish brogue became. "I don't care what you call me. Just tell me *why* you're calling at all. I don't think it's just to compliment me, is it?"

"Well, darlin', I'm after needin' your help."

"My *help*? Why on earth would I help you?"

"First of all, because you know what you're talking about. Not like that fella who said I wrote all the notes. He's dead wrong about that."

"We've established he's wrong. It's not your handwriting on the bomb threat. What else?"

"Meet me and I'll explain it all to yeh."

"You can't be serious," Claudia said in amazement. "I'm not going to meet you, Mr. Odell. How could you even think I would?"

He started talking faster, as if more words could persuade her. "You have to understand, Claudia, it's a desperate situation. Things are not just being blown up for the fun of it."

"It doesn't matter why. There's no good reason."

"It draws attention to the cause."

"A deadly way to get attention, Mr. Odell. Look, I understand you're protesting Agrichem and their pesticides, and I get it. But—"

"Once you know what's going on, you'll *want* to help. Look, I've done a bit of research on you, Claudia. You're a good-hearted lady. From what I've read you've gotten yourself into some hard situations more than once, helping other people who were in need."

"How in the world—"

"I also read you got attacked a few weeks ago in court. Yet you're here, keeping up your work. You're a strong woman. You could do many people a great service, and all we're asking is a bit of your time and that you tell the truth."

"I've already done that. You saw the TV show and the article. I have nothing more to say."

"You don't know that. Just meet me in Cambridge. *Please.*"

The passion in his voice was starting to sway her common sense. Claudia considered herself a good judge of character and she had seen his handwriting, albeit a very small amount. Not ready to give in, she pushed aside the small signs of pathology. "I don't know what you've read about me, but you of all people should know the media routinely tells half-truths and outright lies."

"Yes, I do know that, but I—well, I get intuitions that are not often wrong."

"Regardless of your research, Mr. Odell, you don't know me. What makes you think I wouldn't agree to meet you, then talk to the police and set you up?"

"I just don't believe you would," he said simply, disarming her. "Look, Claudia, I can't stay on the phone. I'm afraid they might have a trace."

Now her curiosity was starting to get the better of her. She plugged in her earbuds to continue the conversation and tap on her tablet at the same time. The Google maps app popped up. She keyed in *distance from Sidcup to Cambridge?* Seventy-five miles was the instant response.

"Cambridge is a long way from where I'm staying—at least two hours. I'd have to go to London to catch a train."

Daphne popped her head around the door, her dark eyes alight with interest. She must have heard Claudia say her caller's name and been listening from the kitchen. "I'll drive you," she mouthed, nodding her encouragement.

"Wait." Claudia paused, hardly believing what she was about to say. "My friend has just offered to give me a lift. That's the only way this might work, and I make no promises about helping you. Take it or leave it."

"I'll take it. *Thank you.*" The relief was plain in Odell's voice. "You can meet me at the Eagle Pub. It's on Bene't Street. Just ask anyone once you get into the area. They'll know it."

She tapped in the name of the pub and pulled up directions. "What's your phone number?"

"You don't need that."

"How will you know when we're there?"

"Don't worry. I'll find ye. Just take a table in the RAF Bar. I'm afraid your friend will have to wait somewhere else while we talk. The fewer involved the better."

Claudia glanced at the clock. "It's 8:30. We could make it by 11:00."

"Excellent. Go in and order a coffee." He was quiet for a few seconds. Then, "I suppose I should say it anyway: Don't bring any coppers with you or the drive will be a waste of your time."

"Don't worry." Claudia ended the call and stared at her phone. Her face was hot and tingly, her hands trembling. She had just arranged to meet a man who was wanted by police around the world. Jovanic would be furious if he knew. *He mustn't know,* a little voice told her. At least, not until she found out what Dax Odell wanted from her.

She would be safe with Daphne knowing where she was. They were meeting in a public place, after all. What could happen? A little thrill ran through her. She glanced up at her friend, who was doing a nervous jig around the room, and asked, "What are you supposed to wear to meet an international terrorist?"

Privately, Claudia thought of Daphne's mustard-colored Fiat 500 as the Clown Car. Daphne kept it mostly for driving to Sidcup High Street or the Tesco for shopping. Squeezing into the front seat, Claudia assured herself that, while it might not be the most comfortable vehicle for a long ride, it beat taking several trains to Cambridge.

They were thirty miles along the M25 when her phone rang with an unknown number. Thinking it might be Dax Odell with a change of plan, she answered, at once regretting it.

"Claudia. Mike Chapman. What the hell's going on?"

"Mike, hi, I tried to reach you. Did Joel tell you we might have seen—"

Chapman broke in. "Why is Dax Odell calling your phone?"

"*What*? How do you—" In the middle of her chagrin at being caught and her dread that Mike Chapman would tell Jovanic, Claudia thought of what Dax had said about a trace on his phone. "If you have his phone tapped, you already know why he called me."

"A trace isn't the same as a wiretap, and I think you know that. Now, tell me what the hell's going on."

"Nothing's going on. He saw what I'd said in the media. He called to thank me for my opinion that he didn't write any of those threats." Why wasn't she telling him the whole truth? She glanced sidelong at Daphne, who gave her a thumbs up. Partners in crime. Could they be charged with obstructing justice, or something of the sort? She wasn't up on UK criminal law.

"That's it?" Chapman sounded skeptical. "He just wanted to say 'thanks'?"

"Pretty much. He was appreciative. I guess when everyone's out to get you, every little thing helps."

"Everyone's out to get him because he's a criminal."

"Yeah, that's what Joel says."

Chapman seemed to accept her explanation and, to her relief, dropped the point. "Look, I need you and your friend to come in and give a statement about what you saw yesterday."

She gave him the rundown about the two bickering men who had departed the train, leaving behind a cell phone.

"I want you to meet with our sketch artist. When can you get here?"

"Sorry, can't now. Late afternoon, or tomorrow would be better. Anyway, I've already told you everything I know."

"Where are you?" Chapman asked, impatience making his tone crisp. "I have to—"

"You're breaking up, Mike. Sorry, I'm losing you." Claudia hit the End button and stuffed the phone in her purse, asking herself what the hell she had just done.

Odell was right when he'd said finding the Eagle would be easy. The 500-year-old pub was in the center of the charming university town, as traditionally British an establishment as any American could wish for. Daphne dropped Claudia at the corner of the street. She was thrilled to have the time to tour King's College chapel. The chapel, constructed in 1446, under the orders of Henry VI, was just down the road from the Eagle. Daphne would wait there for a text message that Claudia was ready to be picked up.

Claudia wended her way through the maze of rooms in the pub, which seemed to be populated mostly by students, and visitors like her. She was ten minutes early for their appointment.

The RAF Bar's claim to fame was its graffiti-covered ceiling. There was a story behind that ceiling, but for the moment, Claudia could concentrate on nothing but meeting Dax Odell. As he had instructed, she got coffee and found a small table in the corner. To hide her nerves, she pretended to study the wartime photos and plaques covering the walls as she sipped her coffee. When she realized she had stared at each photograph a half-dozen times, she stopped looking.

She had anticipated Odell being late, and he was. It made sense for him to stake her out and make sure she had kept her word about coming alone to the pub before he approached her. Yet, even though she was expecting him and her senses were set on high alert, when Odell slipped into the seat opposite her, Claudia was taken off-guard.

A flat, gray tweed cap sat low on his forehead, but the peak could not cover the heavy brows slashed above vivid, violet-blue eyes. The moustache and goatee he'd worn in the photos Jovanic had found were gone, though his clean-shaven chin bore a dark shadow. Patrician nose, firm lips. Handsome enough to leave her breathless.

"Have you been admiring the most famous ceiling in Cambridge?" asked Odell.

"What?" Her gaze automatically went up again to view the words and numbers spread across the darkened plaster.

"This is called the American Room, but both the RAF and the American 8th Air Force inscribed their squadron numbers up there with candle flames, matches, lipstick. Just think of those young men, standing on chairs balanced on a tabletop, leaving a bit of themselves behind. How many of them made it home from the war, d'you suppose?"

"I wish it could have been all of them, but that seems improbable."

"Yes, it is. But they were fighting for a cause they believed in." He waited, letting that sink in. "Thanks for coming, Claudia."

"The FBI called me," she blurted. "You were right about the trace. They knew you'd been in touch with me."

Under the black leather jacket he wore, Odell's shoulders tensed. "What did you tell them?"

"Nothing. Just that you wanted to thank me for giving a correct opinion."

He didn't relax. "That's good. Thanks. We can't stay here. The coppers follow me day in and day out, trying to get something on me, but the nosy buggers don't have a right to know everything I do. If they put a trace on your phone, too, they'll be here before we know it."

"It's all right, my friend and I exchanged phones when she dropped me off here. She's gone sightseeing at the Cathedral."

Odell shot her an admiring glance. "Clever as well as lovely; not a bad combination. But we need to go. There are some people who are very anxious to meet you."

"You didn't say anything about going anywhere else. Or meeting anyone." Alarms started clanging in her head. "I'm not—"

He raised his hands, palms out, with a warm smile that lit up his eyes. "I promise you, Claudia, nothing untoward is going to happen to you. I give you my word."

"The word of a bomber? Of a killer?" She spoke without thinking, saw the flash of pain in his eyes and instantly regretted it.

"Fair enough," he said quietly with a wry twist of his lips. "How about, the word of an Irishman, on me sainted mother's grave."

Claudia sighed. "Where is it you want to take me?"

"Don't worry, m'love, it's a very public place."

Trying not to be distracted by his looks and charm, she gazed into Dax's eyes and, reassured by what she read there, put aside her misgivings. She would have liked to let Daphne know she was leaving the pub, but it might alert the Feds, since they had tracked Dax to her phone. A small lie would have to suffice.

"You'll have to promise to get me back here by 1:30," she told Dax, hanging her purse over her shoulder. "If I'm not here to meet my friend by then, she'll contact the FBI."

"We'll be cutting it close." He rose from his chair. "We'll need to hurry."

Outside the Eagle, Dax threw a furtive glance around and tucked Claudia's arm in his as if they were a couple. Guiding her to the right, he started walking. At the corner she insisted on stopping to gawp at an immense clock built into the wall. Standing atop the gold sculptured clock, which itself was more than four feet tall, was a gigantic insect.

"That's the Corpus Clock," said Dax. "Stephen Hawking inaugurated it a few years ago."

"What's the grasshopper on top?" said Claudia. "I'm not sure I'd mind using a pesticide if I ran into that thing."

"It's a locust. It represents time being eaten up. And *our* time is being eaten up now, so let's go on. You can have a better look at it later."

Turning left onto Trumpington Street, which was crowded with tourists and students. Dax and Claudia hurried along the pavement, soon passing the great churches and colleges for which Cambridge was known; Corpus Christi College on the left, St. Catherine's opposite.

The biting wind cut into Claudia's face and she wished she had brought her scarf. The weather when they'd left Kent in the morning had been warmer, but she had not known then that she would be walking around Cambridge. Hunching into her coat, she glanced up at the growing bank of black clouds roiling overhead. "Where are we going?"

"You're not afraid of the water, are you, Claudia?"

"That's a non-answer," she said, but a kernel of suspicion was growing fast. "You'd better tell me what you have in mind; there's a storm coming."

Dax grinned, showing crooked bottom teeth, a startling imperfection in the handsome face. "Don't worry, luv, the storm won't come before you're back, safe and sound at the Eagle."

She could hear Jovanic's incredulous voice in her head: *Are you gullible enough to believe Odell? You're worse than the teenage girls in those slasher movies. Don't go into the basement, Claudia.*

She told herself she should break away and make a mad dash back to the safety of the Eagle, but her curiosity had gotten the better of her. Besides, as she had lain in bed the night before, unable to sleep, thinking of all she had survived over the past few years, and now, the narrow escape from the

Tube bombing, she was still feeling invincible. It was as if no matter what she did, it would not result in harm coming to her. Was she crazy? *Probably.*

"Just a minute more," said Dax, as though picking up on her thoughts. "It'll be all right. Trust me"

They turned right onto Silver Street, past Queen's College, and came to Granta Place, where he steered her to a punting dock by the Silver Street Bridge.

Claudia gazed down the short flight of steep stone steps at the rows of flat-bottomed boats lined up in the dark green River Cam. What did Dax Odell have in mind for her?

seventeen

JOVANIC

Jovanic turned onto Le Conte Avenue and entered the UCLA campus. Parking was always a challenge at the university, but today he got lucky and found a space in a parking structure near the Biochem building.

As usual, he was running late. He had spent the morning interviewing witnesses in a domestic violence homicide. The husband had called the cops himself. All that was left to do was write the reports. But the victim's mother had not wanted to let him go. He could not very well tell her that while he was genuinely sorry for her loss, he didn't have time to listen to how wonderful her daughter had been. The crack pipe they had found in the young woman's purse did not quite match the mother's story.

So now, here he was, clutching a brown paper evidence bag, trying to keep his cool as he hurried toward the six-story, red brick building. The call he had received from Mike Chapman made keeping his cool easier said than done. What the *fuck* was Claudia doing with Dax Odell? The thought brought the blood rushing to his face and dread to his heart. She had promised to stop letting herself get drawn into dangerous situations, and now she'd gone halfway around the world to do it once again.

Exiting the elevator on the fifth floor, Jovanic stepped into the hallway and searched the names on the row of office doors until he found the one he wanted. Chapman's call had left him infuriated, and afraid for Claudia's safety, but it had also renewed his interest in the Vasquez homicide.

"Enter," a woman's voice called out in answer to his knock. Jovanic did, and found himself in a cubbyhole of an office. An attractive blonde with a big white smile and perky breasts looked back at him from behind a desk piled high with papers and publications. "Come on in, Detective," she said.

"Dr. White?"

"None other," said the biochemist. "Please, have a seat."

Victoria White was nothing like what he had expected when he made the appointment with her student aide. Someone white-haired and stooped, wearing a white coat was more like it. He should have known better than to second-guess. Claudia would tell him he was being sexist if he shared his private thought that the woman was too pretty to be a scientist. He knew it was ridiculous, but as angry as he was with his fiancée for what he deemed her poor judgment in choosing to fraternize with a suspected terrorist, he managed to justify it to himself.

"Thanks for seeing me on short notice," Jovanic said, taking the side chair White indicated.

"Makes a nice break from the routine. Can I get you anything? Coffee, water? I don't have much to offer."

"Thanks, I'm good. I just have a couple of questions I hope you can help me with."

"Hit me."

"Doctor White," Jovanic began.

"Please call me Vicki," she interrupted. "Formality is overrated."

Was she flirting, or did he simply imagine she was shooting him a coy look from under her lashes? Flattered, he squashed a small stab of guilt. Hell, he might be engaged to be married, but he was still a guy, and the truth was, Vicki White looked more like a hot model than his chauvinistic idea of a scientist.

He smiled back. "Okay, Vicki. I'd like to talk about pesticides. As I'm sure you are aware, there have been quite a few protests targeting companies like Agrichem." At her nod, he continued, "The protesters are saying the chemicals are harming, even killing their children, including the unborn ones."

"They're right."

His brows went up. "I'm surprised you're so quick to admit it."

"Well, Joel—may I call you Joel? It may be true, but the fact is, we *need* pesticides. Without them, some vegetable crops would be reduced by as much as half. Even more in the case of cereals, and that wouldn't help world hunger, would it?" Vicki White waved her arms. "There are all kinds of pests attacking our foods: bugs, fungi, weeds. They affect the food supply for vast numbers of people. The bottom line is, if we want our population to have a healthy diet, which means eating a lot of fresh fruit and vegetables, we have to use chemical pesticides. Without them, farmers would lose money and end up being put out of business."

"I'm not sure poison is part of a healthy diet," Jovanic shot back. "And for the people who are affected—well, the little reading I've done talks about genetic damage, reproductive problems, cancer."

"Yes, of course," White stopped him. "From their point of view it's not worth the risk. But what about for the rest of the world?"

"It's a difficult problem with more than one side, I guess."

"Yes, it is."

"Well, we're not going to be able to solve that one," Jovanic said. He opened the paper bag in his lap and removed a small paint can. "There's something else that I hope you can help me with. This is evidence in an incident where an explosive device was left in a mailbox. I'm hoping you can analyze the residue and tell me what it was."

Another dazzling smile. "And here I thought you'd brought lunch."

Now he was sure she was flirting. He opted for the safe course. "The arson guys said there might be something that would give us information about where the device was constructed."

Vicki White raised a brow. "And, they're not doing the analysis, why?"

"Normally, they would, but I'm told there's a backlog at our lab. They've got a reduced staff. One of the regular scientists is on maternity leave, plus they've had budget cutbacks, yada yada. Hey, you work in a university. You know how bureaucracies operate."

"No kidding."

"If you *can* help out, I'd rather not wait a month for results." Jovanic handed over the paint can. "The explosive was wrapped in toilet tissue. It goes off with a big flash-bang, but not everything is destroyed. The paper pretty much turns it into confetti, but there was enough for the arson guys to collect some specimens. This is a little piece of it."

White pried open the can and peered inside at a fragment of red paper half the size of a postage stamp. "I can run this through GC-MS," she said, looking interested.

"Which is?"

"Gas chromatography–mass spectrometry. It's a process that can identify different substances contained in the test sample. There is one problem, though. Spectrographic methods are destructive. They burn or dissolve the paper fibers. Raman testing could give us elemental non-destructive analysis, but our Raman Spectrometer is broken. If you need it fast, we're left with the GC-MS."

"We have enough material left; it's not a problem if it's destructive."

"Good. Now, I hope you understand I can't guarantee the test will give you any clues to where the thing was manufactured. But I'm happy to run it and let you know if we find anything. It'll be two or three days before I can get back to you."

"That's a whole lot better than the crime lab." Jovanic reached a hand over the desk and shook hers. "Thank you, Vicki. I appreciate it."

"Happy to help the local gendarmes." She glanced at the big industrial clock on the wall. "Goodness, look at the time. No wonder my tummy is rumbling. Have you had lunch?"

"I wish."

"Would you care to brave the cafeteria?"

Jovanic hesitated, tempted. Then he thought of Claudia. "Thanks," he said. "It's a nice thought, but I've got another engagement."

eighteen

"WHAT ARE WE DOING here?" Claudia demanded. "You said you wanted me to help you, not go punting on the Cam."

"This is where we're meeting some friends," said Dax, pointing to the dock below.

From their vantage point on the street Claudia could see two groups of tourists waiting their turn to go out on the water. As she watched, a punt slid in at a berth several spaces down from the others, in an isolated spot all by itself. The oarsman jumped ashore and looked up toward them. Dax waved and the man waved back.

"So you planned this all along," said Claudia, fuming at the deception. "Meeting me at the pub was just a ploy. Why didn't you just ask me to meet you here?"

Dax gave a semi-apologetic shrug. "I needed to be sure you weren't being followed. Look, Claudia, I said I'd get you back to the Eagle in time to meet your friend, and I will. Now, come on, easy as you go."

He placed his hand under her elbow and, though she was furious with herself for allowing it, guided her down the steep stone staircase. They walked past the tourists to the punt that had just arrived. It was occupied by six people huddled in the nippy air—a woman, two couples and a small child.

Dax gestured to the couple closest to them: a bald man who looked as if he enjoyed his pudding a bit too much; and his companion, a plain and pleasant-looking woman with short, curly hair. Claudia judged them to be in their mid-thirties. "That's Leigh and Felicia," he said. The pair nodded at her, unsmiling, which made her wonder whether her presence here was as welcome as Dax had made it out to be.

Next, he indicated the woman who sat alone. Late twenties, dark-haired and pale. Her drawn features suggested that, unlike Leigh, she could use a good meal and a good night's sleep. This was Claire, Dax said. Claire nodded, pinch-lipped, in acknowledgment, no more congenial than Leigh and Felicia had been.

Turning to the second couple, Dax introduced them as John and Yvette. John was a man with a high forehead and an expression made stern by his horn-rimmed glasses and big, brushy moustache. Yvette was a freckled redhead with a round face and pink cheeks. Each raised a hand in greeting. The child, a boy, sat on the man's lap, pressing tightly against his chest.

Dax leaned down to ruffle his blond hair. "And this fine young specimen is Colin," he said. "Everyone, this is Claudia."

Little Colin turned large, questioning grey eyes toward her. She gave him a wink and said hello to the adults. It had not escaped her notice that Dax had refrained from giving any surnames, though they knew hers if they were aware of her appearance on *Good Afternoon London.* The five adults stared at her with expressions that varied in their degree of dubiousness. She guessed that the meeting was Dax's own idea.

"We'll move to the back," Leigh volunteered. The boat was formed in two sections with bench seating. In each section two benches faced each other. Leigh and Felicia climbed over to the second row of seats, making room for Claudia to sit in the bow across from John and Yvette and Claire, facing them all. Dax stepped onto the punt and held out his hand to her. His skin was rough, his grip firm, helping her aboard. The boat swayed a little, the water lapped against the sides.

"We'll have more privacy out here on the water," said Dax, as Claudia settled herself on the green plaid seat. "Less worry about the wrong folk showing up or listening in." He stepped onto the till and, with some skill, poled the punt from its berth and onto the river. As if by tacit agreement, no one spoke until they had left the dock and moved past the other boats.

Something in their surroundings stirred Claudia. Despite the angry sky, the nip in the air and the bare trees overhead, it was all ridiculously peaceful—the sounds of the mild splashing of water against the boat, birds chirping, a family of ducks scudding along the water—considering these people were presumed to be behind two of the bombings.

It was not until they passed beneath the Bridge of Sighs at St. John's College that Dax said, "Who wants to go first?"

"We'll start," said John, handing little Colin over to Yvette. The child's thumb went into his mouth and he started sucking furiously as she folded him in her arms.

"Colin is our grandson. He's just turned three. We're caring for him because our daughter can't. She's got the full-time care of her baby, Samuel. Our Sammy's just ten months old. He was born terribly ill and *if* he lives, he's never going to be normal." John's voice cracked with emotion. "He's always going to need special care, and it's down to the pesticides, I can tell you. We live next to a farm. Every time they spray, the kids get sicker." He dipped his chin toward his grandson. "This little one has dizzy spells, he sicks up all the time, can't keep his balance. He has to hold onto the wall or the poor mite falls over."

Yvette took up her husband's narrative, speaking in a strong northern accent. Liverpool or Manchester, maybe. "When the pesticides are in the food, you can change over to organics. Children who have been sickened by the chemicals get better almost right away, within days. But that's not true when they've been exposed inside the womb, like our boys were. And if you're wondering why we don't just move, well, all our money's gone on trying to find treatments and paying the bills. Our house is mortgaged to the hilt and we have nowhere to go. John's been made redundant at his job; we're struggling on the dole. I do a bit of work at the bakery on the High Street now and then, but the point is, something's got to be done about these chemical companies that don't care about the people whose lives they ruin."

As Yvette spoke, pity and compassion welled up in Claudia. She saw that Dax had read her perfectly—she already wanted to do something to help these people's plight. She addressed them all. "I understand your anger and frustration. But blowing things up and killing people isn't going to get the kind of attention you want, is it?"

"It wasn't meant for anyone to be killed," John flared, his gaze swinging to Dax, who was maneuvering the punt to avoid another craft going the opposite direction. "We heard about that poor soul in America. Something went wrong. The device wasn't meant to be powerful enough to do that kind of damage."

"We're not violent people," Felicia said from her seat in the stern of the boat. "We just want those horrid pesticide people to listen and not try to buy us off with a few thousand pounds. Our families are worth more than money, but that's the language they speak."

Claire, the thin woman seated alone at one end of the bench, seemed isolated from the others. Because she did not have a partner like the others did? Claudia wondered. But when she spoke, sounding posher than the others whose accents labeled them as working class, it seemed more likely it was her social status which separated her from the rest.

"My baby died," she said with a touch of defiance in her voice. "So I don't mind terribly much someone else dying if it means these companies will do something about the bloody pesticides."

"The woman who died wasn't involved with pesticides," Claudia retorted. "She was an innocent housekeeper, picking up the mail at her employer's home."

"That's as may be, but this is a war, and in war there are casualties—collateral damage, isn't it?"

"That'll be enough, Claire," Dax interrupted. "Felicia's right. We hate violence, but we also hate what's being done in the name of protecting our food."

Speaking earnestly, Leigh said, "Their sprays don't just stay in the area where they put them down, you see. It spreads all around. More than a quarter of a million people die every year because of pesticides, and too many of them are young children. It's not like you can just wash the chemicals off. Some of them are systemic—they're absorbed right into the plant."

"Yes, and they put horribly strong pesticides on the plants right up to the day they're harvested," added Yvette. "It doesn't help to wash or peel your fruit and veg, either. If it goes through the roots, it's in every part of the plant."

"And it kills more than just the insects it's supposed to target," Leigh added. "It's poison; it's going to affect any organism that's vulnerable, like young children. Or the developing fetus."

Having read about the decimation of the honeybee population due to pesticides, Claudia was not surprised at what she was hearing, nor the passion with which these people spoke. She struggled against letting her empathy get in the way of logic. "I want you to know, I wholeheartedly agree with you about the pesticides. But I don't have any power in the media. I don't know how you think I can help you."

"You might have more influence than you think you do," said Yvette. "You can keep on telling them that Dax didn't write the letter about the train bombing, for one thing. They've got to know we're nothing like those lunatics."

"I can do that if I'm asked. But don't expect me to condone the illegal things your group has done."

"We're not asking you to condone anything," said John. His eyes welled with tears that seemed to hold all the pain his family had suffered. His honest desperation hit Claudia in the heart. She knew better than to open herself up, but here she was, doing it again.

John swallowed hard, and went on, "We need all the help we can get, and like Yvette said, it's vital that we are not tarred with the same brush as the terrorists who blew up that train. Just tell the truth, that's all we ask."

Glancing around at each of the protestors, Claudia thought of the rounded handwriting in the note that had been discovered after the sundial bombing. Had it come from the hand of one of these women? Yvette, the motherly one, seemed the most logical candidate. Claire's manner was too prickly. The handwriting did not seem to fit her. But that was just a guess. It might have been written by another member who she had not met.

"How large an organization is People for Safe Food?" Claudia asked. "How many of you are there?"

"I'm not sure we want to get specific about that," Leigh answered. "I think it'll do just to say we've got affiliated groups around the world. I 'spect you want to know why Dax asked *us* to meet with you. It's because we all live fairly local. There are hundreds of families who could tell you stories just like ours."

"Thousands is more like it," John corrected.

"I'm sure there are, and it's heartbreaking that there are so many." Looking at all of them, she felt a deep pang of regret for what they had endured, and likely would continue to endure. "I'm willing to give my opinion on any handwriting issues that come up, but that's the best I can do for you. I'm not about to become an activist for your cause, regardless of how much I believe in it."

"Maybe if it was *your* family you'd feel differently," Claire sniped with a sullen glare that made Claudia dislike her. Then she remembered that Claire had lost a child, and softened.

"Let's hope it never is," Felicia hastened to add. "We don't wish harm on *anyone,* and we need you on our side."

"I'm sure Dax will find a way to contact me if I can be of use, but you've got to understand, I work in the legal system in the US. I cannot be associated with eco-terrorism—wait—" Seeing them all ready to protest, Claudia held up her hands to stop them. "I know you don't see yourselves as terrorists, but when you blow things up and people die—even one person—that's how you are identified by the world. Besides all that, I'm engaged to a police officer, which means I've got to consider not just myself, but him, too. Our reputations are all we've got. If you want my help, you'll have to accept that."

She glanced behind her at Dax, who stood on the till, silently piloting the boat, letting the others have their say. "Fine, I've got the point. Now, it's freezing out here, and I'd appreciate it if you'd take me back to the Eagle."

"You put me in a rotten position," Claudia admonished as they retraced their steps to the pub. "I'd love to be of help, but—"

Before she could finish, Dax interrupted, "It wasn't just to meet those families that I asked you to come."

"Oh? You have yet another ulterior motive for getting me to Cambridge?"

"I asked those particular people to come and meet you because—"

When he hesitated, she prompted, "Because?"

"I believe one of them is a spy for Agrichem. That's what I really want your help with."

Claudia stopped in her tracks and stared at him in surprise. "Which of them do you suspect?"

"Keep walking. Let's not draw any attention."

"Who do you suspect, and what am *I* supposed to do about it?"

"I have letters from all of them. When someone wants to join the group, they're required to write a letter explaining why they're interested before they're allowed in. Many of the ones we get are handwritten. Everyone is supposed to be thoroughly vetted with a proper background check and all. We have a sort of head office to do things like that. I'm just a front man for some of the protests, but they sent me here to look into one of the newer members a bit more. I turned up some information that doesn't sit right. Will you have a look, Claudia? We'll pay your normal fee."

Anything that involved handwriting naturally piqued Claudia's curiosity. Having just met the person Dax suspected of spying made her even more interested. "Show me the letters. We can talk about payment later."

They arrived back at the Eagle and found their way to an empty table back in the RAF room. As it was past the lunch hour, the undergrads who tended to populate the pub were attending classes.

Dax paid for their coffees at the bar and joined Claudia at the table. He reached into his jacket and removed a manila envelope. He dropped it on the table in front of her and, tapping it with his forefinger, said, "Here are the letters. I won't tell you which is which. That way we can keep it all unbiased."

Claudia held out a hand. "I'll need some time to study them. If these are originals, I'll return them if you tell me where to send them."

His face fell in disappointment. "Isn't there *anything* you can tell me straight away? Just a thing or two?"

Her irritation at the way he had manipulated her made her hedge a little. "I prefer not to do it that way, but let me have a quick look. I can at least let you know if I see any obvious red flags. I have to caution you, though. Handwriting shows *potential*. I'll be looking for signs of dishonesty and lack of integrity, but if the person doesn't feel guilty about their behavior, it may not show up. And even if it does, handwriting can't predict whether the person will or won't act on that potential."

"All right then," said Dax with a nod of agreement. "I understand. Now if you'll excuse me, luv, I'll be off to the loo. It'll give you a minute to have a go at the letters."

Claudia watched him cross the room. His body language broadcast vigilance, the way his head turned from side to side, alert to anything amiss. As he disappeared through a wide archway, she opened the envelope and shook out the contents: several sheets of paper of varying types and sizes. She quickly flipped through all the sheets, getting an initial impression of each before returning to the first page.

Daphne's phone beeped in her pocket. Claudia's stomach curled as she read what her friend had texted her: "Joel called. He knows and he's fit to be tied." Mike Chapman must have ratted her out, damn him. She had hoped to broach the subject with Jovanic in a roundabout way. Now, she had been put on the defensive.

Checking the time, she saw that the eight-hour difference made it five AM in L.A. She closed her eyes and thought it through. Daphne would not have given Jovanic this number, which meant a short reprieve. But knowing her fiancé, who was a pit bull when he wanted a result, he would not give up until he reached her. What she would say to him when they spoke was a mystery to her.

Claudia blew out a long breath through pursed lips, asking herself again whether getting married was such a good idea. Having been single for more than a decade after a brief mistake in her youth, learning how to be a "we" again and share decision-making was something she was still working at. There was no denying she loved Joel with every cell in her body, but there were some big issues between them that continued to cause hard feelings. One of the biggest was what he called her "tendency to go off half-cocked" and put herself in danger. He tended to ignore the fact that on those occasions it had not always been her own doing. Besides, she had always come out unscathed. Just like today. Dax had returned her to the pub as soon as she'd asked him to. Would an unrepentant killer do that?

She texted a message back to Daphne that she would be ready in twenty minutes. They could have lunch at the pub before returning to Kent. Twenty minutes should provide enough time to share her first impressions of the handwritings with Dax. Where was he, anyway? She looked over at the archway as a man came through, but it was not the Irishman, just a patron on his way to the bar.

Returning her attention to the first handwriting sample of the small batch, she noted its strong masculine quality. Dynamic rhythm, clear spacing, a medium right slant and moderately heavy pressure that hinted at someone whose emotions ran deep. From Claudia's point of view, the handwriting had many positive qualities and no major negatives. She made a mental note to ask Dax if the writer was Felicia. Her husband, Leigh, seemed a quieter, milder person than this handwriting suggested. They might have a role-reversed relationship.

The handwriting in the next letter was one she immediately recognized. It bore the softer garland forms of the note that had been discovered after the sundial explosion. This was someone who was motivated by their heart, who had a deep sense of empathy, a sweet, sincere person. Again, no red flags waving.

Claudia glanced up from the letter. What was keeping Dax? He'd been gone a good five minutes. With a twinge of impatience, she went on to the next sample. This one had caught her attention right away. She did not have to look far to find the red flags. Rampant signs of pathology were present throughout the handwriting: unnaturally slow writing due to overelaboration, distorted letters—forms in the middle zone that classical handwriting analysts termed "felon's claws," which pointed to feelings of guilt. The writer was one who would set himself, or herself, up for punishment over and over again. Claudia had not yet read the words, but she fully expected that she would see signs of lying if she did a statement analysis in addition to the handwriting analysis.

A third time, she glanced up, expecting to see Dax returning. The place was virtually empty. He should not have had to wait for the men's room. She refolded the papers and slipped them back into the envelope with a growing sense of unease.

She gathered her purse and the manila envelope and got to her feet, still hoping that Dax would appear and calm a sudden suspicion. Following the route he had taken through the archway, she found herself in a dim hallway where two doors were marked "Gents" and "Ladies."

After hovering there for about a minute, gathering her courage, she knocked on the Gents door and called out softly, "Dax? Are you in there?"

From the tap room came the sounds of glasses clinking and the low hum of conversation. The hallway remained silent. Was he inside...hurt, or worse? As she put her hand on the doorknob, poised to enter and see for herself, a kitchen worker in rolled-up sleeves appeared from around the corner. He grinned at her. "That's the Gents, miss."

"Yes, I know," said Claudia, feeling like a fool. "Would you mind looking to see if there's a man inside?"

He gave a short laugh. "It'd be a surprise if I *didn't* see a man inside, wouldn't it?"

"That's just hilarious. Look, I'm afraid my friend has taken ill."

"All right then." The man opened the door and went inside, returning seconds later. "No one's inside, miss. Looks like your friend has done a runner."

Claudia's heart sank. "Thank you. Is there a way out through here?"

"Go straight along the passage, through that door at the end. You'll come out on the courtyard."

Following his directions, Claudia emerged onto a patio where a few hardy patrons braved the cold. Dax must have gone this way. She made her way around the tables and went out to the street, where she texted Daphne where to find her.

As she watched for the yellow Clown Car, a man in a charcoal pinstripe suit swung around the corner and strode up to her wearing an angry scowl.

"Detective Inspector Ash Hanley," the man said, holding his warrant card high, where she could not fail to read it. "I ought to arrest you on the spot."

nineteen

JOVANIC

Jovanic stared at the ceiling, asking himself what the hell Claudia was doing, and who she was doing it with. He trusted her completely in their relationship. It was the other stuff that drove him crazy. Like going off with a possible killer, if Mike Chapman was to be believed. For such an intelligent woman, she had a bad habit of setting aside her common sense when something fired her interest, especially when children were involved.

He'd called her half a dozen times and left messages. She had not responded and he wanted to know why. Chapman wasn't answering either.

Jovanic had not been sleeping well since Claudia left for the UK. Today he had awakened at dawn after a couple hours of sleep, his body exhausted, his mind refusing to shut down. And tomorrow—no, this morning—he had a nine o'clock appointment with Evan Lockhart at his office in Malibu. He had a strong feeling there was more to learn from the Agrichem CEO about the explosion at his house.

After his initial chat with Chapman, Jovanic had contacted the LAPD task force on terrorism. Given what he knew, and with a homicide that had terrorist potential, they had brought him on board. He was now waiting to hear from Ash Hanley, Chapman's New Scotland Yard contact. It could help push forward his investigation if NSY would release the phone records he had requested.

Giving up on sleep, he crawled out of bed and into the shower. With the rush of hot water soothing his tense muscles, he thought some more about Claudia. Regardless of how much she infuriated him, he could not imagine his life without her. Seeing her lying in the emergency room bed a few weeks ago, bruised and bloodied after the courtroom attack, had made him want to kill Danny Ortiz with his bare hands.

Fury rose in him again that he had been unable to protect his fiancée. If Ortiz had not been in custody, he would have gone after the gangbanger. Jovanic slammed his fist against the tile wall, then cursed his bruised knuckles. It hurt like hell and didn't do much for the wall.

Fifteen minutes later, when he flopped back into bed, he found a voice-mail from Claudia. He listened to the message, cursing himself all over again for missing the call.

"I know you're pissed," said her recorded voice. "But everything is fine. I'm fine. No need to worry. I'll tell you all about it later. Right now, your FBI buddy and his New Scotland Yard pal are going at me with a rubber hose and bright lights. I'll call you as soon as they let me out of here. Love you, baby. Get some sleep."

What the—?

It was early afternoon in the UK. Jovanic listened to the voicemail several times, trying to read something into her voice, her words. When she said something was fine in that tone, it usually meant the opposite.

After that, sleep was more elusive than ever. Ceding the fight, he got up again and took his laptop into Claudia's office. Sitting on the sofa with the laptop on his knees, he did a search on Agrichem. According to Wikipedia, the company was founded early in the 20th century in the Midwest. Among the products they developed first were artificial sweeteners and synthetic materials. In its first fifty years, Agrichem had branched out into pesticides and was among the first experimenters in the genetic modification of plants and food crops.

He browsed through information about the founders, the spin-offs and mergers, and the company's growth into one of the world's largest pesticide producers. He read about the high-profile lawsuits the company had engaged in, both as plaintiff and defendant. It had been sued often in relation to health issues and its products in the US, the UK, and several South American countries.

An article about a worldwide demonstration protesting Agrichem's production of certain pesticides caught his attention. People for Safe Food was among the organizations listed as demonstrators. Dax Odell's name was mentioned, but he was a mere drop in the ocean of protesters the organizers claimed were participating in more than thirty countries.

Then the article started getting into technicalities about chemical formulae and Jovanic found his eyelids drooping at last. He stumbled back to bed, dozing off around five AM.

When the alarm went off, he calculated that he'd slept a total of three hours, and it felt like it. His reflection in the bathroom mirror exposed dark shadows smudging the skin that pooched below his eyes.

Too much beer and pizza, he thought sourly, chowing down on a cold slice of pepperoni for breakfast. Hot oatmeal would have gone down nicely on the cold January morning, but he couldn't be bothered even to zap a bowl. Bachelorhood sucked. He checked his phone. There had been no further contact from the UK.

Opening the refrigerator, he was strongly tempted to crack a bottle of Shock Top. His hand was on the beer carton when he hesitated. It wouldn't do his career any good to show up at his appointment smelling like a drunk.

Donning the shirt he had left draped over the bedroom chair last night, Jovanic checked his tie for stains. Finding none that would show, he slipped the already knotted noose around his neck and tightened it, wishing he could put a noose around Ortiz's neck and pull until the motherfucker's face turned purple.

He had no doubt that if he wanted some "quality time" with the cop killer at the county jail where he was housed, he could wangle a way to get it. But the better side of his nature fought and won. Let Claudia have her day and face her attacker through the legal system.

If by some insane fluke Ortiz got away with it, all bets were off. He stepped into the closet and snatched the first suit he found—the black wool—which fit his black mood.

Since Randy Coleman was scheduled to testify in a trial this morning, Jovanic drove to the Agrichem headquarters alone. The CEO's office was located on a campus above Malibu. Driving north on the Coast Highway, with Queen cranked up, belting out *We Will Rock You,* Jovanic's mood took a significant turn for the better. The Pacific Ocean sparkled on his left, making his heart swell with gratitude for where he lived. He was twenty miles out from his destination when Dr. Vicki White called.

"I know you're waiting for the test results, so I rushed it through for you."

"I appreciate it, Vicki. Were you able to get anything?"

"As a matter of fact, we were. It's kind of strange, but I think it's possible we've identified a chemical that might be helpful. That is, if you have a suspect."

"You've got my curiosity up. What did you find?"

"The GC-MS identifies different substances within a test sample, right? Well, apparently, in the environment where the cherry bomb was made, there was a chemical that's used in a certain pesticide."

Jovanic nearly dropped the phone. "A pesticide?"

"Yes, it's called diethyl axathion. It's a very potent insecticide."

"An insecticide," he echoed. "Is it harmful only to insects, or to humans, too?"

"Oh, definitely humans. And for that reason, it's banned in most countries and restricted in others. There's a movement to get it banned from any use at all, anywhere."

"You said it's restricted. Does that mean it has *some* legal uses?"

"Yes, it's banned on most food crops. It's sprayed on certain kinds of fruit trees and cotton, that sort of thing. Diethyl axathion is among the most toxic pesticides that used to be in wide use. The EPA stopped farmers from using it on vegetables and grasses about five years ago. It's very limited in its use now."

"You're right, that's very interesting. What's the effect of this diethyl—whatever you said—on humans?"

"Diethyl axathion. In plain English, it disrupts the nervous system. Someone who is exposed can have symptoms along an entire spectrum. Headaches, convulsions, vision problems, vomiting, diarrhea, respiratory arrest. Like that."

Jovanic's head was spinning. He pulled to the shoulder of the road and turned off the engine to better concentrate and absorb what he was hearing. "That all sounds pretty nasty. Is it lethal?"

"If it's caught early it can usually be treated, but when someone is poisoned by this particular chemical, the effects can last for months. There have been reports of brain damage and paralysis. It's been used as a chemical weapon in Rhodesia, in the Bush War. People have used it to commit suicide. And, it's been used to poison people by design. Odorless, colorless—cheaper than a divorce."

"Avoid alimony with a few small doses?"

"True love dies hard, Detective."

"How can I find out what companies use it here in the US?"

"That's an easy one. In the US, it's only allowed to be used on cotton crops, and there's only one company producing it. Agrichem. I'm sure you've heard of them. They're almost as big as Monsanto."

"Yes, I've heard of them."

"Well, anyway, my lab assistant identified diethyl axathion residue on the paper fragment you left with me. That means the chemical had to have been in the environment where the bomb was manufactured. Does that help your investigation at all?"

"You have no idea how much it helps. Thank you, Vicki. I owe you."

The flirtatious smile in her reply would have been hard to miss. "Don't worry, I intend to collect."

He clicked off, realizing he was going to have to nip any ideas she had about him in the bud, and tossed his phone onto the passenger seat. Questions raced through his mind as he reviewed what White had just told him. Pesticide residue on the bomb materials. A pesticide used solely by Agrichem. What the hell was going on here?

He thought back to his first interview with Evan Lockhart. What were the chances the CEO was behind the attack on his own home? The property damage had been slight and the death of the housekeeper unplanned. Lockhart and his wife had conveniently been out of the country at the time of the incident. But what motive might he have? The information Vicki White had given him could turn his interview, and the entire investigation, in a different direction.

Negotiating the winding road into the hills, Jovanic soon came to the Agrichem turnoff. He passed a six-foot high, beige and green concrete sign painted with the company's sunflower logo and stopped at the security office, where a metal gate arm barred his way.

Jovanic rolled the window down, as a bulky African-American woman in a spiffy uniform that matched the signage stepped out and strolled over to the car.

"May I help you?"

"I have an appointment with Dr. Evan Lockhart."

"May I see some identification, sir?"

Jovanic flipped open his badge wallet. The guard checked it against her clipboard and, having satisfied herself that the detective's name was on the approved list, pointed a manicured finger east. "Go straight until you see the roundabout. When you get there, turn right and drive until you see a parking garage. Take the second entrance into the garage and park anywhere you don't see a 'Reserved' sign."

"Thanks." When the arm swung up, Jovanic drove onto the property, going over in his head what he expected to accomplish with this visit. With what Vicki White had told him, and having interviewed Lockhart in his home, he was interested in seeing whether the CEO would show a different side of his personality at the office. Too bad he couldn't ask Lockhart for a handwriting sample. He knew Claudia would want one.

Jovanic parked in the garage, then followed a wide footpath to the impressive three-story glass and slate building. He was met inside the door by an armed guard and a metal detector like the ones used in the courthouse.

"No weapons allowed inside," said the guard after Jovanic showed his badge. "If you're carrying, you'll have to leave your piece here, or stow it in your vehicle. Your choice."

He was unnecessarily being a jerk and it rubbed Jovanic the wrong way. He said, "I'm here on official police business."

"So? This is private property. I don't have to allow you through if you refuse to observe company policy."

Figuring him for a cop wannabe who had flunked out of the Academy, Jovanic, who was a touch over six-two, stepped through the metal detector, his weapon setting off the alarm. He thrust his face close to the guard's.

"Listen up, asshole. Check with your boss. If you refuse me entry, you'll be obstructing police business. If you want me to place you under arrest, go right ahead. Meanwhile, your stupidity means your CEO is waiting."

The guard's face, which had drained of color, flushed bright red. He jerked back and reset the alarm. "Wait here," he muttered, then turned to a female guard on the front door side of the metal detector. "Watch him."

The second guard rolled her eyes as her colleague strode away, exiting through a door across the hall.

"I guess somebody pissed in his Cheerios this morning," Jovanic said, recalling his own earlier foul mood.

"I guess somebody be pissin' in 'em *every* mornin'," the guard replied with a grin. "Thanks for the entertainment."

"Happy to oblige."

The door opened several minutes later and the asshole returned, his lips compressed in disapproval. "Third floor, left," he said, refusing to meet Jovanic's eyes.

With a mock salute, Jovanic strode past him to the elevator. He was now ten minutes late.

On the short ride to the penthouse suite, he thought about whether Agrichem's abundance of caution in their security department might be due to the explosion at Evan Lockhart's Venice home, or had it started with the earlier break-ins at the Lancaster facility Lockhart had mentioned?

Evan Lockhart's secretary was a smartly dressed, middle-aged woman who resembled the executive's wife. Accepting her offer of coffee, Jovanic entered the CEO's office.

Evan Lockhart rose from his desk and crossed the room to greet him. Today he wore a crisp white shirt and red silk tie Jovanic envied but could not afford on his detective's salary.

"Good morning, Detective, I've been waiting for you." They shook hands, then Lockhart held up his wrist and tapped the face of his Philippe Patek. "I have another meeting. We won't have as much time as if you had been punctual."

"Your security didn't get the memo that I was expected," Jovanic said, feeling as if he had been called before the principal.

"Ah. Well, we can't be too careful these days. Our policies are not intended to cause problems for our good police officers. We'll do the best we can in the time available."

Jovanic followed Lockhart past his desk, which had enough real estate to plan a small city. They seated themselves at a small, round table.

"Some executives like an office out in the open; one that encourages the employees to stop in and chat," said Lockhart. "I prefer my meetings to take place in a more private workspace."

Jovanic took in the rolling green hills visible through the wall of windows in the corner office. "You've got a terrific view."

"That's why the windows are behind my desk. Otherwise, it would be too distracting."

While they made the usual small talk about the weather and the traffic, Lockhart's secretary returned with a tray bearing two cream-colored ceramic mugs emblazoned with the same sunflower logo as the sign at the gate.

Declining cream and sugar, Jovanic accepted his mug and took a grateful sip. The coffee was strong, hot and delicious, administering the jolt of caffeine he needed. He had noticed an unusual wooden vase on Lockhart's desk. "That's a great piece," he said, looking to create rapport with the CEO. "It has sort of a native quality."

Lockhart reached over and picked it up, handed it to him. "You're right. My wife bought several pieces in the Maldives. You may recall, that's where we were when you contacted us about the explosion."

Jovanic turned the vase over in his hands, admiring the red lacquer work with its intricate black and gold designs. It was exquisite. He handed it back. "The woodworking shows fine craftsmanship. Is this kind of work a specialty over there?"

"Yes, I'm told they start with the lacquer coating and finish by polishing it with coconut leaves. The designs are etched by hand afterwards."

"I see. After our interview I looked at some photos of the area. The water was incredibly clear. The Indian Ocean must be phenomenal diving."

"Yes, it's quite magnificent. The perfect place to get away."

"Had you been planning the trip for a while, or was it spur of the moment?" Jovanic asked, segueing to the purpose for the meeting.

"It was something we'd intended to do for quite some time. I like to plan ahead as thoroughly as possible to avoid problems later. Unfortunately, emergencies can't be planned for." He pushed aside his mug, signaling that the small talk was over. "I assume since you drove all the way out here, Detective, that you have some news for me."

Jovanic took a last sip of his coffee. "As a matter of fact, Doctor, I got some interesting news on the way over here. What can you tell me about diethyl axathion?"

The other man's eyes widened in surprise. "Why on earth would you ask about that?"

"I understand it's a chemical that's manufactured in your plant. Is that correct?"

"Yes, it is. What about it?"

"Residue of that chemical was found on a fragment of the explosive device from your mailbox."

"What? I don't understand. You're saying that one of our products..." Lockhart broke off. "I'm confused, Detective."

"I took some of the material that was left after the explosion to a lab for chemical analysis," Jovanic explained. "There were traces of diethyl axathion on that material. I'm wondering, do you have any idea how that might have come about?"

The CEO was quiet for a long moment. "Diethyl axathion is restricted in its use," he said at last. Jovanic did not tell him that he already knew this fact. "It's used in a very narrow range of operations because it's a somewhat dangerous organophosphate. People who handle the products made from it, or who apply it in the fields, have to be very careful. For that reason, relatively few employees have access to it. I'll have our HR department pull the file of anyone who might have had an opportunity to come into contact with it." The muscles around Lockhart's electric blue eyes tightened as he must have calculated how many files that could mean. "We have hundreds of employees at dozens of facilities around the world," he said with a sigh. "I'll ask our security department to start going through the local ones."

"I suggest you look for any disgruntled former employees, or current employees who might have ties to a protest group that calls itself People for Safe Food."

"I'm familiar with the group. They're as bad as those Occupy people who cropped up a few years ago."

"We believe they're behind a note found after the incident at your house, near the Playa Lagoon."

Lockhart was beginning to look concerned. "What did the note say?"

Jovanic got out his cell phone and thumbed through the photos to the series he had taken of the geocache note. He turned the screen toward the CEO. "Here, you can see for yourself."

"Something similar happened in the UK," Evan Lockhart said slowly after reading the note.

"I've seen the UK note."

"Obviously, the two incidents must be connected."

"Yes, they are. Have there been any other notes like this?"

"None I'm aware of." Lockhart pressed his lips together tight. "This adds hundreds more employees to the mix. We're already having a handwriting expert in the UK compare it with the writing style of all the employees in England who are involved with the product."

"I'll send you a copy of this one," said Jovanic. "Our expert has examined the available handwriting, but she didn't have the opportunity to compare the note to your employee files. To be frank, I think that's a long shot, Dr. Lockhart. We believe the handwriting in the note we found here to be that of a man named Dax Odell. He seems to be a leader in the People for Life protesters. Does that name mean anything to you?"

"Dax Odell," Lockhart repeated thoughtfully. "Sounds vaguely familiar, though I can't say why."

"He's been in the news lately, associated with the Tube bombing in the UK."

"And you think the person who is responsible for the Tube bombing blew up my mailbox?" Lockhart sounded alarmed.

"No, Doctor, but we are exploring all avenues." Jovanic took his notebook from his coat pocket and flipped to the page from his conversation with Roland Sparks, the FBI SAC. "There's another name I'd like to run by you. Garret Lashburn."

"Dr. Lashburn is our chief scientist. Why are you asking about him?"

"He's been in communication with some of the people we're interested in. What can you tell me about him?"

Lockhart's expression of bewilderment changed to a concerned frown. "Garret has been with the company for more than twenty years. He's an odd duck, but a very talented scientist, which is why he quickly distinguished himself."

"What about friends and acquaintances in the company, or outside, if you know?"

Lockhart lowered his voice as though someone might be listening in and could overhear an unfavorable remark. "Garret isn't exactly what you'd call sociable, Detective. He keeps very much to himself, kind of an 'absentminded professor' type, you know? Walks around with his head in the clouds—a pretty typical scientist."

"You don't know him to hang out at the local bar, or—"

Lockhart barked out a laugh. "Hardly. I used to work with him in the lab years ago, before I was promoted to the board. He was always a solitary type, even before his wife died."

"What happened to his wife?"

"It was four or five years ago. She evidently contracted a rare form of blood cancer. A sad thing. Bridget was the glue that held Garret together, I think. As I said, he was always something of a loner, but after she passed, he became a complete hermit. From what I hear, you're lucky to get a grunt out of him these days, even in the lab."

"You said he's your chief scientist? Doesn't he need to communicate with others in the lab?"

"Well, no. He no longer directly supervises the other scientists. He became too difficult to work with. A few months ago, he was assigned duties that allow him to work on his own projects. He posts progress reports when appropriate and we speak regularly."

"I'll need to speak to him."

"He works at the Lancaster lab. Detective, you can't possibly think *Garret* was involved in some way?"

"I'm not thinking anything at this point. I'm gathering information. What I'd like to know is how that particular chemical, which is as I understand it a proprietary pesticide, came to be on an explosive device that was detonated on your personal property."

"It just doesn't make sense."

"I've asked you this before, but once again, who can you think of who might have a beef with you?"

Lockhart paused to clear his throat, which sent a message to Jovanic that he was uncomfortable with what he was about to say. "Look, I'm sure this doesn't have anything to do with the situation you're investigating, and maybe I shouldn't say anything, but since you've brought up his name..."

"Anything at all that comes to mind could help," Jovanic prompted when he hesitated.

"All right. A while back, Garret was doing some experimenting with diethyl axathion. He was attempting to develop a mutation on one of the molecules, hoping it would have a beneficial effect—kill the pests it was intended to kill but remove the toxicity to humans."

"I see. And what happened?"

Lockhart flapped his hand dismissively. "Oh, nothing worth talking about. The project was a wild hair; nothing of any value came of it. That's why I wasn't going to mention it. But the diethyl axathion connection is strange."

"You don't think there could be any connection between Dr. Lashburn's experiments with this chemical and the explosion at your house?"

"I can't begin to imagine such a thing." Lockhart rose and offered his hand. "Thank you for coming out, but I need to end this. I'm sorry I have nothing further for you."

twenty

CLAUDIA SUSPECTED THAT DCI Hanley's earlier threat of arresting her was not an entirely idle one. Mike Chapman had already read her the riot act about fraternizing with a terrorist, and now he had been giving her the cold shoulder for the last twenty minutes while he tapped on his tablet. She was torn between making a snippy remark and keeping her mouth shut. It had not seemed prudent to argue that since Dax Odell had not been arrested and charged with a crime, there was nothing to stop her from meeting with him.

Daphne had been sent home hours ago with a stern warning, leaving Claudia stranded in Cambridge. She was going to have to catch a train to London and backtrack to Sidcup. Assuming they let her go. Joel had been right again, damn him. How the hell did she keep getting into these situations?

"Are you going to tell me how you managed to put my phone number together with Dax?" she asked Chapman when she could keep quiet no longer.

The FBI agent glanced up from his tablet. "Have you got any idea of the amount of trouble you could be in?"

"From the way you're looking at me, I'm guessing it's a lot."

"You're a real smartass, Claudia, you know that?"

"Yes, I do know that. I'm sorry, Mike. Thank you for rescuing me from that New Scotland Yard guy. He looked like he was out for blood."

Mike sucked in a deep breath and blew it out hard. "I didn't do it for you. I did it for Joel."

"For Joel?"

"Yeah, he'd asked for Odell's phone records, which I got for him from New Scotland Yard," Mike said. "Here I am, scanning through dozens of Odell's phone calls, when imagine my surprise. Look whose number appeared—my old pal's girlfriend."

Fiancée, she wanted to correct him, but thought better of it.

"Lucky I recognized your number. At first, I couldn't believe what I was seeing. What the hell were you thinking, going off to meet with Odell like that?"

"You've asked me that question sixty different ways, Mike. Do you think I'm about to give you a different answer? You can see for yourself it was just the one call and it was *in*coming to my phone. I never called him."

"That so? We haven't checked the US records yet."

"You won't find anything when you do. I've never spoken to him before."

"Fine and dandy, but you *did* come to Cambridge and meet him in person. I'm still waiting to hear the truth about *that* story."

"I've already told you the truth," Claudia responded hotly. "I have no reason to lie, Mike. I've told you over and over *everything* that happened today. I'm not hiding anything." She could see he was practically grinding his teeth, probably wanting to shake her like a terrier with a rat, but she was not about to feel an iota of guilt when she had done nothing wrong.

Chapman glared at her, his eyes narrowing in his thin face. "I'm stepping outside my authority here, Claudia. Maybe you don't respect my position, but the fact is, I represent the United States of America. I'm here at the pleasure of the Ambassador, and if he sees something he doesn't like, trust me, I'll be out on my ass in a hot minute. I'm supposed to get his approval for things like what I did today, but I didn't. I could be screwed."

"I didn't ask you to come chasing after me and report me to New Scotland Yard."

"What was I supposed to do when I saw you were making contact with Odell—"

"Wait a minute," she cut in. "That's not fair. I've told you I didn't make contact with him—"

"Right now, you should be worried about your name getting onto an FBI list. That would make your future travel no fun, I can promise you. Plus, I still have no idea whether NSY is going to jam you up, or—"

The door opened and Ash Hanley strode into the room. Claudia was quite certain the Detective Chief Inspector had been watching through the two-way mirror that stretched along one wall of the interview room. Hanley had borrowed the room at the local constabulary, a modern office building a few miles from the Eagle Pub, where they had grilled Claudia about her meeting with Dax Odell. She was undecided whether they were doing the good cop/bad cop routine to get more information, or if they truly did not believe her story.

"Let's go," Hanley said, holding the door open.

Oh god, was this where they arrested and booked her for consorting with Dax? He hadn't seemed like a terrorist. Neither did the people she had met in the punt. Definitely not little Colin, she thought wryly.

"Go where?" she asked.

To her surprise, Hanley said mildly, "I thought we might have a cup of tea. God knows, I need one."

Without waiting for a second offer, Claudia snatched up her coat and followed him out into the hallway, leaving Mike Chapman to hurry after them. She had been trapped in the little room all afternoon. Too nervous to eat, she had refused their offer of a snack, but now that she could see freedom on the horizon, she was starving.

They walked in silence to a nearby coffee shop, where Claudia and Mike ordered sandwiches and coffee. DCI Hanley requested tea, along with two hardboiled eggs, shells off, please, with cream scones and jam.

Once they were seated with their food and drink, Hanley leveled a serious gaze at Claudia. "You're quite lucky you've got Special Agent Chapman to vouch for you," he said. "But your actions have put him in a rather delicate situation."

"I'm sorry if that's the case," said Claudia, biting into her egg and cucumber sandwich. To her empty stomach, the plain food felt like manna from heaven. "But it seems to me he made his own decision to follow me." In her head, she was rebelling. Why did Mike have to contact Joel about what she had done? She took another bite, darting a glance at the FBI agent. She didn't believe he was as impassive as he looked in his drab brown suit. Seated against the wall, he stared past her and would not meet her eyes. He might be trying to hide it, but Claudia could feel him bristling with anger.

DCI Hanley stirred milk and sugar into his tea and sipped. He took his time devouring one of the scones, giving her time to think about what he was saying. "Have you given any consideration to this Odell fellow and who he is?" he asked after wiping his lips on a paper napkin. "Yes, he's got loads of Irish charm and blarney; we've heard that before. And I expect you're not the first woman to be bowled over by those 'roguish eyes.' "

"Don't be ridiculous."

"The fact is," Hanley said. "He's following the footsteps of his IRA grandfather, who went to prison for crimes against the government. Odell could be brought up on any number of charges in both the US and the UK, including aggravated assault with a deadly weapon, financing a terrorist act, murder."

"*Could be,*" Claudia said, stone-faced. She was not about to let them see her sweat. "But he *hasn't* been brought up on charges, has he? That means you don't have anything. Who did he kill in the UK? You aren't trying to tie him to the Tube bombing, are you? That wasn't his handwriting in the note, I don't care what that idiot Hewett Pflueger said."

Hanley looked at her curiously. "What makes you disagree so strongly with Mr. Pflueger? It's a matter of opinion, isn't it?"

"Have you checked out that man's reputation? He's nothing better than a hired gun. He ought to be tossed out of the field. Have you had a second opinion on the handwritings he's so eager to claim are Odell's? I'll be happy to refer you to a competent handwriting examiner in London. You don't have to be a trained professional to see that the writings weren't done by the same person."

"I'll have someone look into it. We have our own experts."

"You haven't answered me about Dax. What does he deserve to be charged with?"

Hanley gave her a cold stare. "Our investigation is confidential, Ms. Rose. I'm not going to discuss our strategy with you. But I do have a proposition, and I would advise you to consider it very seriously." He paused, the silence going on long to make Claudia uncomfortable. But her courtroom training had taught her to sit still and not fidget, not volunteer additional information without being asked.

Hanley must have eventually realized that he could not rattle her into talking. "You do see that you have allowed this man to involve you in his criminal activity?" he said at last, raising his hand to stop her when Claudia started to protest. "He's already introduced you to some of his cohorts. He's taken you into his confidence. That's something we can use to our advantage."

Speaking for the first time since they'd ordered their food, Chapman added, "We'd like you to become a confidential informant for us."

"A confidential—" Claudia stared at the two men. "No. I won't do it. You can't ask me to betray those people. They're not terrorists. They're ordinary families who have already suffered enough. They have a legitimate right to protest what's happened to them."

"They don't have a right to blow things up and kill people," said Hanley.

"Killing people wasn't their intention. It was a horrible accident that the housekeeper died."

"I can't believe you're defending the terrorists," said Chapman, frowning. "How would Joel feel about that?"

"Don't try to guilt me, Mike. I know you've already told him that I met with Odell. However he feels about it, whatever damage it's going to do to our relationship, is done. Thanks a heap."

"Now, just a—"

DCI Hanley cleared his throat loudly, putting a halt to the heated exchange. "Ms. Rose, all we're asking for is information. What we are asking you to do is contact Odell and set up a meeting, see what you can get out of him. You'll wear a wire and we'll monitor you the whole time. You should be able to get him to share names, plans, dates."

"Excuse me, but being a CI is pretty damn dangerous. I just testified in a case where one was killed and I was attacked."

"But if these people are as harmless as you would have us believe, there should be nothing to fear."

"It's not a matter of being afraid. I just don't want your thirty pieces of silver."

Chapman took his turn. "Look, you said he wanted your opinion on some handwriting, it makes sense that he'll expect you to be in contact."

"That was before he disappeared, and *that* had to be because something tipped him off that you were watching us. Besides, I have no way to contact him. I've told you he didn't give me his phone number. It came through on the phone as '*Unknown.*'" Secretly glad that Dax had escaped without telling her how to find him, Claudia straightened in her chair and tried to sound more powerful than she felt. "I'm going home to California the day after tomorrow. I have no desire to speak with Dax Odell again, let alone meet with him and pretend to be his friend, then turn him over to you."

Mike Chapman leaned his elbows on the table hard enough to make his coffee cup rattle on its saucer. "If you do want to go home, honey, I suggest you think very carefully about this offer. As DCI Hanley has told you, there's already enough to charge you under the Anti-terrorism Act if he wants to, as an accessory after the fact to Odell's crimes. As a handwriting expert, you work in the legal field. I'm pretty sure you know what that means."

"Yes, I know what it means," Claudia said. "And you haven't given me reason to believe that Odell has committed even one crime in the UK that you can charge him with." She looked them each directly in the eye. "Am I under arrest?"

She counted to five in her head, pretty certain they were just trying to scare her into doing their work for them. When neither responded, she got to her feet and slung her purse over her shoulder. "I assume since we left the police station and are talking in a café, I'm not. Therefore, *boys,* I'm leaving."

Holding her breath, she strode to the front door. She could feel their eyes following her, but neither man tried to stop her from leaving the café. Taking with her the hope that Hanley and Chapman were now reviewing how badly their tactic had failed, Claudia called for an Uber to take her to the railway station.

By the time she had caught the London train to Sidcup, where Daphne picked her up, it was late in the evening. On the ride down from Cambridge, she had changed her airline reservations to match what she'd told Chapman and Hanley, and Daphne had called the car service she used to get to Heathrow. The car would be waiting for her at Daphne's house by nine AM the day after tomorrow.

twenty-one

AIR TRAVEL MIGHT NOT be as pleasant as it used to be before 9/11, but Claudia had always been like a cat when it came to sleeping on a plane. The instant she fastened her seatbelt and pulled on an eye mask; on most long flights she would be sound asleep for the duration. Not this time.

For the past two days since her interview with Chapman and Hanley, Claudia and Jovanic had been playing phone tag, exchanging only a few terse words via text message. Secretly, she was relieved when he did not answer her phone calls, and just as relieved when she missed his. Before departing Heathrow for Los Angeles, she had texted her arrival information, but by the time the plane took off, there had been no response.

When the flight attendants came around for drink orders, Claudia requested a screwdriver, then another, earning a nasty headache by downing them too quickly. She spent most of the ten hours aloft wakeful and worrying, fretting about what they were going to say to each other when she landed in L.A.

A text was waiting when the plane touched down and phones switched on. Jovanic was outside the Virgin Atlantic baggage claim area. In the airport, Claudia stopped in the ladies room for a quick spruce up. She looked as tired as she felt. She dragged a brush through the long auburn hair, added a little blush and a touch of lipstick, and headed for customs. Having only carry-on luggage, there was nothing to delay her.

She saw him almost immediately, standing at the open driver door of her Jag. It was more comfortable than the Jeep, and he was never short of an excuse to get behind the wheel. He must have shown his badge to the security cops or he would not be allowed to wait at the curb.

Their eyes met across the vehicles lined up outside the terminal. All the worry and stress of the past few days washed away. He was still the man she loved and everything was going to be okay.

Jovanic must have felt it, too. He seldom showed affection in public, but tonight he swept her into a hard embrace and whispered into her ear that he loved her. "I'm glad you're home," he said, navigating into the ever-present gridlock around LAX. "God, I missed you."

"I missed you, too. Daphne's spare room got pretty lonely."

"So did ours. I never knew how big that bed was."

"I can't wait to get into it. A little snuggling is in order."

"I was hoping for more than a little snuggling."

"Keep your hopes up—you might get more than you bargained for."

He grinned. "You're pretty perky after a long flight."

"Hey, it's been a long ten days."

"I've got to get up at 0-dark-thirty tomorrow for a drive up to Lancaster. That means an early night."

"Sounds good to me. The early night, I mean, not the early morning."

Jovanic reached over and took her hand. "Mike told me what they asked you to do."

"And I'm sure he told you that I declined."

"Yeah, he wasn't too happy about that."

"Tough shit. Let's not talk about this right now. I couldn't sleep on the plane. I just want to relax with you and not think about that mess."

"Sure, but we'll need to discuss it sooner or later."

"Why will we?" A light clicked on in her head. "Oh hell, you're not going to try twisting my arm to do it? I don't want to be a CI, don't you get it?"

"You could be a big help to us, babe. This trip to Lancaster is to meet a scientist who's a contact of Odell's. If you could find out something about their connection, it could help break my homicide case, and help the UK side, too."

Claudia stared at him across the dark interior of the car. "You can't be serious? I just got off a ten-hour flight. I've been awake for more than twenty-four hours, and you're already pressuring me about this?"

He shot a sidelong glance at her. "What's up, Claudia? Why are you trying to protect this guy? You got the hots for him?"

Claudia's jaw dropped. "Oh. My. God. I cannot believe you just said that. It's not like you to be jealous. What the hell did Mike say to you? He implied to me that I must be attracted to Odell, but I thought it was just a tactic to get me going. Dax may be good-looking, but I'm not interested in him." Even as she said the words, she fully realized she was being so emphatic because she *had* been attracted to Odell and she did want to protect him. And now, she and Jovanic weren't even home and they were already arguing.

Jovanic flung his razor into the sink in disgust and scowled at his image in the mirror. He tore off a tiny corner of toilet tissue and stuck it to his chin, which he had nicked hard enough to draw blood. He was kicking himself for picking the fight with Claudia the night before. Instead of holding her in his arms as he had wanted to, they had rolled away from each other, the tension in the bed making sleep impossible.

He had not even known he was jealous of Odell until the words fell out of his mouth. Mike Chapman had planted the insidious seed and Jovanic had let it grow like a poisonous weed, choking out what he knew to be true about his fiancée and leaving behind foul suspicions. Now he stood by the bedside looking down at her sleeping form, tearing himself up inside with questions. Was Chapman right? Had Claudia given in to Dax Odell's Irish charm? They were aware she had met with him, but what they did not know was whether it was the only time, or what had taken place at the meeting after they had lost track of them.

When his FBI buddy had told him of the plan to make Claudia a CI, Jovanic's first instinct was to reject it out of hand. After thinking on it, though, he recognized that despite it being a form of blackmail by Chapman and the inspector from New Scotland Yard, it could be a means of protecting her from getting on an FBI list.

He had always tried to protect her, even when she rejected his efforts. Now here he was, encouraging her to do what he had discouraged—become involved in something that could potentially hurt her, if not physically, then emotionally. He cursed himself for a selfish bastard, but the truth was he wanted more than to keep her off a list. He wanted to resolve his case, too, and he wanted to get Dax Odell for Sylvia Vasquez's sake.

His great misgiving was that the plan required Claudia to once again be in the company of the terrorist. A charismatic terrorist.

The traffic app on his phone promised a grinding seventy-mile commute. In the morning drive that could mean two-hours. Jovanic entered the bedroom, still dark at six-thirty. He listened to the steady cadence of Claudia's breathing, pretty sure she was just pretending to be asleep. He hated to leave without making peace, but when he said her name quietly, it was met with silence. Deliberately bumping against the bed didn't work, nor did dropping a shoe to the floor or turning on the bathroom light. It looked like he was going to have to do some serious groveling. But first, he had a scientist to see.

Jovanic drove north to the Santa Clarita Valley, then got onto the Antelope Valley freeway and headed east, where the landscape grew desolate. For miles on either side of the highway, there was nothing to see but scrub and brown hills. The long drought had been hard on the scenery. Though El Niño had brought some precipitation, it would take a while for much of the vegetation to return. With little in the way of plants and roots to hold back a heavy rain, mudslides were a more pressing concern.

Lancaster had begun as home to the Paiute Indians. Then the railroad came along and the settlement became a station house and residence for the track layers. Now one of the largest cities in Los Angeles County, it was home to a maximum-security prison, major defense contractors, and more than its share of gang activity.

Agrichem's Lancaster facility was set just outside the city. Despite the dearth of water in the area, the lab was surrounded by lush farmland, which Jovanic presumed were test zones for their products.

Security must have gotten the memo this time. Jovanic was ushered straight through and greeted by Dr. Garret Lashburn's lab assistant, Tom Sharp.

With his round eyeglasses and earnest air, Sharp reminded Jovanic of Harry Potter in the movies Claudia had dragged him to. The young man led the way to the second-floor lab, jabbering nonstop.

"I bet you're here about the explosion at Dr. Lockhart's house, huh? I saw some video on the *L.A. Times* website; it looked pretty gnarly, nothing left of that mailbox. Though maybe not, when he lives in L.A, right? Why would you come all the way up here? We've been talking in the lab about whether it might have been a disgruntled employee looking for revenge. Or is something else going on? There's always something going on around here..."

"I've heard there were some incidents at this facility," Jovanic said without answering the barrage of questions. "I understand some vandals broke in a while back and did some damage?"

"Oh, that was a different department, downstairs. I heard they made a big mess of the lab. You know these protesters—they don't think twice about the people who work here. They're not hurting the big bosses when they do this stuff, they're hurting the worker bees. Us."

"What was it they were protesting? Do you know?"

"It's always the same thing. They hate us because we produce pesticides; think they're too harmful to the environment. But there are some things that just can't be helped. It's like with war, you know? There's gonna be collateral damage. You reduce it to whatever degree you can, but hey, without the products we make, there wouldn't be the same quality of food and then they'd be upset about *that*." Sharp was echoing what Vicki White at UCLA had said. He continued without taking a breath. "Without the work we do, millions more would be starving."

"Maybe someone could find a safer way to do it."

"If there were, don't you think we would?" Sharp snapped, not trying to hide his offense at the comment. "It's not easy, you know. Research is super expensive, Detective. Really super expensive. Nobody seems to get it."

"I'm sure it is," Jovanic said, taken by surprise at the lab assistant's strong reaction.

"It's our job to keep coming up with new products that *don't* harm the environment. That's why I work where I do. Dr. Lashburn may not be easy to work for, but nobody can say he's not passionate about trying to find a better solution. He's totally dedicated to his work, and after his wife died—that was before I came here—he was working on a new pesticide that—" Sharp caught himself. "Oh man, I shouldn't be babbling on like this. Dr. L. is paranoid about anyone knowing anything about him. Please don't repeat what I've said. I'd get into a ton of trouble." He stopped before a closed door. "Here we go; this is our lab."

He unlocked the door with a card key and allowed Jovanic to go through first. Inside, Sharp led the way to a man so tall and thin that 'cadaverous' came into Jovanic's mind.

The lab assistant came to a halt about five feet away from his boss, who was stooped over a trinocular microscope. "Uh, Doctor—Doctor—you have a—"

Garret Lashburn ignored Sharp's timid attempt to get his attention, but his bunched jaw gave away his irritation at being disturbed. If the scientist remembered or cared about the appointment that had been made the day before, he showed no sign of it.

"Doctor—"

"*Shut up,*" Lashburn hissed, not looking up.

Sharp darted an apologetic glance Jovanic's way and gave a helpless shrug, mouthing, "Sorry."

Jovanic stepped forward. "Dr. Lashburn, I'm—"

The scientist, his eyes still glued to the microscope's eyepieces, shooed him with his hand. "What's the matter with you? Can't you see I'm busy? You'll have to wait."

This is what I drove seventy miles for, Jovanic thought, miffed. He waited a full two minutes, counting off the seconds in his head, then abandoned his cordial tone for more of an edge.

"We have an appointment, Doctor. Is there someplace we can talk in private?"

A lengthy silence followed in which Jovanic ran through his options if the scientist persisted in giving him the brush off.

With an exaggerated sigh, Lashburn made an adjustment to the third eyepiece tube of the microscope and triggered the camera with an audible click. He jerked his head up and quickly looked away. Jovanic caught an impression of a clean-shaven face creased with resentment. Lashburn stared at the hand he extended as if it were an alien thing that he could not bear to touch. Then abruptly, he pivoted on his heel and strode off down the lab.

"You'd better follow him," Tom stage-whispered. "He's going to his office."

Thanking the young assistant for his help, Jovanic hurried past several other white-coated technicians who were at their stations, watching with interest. He reached Lashburn just as he threw open a door at the far end of the lab, and followed the chief scientist inside.

Along with the standard desk and chairs, filing cabinet, and computer table that held a closed laptop, the length of one wall was a whiteboard covered in mathematical notations far beyond Jovanic's ken. Except for a photo frame on the desk, which he surmised might be a picture of the man's late wife, there seemed to be nothing in the way of personal effects.

Lashburn dropped into his chair and clasped his hands on the desktop, staring at them as if they held the key to the mysteries of the universe. When an invitation did not follow, Jovanic seated himself in the guest chair and thrust his hand into his pocket to switch on the voice recorder he carried for some interviews. He couldn't use the recording as evidence in a court of law without the other person's permission, but he would review it later and listen for any voice inflections, missing words, and half-finished sentences that might be significant.

"Why are you here?" Lashburn asked before Jovanic could start the conversation. "I'm running an important experiment and I must be present because these young people are incompetent. They live in a virtual world. All they care for is communicating electronically." His words seemed to rush from one to the next without punctuation, as if an entire statement was made up of one sentence. The strange thing was, he never looked away from his hands.

"It's different from the world you and I grew up in," Jovanic agreed.

"Seeing that I'm at least twenty years older than you, Detective, I'm not certain that is an entirely apt comparison, but I suppose it's true enough in its way. Again, why are you here?"

Jovanic, who was in his early forties, gave a thin smile. "How long have you worked at Agrichem, Doctor?"

"If you had taken the time to review my personnel file, which I'm fairly sure you did, you would know I have been here for twenty-eight years. Fifteen of them as chief scientist. I'm sure you already know that, too. Please do not bother to try to create rapport, Detective Joel Jovanic, I don't have the time or interest. What is the purpose of this visit? Why is a homicide detective driving all the way out here from Los Angeles to interrogate me?" Although his words were brusque, his voice was without inflection.

"This is not an interrogation, Doctor Lashburn, just a friendly interview."

"Since when do homicide detectives concern themselves with making friends of strangers?" Jovanic caught the brief glance Lashburn flicked at him before he looked back down at his hands. "I've heard from Dr. Lockhart that you are investigating the death of his housekeeper. Why are you *here*?"

"You're correct that I'm looking into the death of Ms. Vasquez. You know that an explosive device was left in Dr. Lockhart's mailbox. Our forensic lab tested the residue and found particles of a proprietary chemical substance that belongs to Agrichem." He waited for a reaction that did not come. The scientist did not look up again, but Jovanic observed that his lips pursed. After a lengthy pause during which nothing changed, Jovanic prompted, "Doctor?"

"What?"

"Do you have any response?"

"To what? You made a statement. You asked no question."

Jovanic suppressed a sigh. "You're right, I didn't. Here's the question. Do you have any ideas about how this particular chemical—" He paused to consult his notebook. "Diethyl axathion—I hope I'm pronouncing it correctly—came to be in the vicinity of the mailbox bomb at your boss's home?"

"Diethyl axathion?" Garret Lashburn echoed faintly. "How strange. Perhaps someone who works with the product carried it home on their clothing."

"Isn't it a toxic product that requires protective clothing?" Jovanic pressed, wondering whether the scientist had made such an absurd statement to mock him.

"You clearly know it is. It was taken home willfully, then. It sounds as if they wanted to kill something in the insect genus—cockroaches, perhaps." Lashburn paused, then added, "Or children. Who knows?"

His tone, flat and devoid of emotion, chilled Jovanic even more than his words. "You would agree doctor, that this substance is lethal?"

"There's no question it's lethal, Detective Jovanic. Why else would the FDA ban its use in most applications?"

"Dr. Lockhart mentioned you had been working on a similar product that would be less toxic."

"Oh, he told you that, did he?" Anger burst across the scientist's face like the fiery tail of a comet. "Did he also tell you that—" Lashburn interrupted himself. "Do I sense a trap? Evan would not have given you any details of what happened between us. He could not, any more than I can."

"Something happened between you?"

"Not that I wouldn't be quite glad to discuss it, Detective, but as I said, unfortunately, I cannot. There's a rather troublesome binding nondisclosure agreement that prevents me from discussing that which I would otherwise be quite happy to talk about." Lashburn's sudden animation ended as he fell silent and seemed to turn inward again.

Jovanic waited in silence, hoping to prompt something more. At last, the scientist shook his head decisively. "I wish I could explain further, but I cannot talk about it. I simply can't."

Jovanic, deciding to try changing the direction of the conversation, said, "I understand you lost your wife several years ago."

Lashburn lifted his head and for an instant stared as if in shocked disbelief. "*Lost my wife*? I didn't *lose* her, Detective." His gaze went to the photo frame on his desk and he blinked rapidly. "She was not like my house keys that I continually misplace, then find again." As though he had taken a bite from a particularly sour lemon, his lips puckered in distaste. "My wife was *taken* from me. Evan Lockhart and his fiendish love of the almighty dollar is at fault."

He choked on the last words, giving Jovanic a sudden insight. The man was not lacking feelings. They were solidly tamped down, so that letting them rise to the surface brought great pain. He found himself wondering what Claudia would say about this enigmatic man. The first thing she would ask would be, "What does his handwriting look like?"

"I'm very sorry," Jovanic said. "It must have been a terrible loss. Would you care to tell me more about why you feel Dr. Lockhart is responsible?"

"Yes, I would care to very much, but—" Lashburn gave a plaintive sigh. "Oh, how I wish I could."

Jovanic could see that an internal war was raging inside Garret Lashburn. He meant what he said. He wanted to talk. Needed to talk.

Abruptly, he stood. "My experiment calls. Unless there's anything else…"

"As it happens, there is one more thing, Doctor Lashburn. Does the name Dax Odell mean anything to you?"

Lashburn sat back down. "Obviously since you are asking, you know it does."

"How are you and Odell connected, Doctor?"

"Ah. The knowledge stops there." Lashburn paused with a bitter half-smile. "Or do you know the answer and just want to see whether I will tell the truth? I have no reason to lie about that, Detective. Dax's parents, Sean and Maeve, and I, were quite close growing up together in Ireland. That was before they were assassinated by the government. I virtually lived with the Odells when I was a child, my own parents being unavailable much of the time. Later, when Dax was born, Sean and Maeve made me their boy's godfather. I've stayed in contact with his grandparents through the years, followed his progress. I must say, I'm quite proud of the man he's become."

Jovanic tried to hide his surprise. He had noticed the scientist's very slight accent, but had been unable to identify it. Now he realized it must be what was left of his Irish brogue after all his years in the US.

"Are you in contact with your godson, too?" he asked.

"What does that have to do with this conversation?"

"He's a person of interest in the bombing at your boss's home. I guess Dr. Lockhart didn't mention that?"

The scientist unclasped his hands. The long, thin fingers began restlessly tapping the desktop. "No, he did not. A person of interest, why? What makes you think Dax was involved in that incident?"

"He was implicated in some handwritten material related to the case."

"I assure you, Detective, the lad is not a killer. He's very much like his father, who was a peaceful activist."

'Peaceful activist' sounded like an oxymoron to Jovanic, but he kept the thought to himself. "Whether or not this was a deliberate killing, Doctor Lashburn, a woman did die. And isn't it interesting that the explosive was set at the Lockhart's home, when you and Dr. Lockhart apparently have some kind of animosity between you?"

Lashburn frowned. "'Interesting' is not the word I would use to describe it, Detective." The sigh came again. "It's such a pity you don't have a warrant."

"What would I find if I had one?"

"So much, Detective, so much. But would it lead you where you want to go? No, I don't think so."

"If I had a reason for a warrant—"

Garret Lashburn shook his head to stop him. "I wonder if—perhaps there's a way—" He swiveled his chair to the file cabinet behind the desk, leaned down and pulled open a drawer. Riffling through the manila folders until he found what he wanted, pulled it out and slapped it on his desk.

"Are you much of a reader, Detective Jovanic?"

"I like to read whenever I get a chance."

"How nice for you. Now, I have to take care of—" Lashburn broke off and rose. As he edged around the desk, he slid the slim folder to the center and, without another word, left his office, pulling the door closed behind him with a quiet click.

Jovanic, not about to wait for a bigger hint, switched off the voice recorder and reached for the folder. Under the "plain view doctrine," the law allowed him to take a look at the file. If he found anything he could use in his case, he would return with a warrant.

Keeping his back to the door, he flipped open the folder and found a three-page document with slightly yellowed edges. He captured each page with the scanner app on his phone and hurriedly closed the folder.

His hand was already on the doorknob when his curiosity got the better of him. He spun back around and reached across the desk to turn the picture frame toward him.

Evan Lockhart had been right, Lashburn was an odd duck.

The frame was empty.

twenty-two

CLAUDIA SPENT THE MORNING catching up on email and cases that had accumulated in her absence, letting clients know when they could expect results. She also surfed the web for information about Dax Odell, not finding much more than she had seen before. A few UK tabloid sites speculated about his supposed involvement with the Tube bombing, which irked her all over again because they quoted Hewitt Pflueger. The man's ridiculous pronouncements incensed her. She made a note to herself to file an ethics complaint against him with the British Institute of Graphology.

She also found herself quoted in some of the larger British newspapers and websites, and wondered fleetingly whether the FBI was monitoring her emails and surfing history. She was too depressed to care. She hated it when she and Jovanic were on the outs. This morning, she had fought a temptation to laugh at his obvious attempts to get her attention. But she had not been ready to talk then. She had no heart for the argument, and after last night's harsh words, she was afraid that any conversation would lead them there.

From her office window she gazed across the highway at the ocean, her thoughts racing around her head like a puppy chasing its tail. The situation with Dax Odell was not as cut and dried as Jovanic would have her believe. The way he saw it, Dax deserved to be charged with a serious crime, and maybe that was true. A woman had died because of his actions. He should be held to account. But even if Dax accepted a plea of manslaughter, he would be sentenced to at least ten years in prison.

In her heart Claudia believed that he was basically a decent person who was trying to do something to help others; that the protestors he was helping deserved some kind of recognition for what they had suffered. Not that they could ever be compensated for their losses. No amount of reparation could pay for the lives of their loved ones. But the pesticide company could at the very least admit its culpability and help them through the difficult time, financially, if nothing else. Dax had introduced her to a few of the many who were affected by the pernicious chemicals being circulated in the environment, but she knew that *every* story was as heartrending as the ones she had heard in the Cambridge punt.

Around noon, buffeted by her conflicting thoughts and emotions, she decided to pull on her boots and brave the rain. On a raw day like this, comfort food was in order. Remembering the saying that the way to a man's heart was through his stomach, she drove to Gelson's Market in Marina del Rey and filled her shopping cart with items to make a delicious pot roast and a bottle of good Merlot to go along with it. She was going to make it impossible for Jovanic to harangue her about Dax Odell. She would kill him with kindness.

Despite his curiosity about the papers he had photographed in Dr. Lashburn's office, Jovanic made a detour to Santa Monica Airport before driving to the police station. RJ Scott had researched where Agrichem moored its corporate jet fleet and who the pilot was for the Lockharts' flight to the Maldives.

He spotted the Spitfire Grill behind a long white picket fence on Airport Avenue and drove into the large parking lot. Guided to his table by a waitress, he found Captain Darrell Brown already waiting for him on the patio of the unassuming restaurant.

Trim and slim in a smart black uniform whose rank was displayed in the four gold stripes on his cuffs, Captain Brown rose as Jovanic approached. His handshake was firm and confident.

"Have a seat, Detective. I hope you don't mind sitting outside."

"Not at all. I spend far too much time indoors."

"Good. What can I get you?"

"Coffee, thanks."

The waitress topped off the pilot's cup and went to get one for Jovanic. Brown closed the logbook he had been writing in and leaned over to place it in the leather flight bag perched on an empty chair next to him. He went straight to the point. "What's this about, Detective? You didn't say a whole lot on the phone. How can I help you?"

"I appreciate you seeing me on such short notice. As I mentioned, I'm investigating the death of Dr. Lockhart's housekeeper, Sylvia Vasquez. I need to fill in a few blanks for my report."

Brown shook his shiny bald head with a regretful sigh. "Man, that was tragic. Can you imagine—a bomb in the mailbox? Do you think it was a kid's prank? That's what the doc said."

"We're looking into all the possibilities. I understand you had flown Dr. and Mrs. Lockhart to the Maldives for a vacation, Captain. That's where you were when it happened?"

"That's right. We'd been down there a few days. Took the Gulfstream."

"That's one of the longer-range jets, isn't it?"

"Yessir, one of the larger planes owned by the company. Couldn't get to the Indian Ocean in one of the Cessnas without several layovers."

"Nice to have the option."

"Dr. Lockhart often visits some of the remote plants and combines it with a vacation."

"I see. It's too bad they had to cut the trip short."

"The doc's missus took it real hard about their maid. After our return, the flight attendant told me she'd cried her eyes out on the flight back home."

"She was close to Ms. Vasquez?"

"She's a kindhearted soul, that lady. The type who sheds a tear if you swat a fly, know what I mean? Didn't even want her husband comforting her. I guess you could say she was inconsolable."

The coffee arrived and Jovanic took a moment to drink some, contemplating Lisa Lockhart and her tears. Over his long career in homicide, Jovanic had learned that there was no such thing as a "normal" reaction. Everyone bears the news of violent death in their own way. He set down his cup. "You flew them right back to L.A. after they were notified, is that right?"

"Yessir, I surely did. Dr. Lockhart phoned and wanted me to have the aircraft fueled and checked out, ready to go at 0600 the next morning. Good thing he called when he did. It had already been a long day and I was fixin' to go down to the bar for a cocktail or two." At Jovanic's questioning look, the pilot added, "FAA regs forbid the imbibing of any alcohol within eight hours of flying, but Agrichem has its own rule of twelve hours. I would have had to find a replacement pilot."

"I'm sure you're used to last minute changes."

"I fly the doc a lot of interesting places; it doesn't matter to me. When the doc calls, I've gotta be ready to go." Brown smiled. "That's why they pay me the big bucks."

"Was this trip on the spur of the moment, or did you have advance notice?"

Captain Brown scratched his nose while he thought about it. "I had about two days' notice, as I recall. We left on Friday. I guess he decided and away we went."

Lockhart had said the vacation was planned ahead. Had he 'suddenly' needed to be out of town while Dax Odell was setting the explosive? The cherry bomb had sat in the mailbox since the Saturday delivery. With the Lockharts out of town, the housekeeper had not picked up the mail until Monday morning. Coleman was checking out Lockhart's financial situation. Maybe that would produce some answers.

Jovanic drained his cup. He dropped some bills on the table and extended a hand. "Thanks again, Captain. I think I've got everything I need."

The pot roast had been simmering in the crockpot all afternoon and was fall-apart tender in its dark glaze gravy; the potatoes, carrots, and onions cooked to just the right texture. The aroma of baking bread permeated the air. The bread was from frozen dough, but smelled as heavenly as if Claudia had spent all afternoon kneading it with her own hands.

Jovanic had texted that he would be home by seven. She texted back to come hungry. An unspoken truce had been declared; any discussion of work a no-fly zone.

At ten minutes before seven, she uncorked and decanted the Merlot into two of her grandmother's crystal wine glasses on a dining table covered with her best damask tablecloth. This was not an evening where they would eat, as they usually did, in the kitchen. They were going to dine in candlelight, phones and T.V. turned off.

Dressed in a heather-colored cashmere sweater dress over black leggings, Jovanic's favorite perfume dabbed on her wrists and throat, Claudia was ready to do battle in her own way.

She breathed easier when she saw his look of relief chased by pleased surprise. She sensed that Jovanic had been as strained as she had, and as happy to let last night's argument go.

"What have you got cooking?" he asked, shrugging out of his jacket and draping it over a chair. "The smell is making me drool." He turned back to her with a wolfish leer. "And you look good enough to eat, too."

Moving close to him, Claudia put her arms around his neck and lifted her mouth to meet his. The kiss deepened. His hands dropped low, pressing her hips against him.

"Later," she murmured, moving away with a smile. "We have wine to drink, pot roast to eat. Tiramisu for dessert."

Jovanic gave a small groan. "You're a tease, GraphoLady, but my stomach is grumbling, so I'm going to let you get away with it—for now."

"That's okay. I have plans for you."

Their relationship was tied in to their work, and making small talk during the meal was harder than it should have been. Several times, Claudia found herself biting off what she wanted to say because it broke the rules of engagement for the evening. She could tell Jovanic was in the same bind. Halfway through dinner, she set down her fork. "This is too hard. I keep wanting to ask about your day. If you're in the mood to tell me about it, go right ahead."

Jovanic laughed, and she was glad to see it. In his line of work the opportunities to laugh easily were often stretched thin. "What a pair we are—the *all work, all the time couple.* You're right, I do want to tell you about it. I need your opinion."

"Go ahead."

"This guy I saw today in Lancaster—the scientist? There was something 'off' about him. You would have picked up on it right away. It was something..." Jovanic hesitated. Putting his impression of Garret Lashburn into words was harder than it should have been.

"Is he a suspect in the bombing?" Claudia asked.

"If I had to put a number on it, I'd say, maybe ten to fifteen percent suspect, but for now, let's just call him a person of interest." He speared a chunk of beef and chewed thoughtfully. "I couldn't get him to look me in the eye. Even when we were alone in his office, he kept staring at his hands almost the whole time we were talking—his hands were on the desk. I don't know, something just didn't feel right."

"You mean, he couldn't look at you, like he was feeling guilty?"

"No, not like that. He was abrupt—pretty rude, in fact. His lab assistant was scared to death of him. And get this, his wife died a few years ago and he has a frame on his desk."

"What's wrong with that? Lots of people keep their dead spouse's photo on their desk years later."

"There's no photo. The frame is empty."

Claudia's brows shot up. "That's more than a little creepy." She frowned, trying to picture the man Jovanic was describing. "What about—"

"His handwriting?" Jovanic finished for her with a sly grin. He fished his phone out of his pocket and switched it on, thumbing to the photo gallery, where the phone had stored the pages he had scanned.

Claudia's eyes lit up. "You got some handwriting? Well done, Columbo." She took a quick look at the screen, then handed back his phone. "Email it to me and we can print it out after dinner. I'll tell you what I find."

"You got it."

The rest of the meal passed in a lively discussion that managed to skirt around the topic of Dax Odell and the FBI, sticking to less fraught areas of the case. Sated after tiramisu and coffee, they went upstairs and Claudia printed the sheets Jovanic had emailed.

The text of the document, which was titled *Binding Confidentiality Agreement* in capital letters, was printed, but the margin and lower half of the last page were dotted with handwritten notes. That was what interested Claudia, but before she began to analyze the handwriting, Jovanic wanted to know the terms of the agreement.

He leaned back on the office sofa and listened as she skipped over the mundane data and read aloud the parts that seemed relevant.

"This Agreement is entered into—yada yada, dates, names of the parties, Garret Lashburn, PhD, Agrichem and its affiliates and subsidiaries, at their corporate headquarters address." Claudia paused, her eyes running down the page. "Here are the Definitions. In this context, *'Confidential Information'* refers to *anything* related to any product, chemical compound, or process created or developed by the party (Lashburn)." Another pause as she read through the next section. "There's a 'No Use' clause..."

"Wait, what's that mean, Ms. Legal Eagle?"

"I believe 'No Use' literally means that Lashburn can't use anything the agreement covers for any purpose other than what's set forth in the agreement."

"It's a narrow interpretation of what that information includes."

"Yep. Even if Lashburn already had something in the works and it ended up at the lab, he can't disclose it to anyone outside the company. Let's say he was playing around with his mega-science chemistry set and he came up with a fabulous new product he wanted to develop on his own time, he couldn't do it."

"Are you psychic? Lockhart told me Lashburn had been working on something that would improve a chemical compound they sell for use in pesticides, which is lethal in its present form. Lockhart didn't seem to think much of whatever it was he'd come up with."

Claudia continued skimming through the legalese. "If Lashburn were to break the agreement, he agrees to forfeit his pension and will be named in a lawsuit." She whistled. "He's liable for a minimum of a million bucks. The term of the agreement is *Indefinite,* which means Lashburn is stuck with it forever. And there's more. Under 'Other Provisions,' it says even if a portion of the agreement is found to be unenforceable, all the rest of it stays in effect. And it's binding on heirs and assigns. Agrichem owns all confidential information. Jesus. I'm not an attorney, but this sounds vastly unfair to me. It gives everything to Agrichem and basically nothing to Lashburn." Flipping back to the first page, she looked at the date, did a quick calculation. "It's dated more than twenty-five years ago. They must have required him to sign it when he first joined the company."

"I guess he must have wanted the job pretty badly. What about the handwritten notes? Can you tell when they were written?"

"No, and especially not from a photograph. Let's see what I *can* tell you." Claudia selected an electronic microscope from the cabinet behind her desk and plugged it into a USB port on her computer. She placed the lens over the area on the first page where there was handwriting and studied the projected image on her computer monitor.

"I'm not looking at an original, but from what I see here, the hand-written parts appear fresh compared to the printed text, which could have been toner or ink jet—I can't tell well enough from the photo. The handwriting doesn't look at all faded, as it might if it were close to thirty years old."

"The original pages were slightly yellowed."

"There you go. We can surmise that it was probably not done at the same time the document was signed." She turned to the signatures on the last page. Evan Lockhart's was an illegible scrawl that took up more space than it warranted—a narcissist, as CEOs of large companies often were.

Garret Lashburn's signature was a mixture of print and script, small, precise, with large spaces between the words; an upright slant and an emphasis on the upper extenders. To Claudia, it said he was shy, retiring, a loner. The two men had polar opposite personality types.

She started to read the handwritten notes. "Assuming it was Lashburn who wrote these notes—and they are consistent with the signature—it's a rant against Agrichem. It's basically saying Lockhart rejected Lashburn's new formula because it would cost too much to produce, even though it could potentially save many lives. He talks about wanting to expose them, but Lockhart reminded him of this agreement he'd signed all those years ago." Claudia looked over at Jovanic. "Lashburn would be totally screwed if he blew the whistle. Bye-bye pension and a big lawsuit to boot. I guess he thought he could avoid the consequences by leaving this folder for you to see, but not directly showing you."

"The lawyers would have to fight that one out."

"Is he credible in what he says about his new formula?"

"He's their chief scientist. I assume he's credible. That is, unless Lock-hart has just kept him on staff to monitor him and make sure he didn't throw caution to the wind and blow the whistle. There could be serious negative consequences for the company if the media got wind of it—saving money is more important to them than the consumers."

"Even more so when the people who die are kids," Claudia said, thinking of little Colin from the Cambridge punt, and his baby brother who was suffering due to Agrichem pesticides. She had not yet told Jovanic about them. "Between what you've told me about Dr. Lashburn and what I see of his handwriting, I think he might be on the autism spectrum. Asperger's maybe."

"That's a social problem, isn't it?"

"That's part of it. Asperger's people have trouble with social cues; they don't know how to pick up on body language. They also like to have a steady routine; they don't like having it interrupted or changed."

"I can see that with Lashburn," said Jovanic. "He was pretty resistant when I wanted him to leave what he was doing and talk to me."

"Not having much empathy can make an aspie appear cold—a lot depends on how severely autistic they are. On one end of the spectrum, you have people who are nonverbal and can't live on their own. On the other end, there are the high-functioning people like Temple Grandin—remember that movie about her life? She says that *normal* people have a lack of empathy when it comes to understanding autistic kids."

"Didn't she say Einstein had mild autism?"

"I think she did. But there are many factors. The symptoms you described, plus the handwriting, also partly describe the Schizoid Personality Disorder."

"You mean he's a split personality?"

"No, that's a totally different diagnosis. Schizoid people are happier being alone and independent. They don't seem to experience pleasure like other people do. In that way, they're like the Asperger's person. They can seem indifferent or cold. Sex isn't a big motivator for them, either." Claudia pointed to Garret Lashburn's handwriting on the monitor, which Jovanic could see from where he sat.

"His writing has a strong degree of angularity and narrowness, but there are wide spaces between the words. The lower zone—the g's and y's—have angles in the lower loops, which points to hidden hostility. The overemphasis on the upper zone, l's, b's, and h's, etcetera, show he's more intellectual than physical. It's also an extremely simplified writing; it's stripped to the barest essentials—no extra loops or strokes at all. It's almost skeletal.

"From what I can see, though he may come across as arrogant to you, it's more a case of not knowing how to connect socially. And that's literal, too—many of the letters are abruptly *dis*connected. I don't suppose he sees himself that way. He's living in his own world."

Claudia sighed, her own empathy kicking in. "Poor guy. People like this tend to have one significant relationship, and that most likely would have been his wife. If he didn't have anyone else in his support system—and we don't know that for sure—when she died, he might have been set adrift. He might be alone now."

"Except for Dax Odell."

Hearing Jovanic say the name startled her. "Did you find out how they're connected?"

Jovanic explained the association. Claudia kept her face bland, but her thoughts were running wild. "But if he's Dax's godfather, that explains why money is changing hands. It's not because he's some kind of terrorist."

Jovanic's expression darkened. "Claudia. Doesn't it seem a little coincidental that Lashburn has a beef with Lockhart over this formula Lockhart rejected, and Lashburn gives Odell money? Odell comes to the US, and Lockhart's mailbox gets blown up? And you identified his signature in the logbook."

"But you said before that you thought Lockhart himself might be in on the bomb."

"I know I did, but the more I learn about him, the less that scenario makes sense."

The conversation was turning in a direction Claudia wanted to avoid. Before it deteriorated beyond repair, she rose from the computer and stretched, making sure Jovanic got a good look at her breasts swelling against the soft cashmere. "Why don't we put the case on hold for now and I'll give you your dessert."

His left brow rose in the sardonic way that turned her on. "You mean the tiramisu wasn't dessert?"

"Nope." Claudia went over and tugged at his tie, which he had loosened. "Come on, Columbo. Let me show you what I have in mind."

twenty-three

THE NEXT MORNING, CLAUDIA was intrigued to find an email from
Elliott Field, the reporter in England. He was writing to let her know
that another note had been found in another geocache. He had sent an
attachment, too: a photograph of a tiny blue door at the base of a tree
trunk. Surrounded by tiny flowers, painted toadstools, and a miniature
watering can, there was a hand-painted signpost that announced: "A
fairy lives here." Claudia smiled, charmed by the scene.

"It's a fairy door," Elliott explained when she phoned him. "It was
found in Pitminster. There are hundreds of them on the trees near
there."

"Where is Pitminster? I've never heard of it."

"It's in Somerset on the west coast, quite a distance from the last
communication. That one was in Norfolk on the other side of the
country. So far, nothing has been blown up, but everyone's pretty
nervous, waiting to see."

"I've never heard of a fairy door, either, but I love the idea."

"They're quite popular over here. Lots of people believe in fairies.
Don't you?"

Claudia ignored the mild sarcasm. "What's the story, Elliott?"

"The doors can go anywhere, really. People install them near the floorboards against a wall in their house, or in a rock garden, or on trees like in
the photo I sent you. Supporters are saying with all the urbanization going
on, the fairies have nowhere to go and they're moving into the woodland

areas." As he warmed to his theme, Elliott's enthusiasm grew. "There have been several stories about them in the news."

"Is there anything behind the doors?" Claudia asked.

"Not always, but sometimes, a space has been carved out behind them and a little room made up. You know—a bed for the fairy. Children leave notes for them. The trouble is, it's gone absolutely out of hand. The Pit-minster county council is trying to put a stop to it, which isn't playing well with the residents. They've said publicly it's not that they're anti-fairies, but having little rooms carved out of trees is bad for conservation purposes."

"You're telling me this note was found behind a fairy door?" Claudia had already read the second attachment, a photograph of a handwritten note: *"We don't like violence, but if you harm our woods, we will hurt something precious of yours. Signed, the Fairies."*

"Yes, it turned out someone had put this particular fairy door in front of a geocache. A player discovered it. Like the others, they contacted the authorities."

"And now you expect me to tell you whether the handwriting matches any of the earlier ones, is that it?"

"Yes, please. As usual, if you can say something about the personality of the writer, that would be brilliant."

"Well, first, it doesn't take a handwriting expert to see that it's not Dax Odell's handwriting."

"I had a suspicion you might say that."

Claudia's heart sank. "Oh lord, why? Don't tell me Pflueger said it was?"

"Course he did."

Even though Elliott Field could not see her, she curled her lip in distaste. "Mr. Pflueger suffers from a serious case of confirmation bias. He sees what he expects to see—or what his client wants him to see. There's absolutely zero evidence to suggest this writing is Dax Odell's. Quite the opposite, in fact."

"Can I quote you on that?"

"No, you cannot. Silly me, I should know better than to speak to a reporter. Goodbye, Elliott."

"Wait, don't ring off, Claudia. I was just taking the piss. I promise I won't quote you on anything you call off-limits."

"Fine. Let's stick to the handwriting and leave Pflueger out of it. What you *can* say is, this handwriting is nothing like the last one you sent me. There's no way it was written by the same person."

"You're talking about the one found after the sundial explosion?"

"Yes. The style of writing and the letter designs in this note are very different from that one, not to mention the spatial pattern, which is an unconscious element of handwriting and can't easily be simulated."

"What about personality traits?"

"Again, opposite ends of the spectrum. This new one is someone who tends to be subjective in her—" Claudia interrupted herself. "I'm just guessing at gender—*her* point of view. The writing size is pretty large, with elaborate, showy capital letters. The middle zone—the vowel letters, have extra complications, double loops in the o's. By itself that doesn't mean anything, but in this handwriting, it suggests someone who doesn't always tell the truth. The words and lines are a bit crowded, too, which indicates a tendency to not see the forest for the trees. Oh, I suppose that's an apt idiom under the circumstances."

Elliott snorted. "Yeah, I suppose it is. You believe it's a female who wrote this note. Is she the type to work in a group, to take direction? Or would you expect her to go out on her own?"

Claudia took time to consider the question. "With all that elaborate, showy stuff going on, this person needs as much attention as she can get. Even if it's negative attention, she wants all eyes on her. I can't see her being willing to work with anyone else who might want to share the limelight. You know, Elliott, the more I look at it, the more I doubt this is connected to the other geocaches. More a case of someone jumping on the bandwagon; a copycat, perhaps.”

“Mmm. That's what the police are saying, particularly since, as I mentioned, nothing has exploded. At least, not yet. Sounds more like a conservation protester, doesn't it?”

“With this level of neediness, she might be jumping onto the conservation bandwagon. But in my opinion, it's just a means of making sure she's in the spotlight.”

“Well, then, would you say she's dangerous?”

“I would have to see the original writing to make that kind of judgment, but from what I'm seeing here, I think she's more talk than action. The thing is, even though no one knows who she is, she has the satisfaction of watching the stir she's caused in the media. She might escalate, but I wouldn't expect her to do anything all that harmful.”

Claudia could hear Elliott tapping away on his keyboard. “By the way,” she added casually. “Have you heard whether there was anything left behind in the geocache besides the note?” The cherry candy and the slashed hedgehog that had been found with the earlier notes were pieces of evidence the police had not released to the public.

“No, I've not heard about anything else,” Elliott said. “And my source is very close to the investigation. I'm sure they would tell me. Why do you ask?”

“Never mind. Just curious,” said Claudia. “Keep me posted if anything else happens.”

She refrained from telling him that she had seen the handwriting before.

As she ended the call, the phone rang. A man's voice said, “Claudia, this is Investigator Alvarez calling from Paul Feynman's office about the Ortiz matter.”

Hearing Ortiz's name started Claudia's heart racing. She knew from media reports that Danny Ortiz had been convicted of murdering the undercover detective and was awaiting formal sentencing. Alvarez was referring to a separate trial to deal with the assault on her. Ortiz was being charged with attempted murder, including assault with great bodily injury. Having three strikes already, under California law he was already facing life in prison for the cop. Whatever sentence he received for attacking her was moot.

Claudia was tempted to tell the investigator that she did not want to be present at the trial, but she knew that if she stayed away, she would feel like a coward. Jovanic had made clear his intention to accompany her in the event Danny's supporters decided to show up. Still, the very thought of having to face her attacker again made her feel sick.

"Can you ask the DA to have the judge bar spectators from the courtroom?" she asked Alvarez.

"That shouldn't be a problem."

"Thanks, Jesse." She ended the call and made a note of the trial date, which was scheduled for next month. It wasn't fair that she felt like it was she who was in prison and not Danny Ortiz. On impulse, Claudia grabbed her purse and jacket and headed for the garage. The Century City Mall was holding a post-holiday sale. A new suit for the trial would cheer her—a *pants* suit that would not show her ass if anyone decided to kick it.

The sensation of being followed started soon after she left the house and drove down the hill to Jefferson Boulevard.

She had spotted a dark car in the rearview, turning from her street right after she did. She didn't know how long it had been parked near her house, but it was keeping two car lengths behind her. Would Danny Ortiz bother sending his homies to intimidate her over the upcoming trial? That seemed ridiculous. The call from the DA's investigator had rattled her and made her paranoid.

Her eyes kept flicking to the mirror, but by the time she reached the mall and parked in the garage, Claudia had lost sight of the car. It might have been her imagination that she was being followed, but she was not convinced. When the mall doors swung closed behind her did she breathed easier.

She browsed Macy's racks and found a tan herringbone tweed jacket that would go with a pair of tailored black trousers already hanging in her closet. She slipped into it and found a full-length mirror. Turning to view the back, her eye caught the reflection of a thirtyish woman watching her from a few feet away.

The woman's coloring was not so different from Claudia's own, though her short, spiky hair was a brighter shade of auburn. Stylish jeans with boots and a white silk blouse, a purse on her arm. No mistaking her for a store clerk wanting to offer help.

Their eyes met in the mirror and the woman sauntered over, and said with an admiring smile, "That looks awesome on you. It's hard to find the right shade for coloring like yours and mine." She pointed to her pale skin, the light dusting of freckles powdering her cheeks, and grinned.

Claudia turned away from the mirror to face her. "I'm looking for something to wear to court with black pants."

"That will be perfect. Now all you need is a cream shell to wear underneath."

"And I just happen to have one." Claudia shrugged out of the jacket and back into her own. She draped her intended purchase over her arm and thanked the woman for her opinion. As she turned away to look for a cashier, the woman said, "Claudia, wait."

Claudia whirled back around. "Do I know you?"

"Not yet. But I have a message for you. From Dax."

Perhaps she should have, but Claudia felt no surprise. "You followed me from my house."

A perky grin brightened the other woman's face. "Oh, jeez, you mean I was that obvious? Let's just say I was looking for an opportunity to talk to you. I gotta tell you it was a huge relief when you decided to go shopping.

I was getting kind of antsy, just waiting until you went someplace where I could talk to you."

Claudia narrowed her eyes. "You know where I live. Why didn't you just phone, or come to my house?"

"Dax thinks the feds could be listening to your calls and watching your house. That's why he asked me to find a neutral meeting place, rather than just showing up. God, I hope *they* didn't pick me out as easily as you did."

"I strongly doubt anyone's watching me. My fiancé would know if they were, and he would certainly have told me."

"Are you sure? Isn't he the guy who's leading the police investigation against Dax here in the US?"

"How did you know that?"

"Dax has his sources. He stays pretty well-informed."

"You said you had a message for me. What is it?"

"He wants to meet with you. Will you let me take you to him?"

"Not a good idea. I already got in some serious hot water with the FBI *and* New Scotland Yard because I met with him in Cambridge."

"That bites. But seriously, how could it hurt? Nobody will know. Today, it's just you and me and Dax."

"That's what I thought the last time I met with him. Didn't turn out to be true."

The interview with Mike Chapman and Ash Hanley was still fresh in Claudia's mind, as was their request for her to become an informant. It occurred to her that they had asked her to meet with Dax, and so had Jovanic. She would never agree to let them wire her up and betray Dax. But in the absence of a wire, she could determine for herself whether there was anything that should be shared with Jovanic. "Where is he?" she asked.

"I called him when we got here. He's in the mall now, ready to meet us."

"As long as we're not leaving the mall, I'll go with you."

"Thank you," the woman said, her smile one of relief. "My name is Jade, by the way."

"You must have been named for your eyes," Claudia said, admiring their smoky green color.

Jade smiled. "That's what they tell me."

While Claudia purchased the jacket, Jade texted Dax that they were on their way. The two women left the store, walking into the mall together like two friends on a shopping trip.

He was waiting for them in the Coffee Bean & Tea Leaf, nursing a steaming mug at a small table in the rear of the store. He rose as they entered, and raised his hand to get their attention.

The goatee was back, and unwashed hair that hung lankly over the collar of his green army jacket. Claudia hoped the scruffy look was intended to serve as cover, but though it had been less than a week since she had seen him on another continent, something about Dax had changed. He had been hyperalert before, but now he was jumpy. His eyes constantly darted this way and that, checking the windows that faced the mall.

The fact that Odell had been allowed back into the country indicated that law enforcement either had nothing to hold him, or were continuing to watch for a good reason to nab him. Or maybe he had traveled on a false passport.

Dax's beard grazed Claudia's skin as he brushed his lips against her cheek. "Hello again, Claudia. I'm sorry I had to leave you so abruptly last time we met."

"How did you know the police were waiting for you outside the Eagle?"

"I spotted the bastard through the window when I went to the loo. There was no mistaking he was a cop; I can smell the bloody buggers a mile away. I didn't want to leave you in the lurch, Claudia, but you must see I had no choice."

"They grilled me all afternoon. Trust me, it wasn't fun. But I didn't have anything to tell them, and I *am* glad you got away."

He grinned, reminding Claudia of the charm that had attracted her. "We'll make an outlaw of you yet."

"Uh, no, thanks. This is as far as I go in the outlaw business."

"Can I get you a drink?" Jade asked.

"I'll have a chai latte, thanks." As Jade walked away Claudia asked whether she was his girlfriend.

"No, she's the niece of a friend," he said, offering her a seat and taking the one beside it. "She wants to help the cause."

Claudia filed away the information in case it might be of some use. "I suppose you've called this meeting to find out what happened to the packet of letters you left with me at the pub."

"The bastards took them for sure."

"Yes, the police have them."

Dax tapped restless fingers on the tabletop. "There were no addresses, nothing to identify who'd written the letters. Did you get any impressions from the handwriting at all?"

"I'd had a quick look through them. One in particular stood out as being dishonest, plus there were signs that the writer felt guilty about something. And Dax—"

"Yes?"

"I've seen that same handwriting again since then. At least, I'm 95% sure it's the same handwriting, though I wasn't able to compare them side-by-side."

"You've seen it where? How?"

"You've been traveling, but have you heard about the new geocache?"

"No, I haven't. What's happened?"

Claudia repeated what Elliott Field had told her about the fairy door. "The note in the fairy door geocache was written by the same person who wrote one of the letters you showed me."

He slammed his fist on the table, causing nearby customers to glance up in alarm. Seeing their reaction, he leaned closer to Claudia and lowered his voice.

"Damn the woman, she's setting us up to take the blame for more than we've done. God, she'd better not do anything to hurt anyone. We've had enough of that."

"It's Claire, isn't it?"

"The writing you described sounds like hers, for sure."

"You think she's the traitor, and it seems the fairy door confirms it."

His eyes contracted to angry slits. "She's working for Agrichem, I'm positive of it. They're trying to make us look like criminals."

Claudia did not remind him that his involvement in the housekeeper's death, unintentional though it had been, made him exactly that. "Why don't you just kick her out of the group?" she asked.

"It's more useful to keep an eye on her. That way I can feed her bogus information to take back to her bosses. The hard part is not letting her in on anything important we're planning."

Claudia had to admire the strategy. Jade returned with their drinks and sat on the other side of Dax. The warm glance she threw at him told Claudia that whether he realized it or not, her interest was in more than just the protest movement. Jade reached out and touched his arm. "Are you okay, Dax? You look worried."

"Why should I be worried? I've got a pair of loose cannons on my hands and I'm trying to avoid going to prison."

"A pair?" Claudia echoed. "Who else?"

"Oh," Jade said, "he means my uncle—"

"Shut it, Jade," Dax warned. Then, seeing how hurt she looked, gave a forced smile. "There are some things Claudia doesn't need to know, for her own sake as well as ours."

"You're right. I'm sorry. I didn't mean to put either of you in a bad position." Her voice wobbled on the verge of tears.

He reached over and gave her hand a reassuring squeeze. "It's all right, luv."

"So why did you go to such extreme lengths to meet with me today, Dax?" Claudia asked, defusing the moment.

"It's the kind of precaution I have to take. I have no interest in getting arrested, which your boyfriend would be happy to do."

"It's his job to investigate homicides and that's what he's doing. I'm sure if you could talk to him and let him see it wasn't your intention to hurt anyone—"

"Then what? He'll charge me with a lesser crime? Second-degree murder? Manslaughter?" His short laugh held no humor. "I have no desire to be put in prison on *any* charge. I saw what ten years in Portlaoise Prison did to me granddad."

"Then why are you here? Being back in the US has to put you at greater risk." She suddenly understood. "It's the other 'loose cannon'—Jade's uncle. He's acting on his own and you're here to stop him, right?"

"I'm not going to discuss it with you, Claudia. I wanted to see for myself that you were all right, and to get your thoughts on the letters. You've confirmed for me that Claire is the one behind some of our problems, and that's that."

Claudia took a business card from her pocket and extended it to him. "This is Joel's card. Please just take it and at least *consider* talking to him. Even if you don't tell him where you are, it can't hurt to talk."

Dax took the card and stuffed it into his jacket pocket. "You've been kind enough to me; the least I can do is say I'll think about it." He stood and gave her his hand. "I don't suppose we'll see each other again, so, I want to thank you for trusting me. I hope you'll keep this little tête-à-tête between us."

With a nod to both women, he grabbed his backpack and was gone almost before Claudia could draw her next breath.

twenty-four

JOVANIC

"Hey buddy, you still engaged?" Mike Chapman sounded as though he were around the corner, rather than on the other side of the world.

No thanks to you, 'buddy.' "What's up, Mike?" Jovanic responded.

"I thought you ought to know that our Mr. Odell is back in your neck of the woods."

"Sonofabitch. Where's he staying?"

"He listed the Motel 6 in Granada Hills."

"Granada Hills? Not Garret Lashburn in Lancaster? Lashburn's his godfather. And remember, my local feeb contact said they've shared some financial transactions."

"Maybe Odell didn't want to implicate him. We've got him in our sights, but we still don't have anything concrete to pick him up."

"Thanks, Mike, I appreciate it. I'll head over there right now, see if I can grab him for a chat."

"How close are you to filing paper on him for the homicide?"

"Not close enough. No point in getting a warrant. I can't put a case together yet. The team is working it. If I can at least get him to talk to me, convince him to take a plea for manslaughter..."

"Good luck, guy."

The desk phone rang. "Gotta go, Mike. I appreciate the heads up. Let me know if you hear anything else." He clicked off the cell phone and answered the call from the duty officer at the front desk.

"Joel, you've got a call on line one. Dude sounds pretty upset."

"Got a name?"

"Yeah, Tom Sharp. Says you know who he is."

It took a few seconds to process the name. Then a memory jog attached it to the eager young lab assistant he'd met at Agrichem. "Got it, thanks." He pressed the button on the phone and announced himself.

"Oh my God, I'm so relieved you're there, Detective Jovanic," said Sharp. "We met when you came to see Dr. Lashburn, remember?"

"What can I do for you, Tom?"

"I'm not sure whether I should be calling you about this, but something very wrong is going on here. I guess I should be calling Security, but after your visit the other day, I thought—I mean—I can't believe he'd do this. He must've gone over the edge. They're just innocent people…"

"Hold on, Tom, calm down and tell me what's going on."

"Yes, yes, I'm sorry, I'm sorry."

Jovanic heard the young man pull in a deep breath and let it out on a shaky sigh. What he heard next made him sit up straighter and pick up his pen, ready to jot notes.

"He's poisoned most of the department. Five people. I'm at the hospital. I drove Jason and Chellie over first, then when I came back, Roxanne was sick, and Carlos. George, too, but he's big and kind of obese, so it took longer to affect him, but—"

"Hold on, Tom, slow down. Why don't you take another deep breath and tell me all about it from the beginning?"

"Sorry," Tom said again. "I'm sorry. I'm just really upset. Maybe I'm imagining things and I'll feel stupid later, but to be honest, I don't think so." He stopped talking and took another deep breath, holding it longer this time, sounding marginally calmer when he took up his story again.

"I had a dentist appointment this morning, which made me about an hour late to work. It's the day of our weekly departmental meeting, but it was the only time I could get an appointment. I'm obsessive about keeping my teeth clean and—I'm sorry, I'm getting off track."

Jovanic rolled his eyes. If the guy apologized one more time, he was going to stick a pencil in his eye. Recognizing the look, RJ Scott, sitting at her desk, snickered.

"Go on, Tom," Jovanic said, hoping he sounded more patient than he felt.

"Everyone was in the conference room as usual—this is what I was told of course, since I wasn't here. They all sat around drinking coffee, waiting for the meeting to start, but Dr. Lashburn never showed up. When I arrived they were already getting sick."

"When you say 'sick,' could you describe what you mean?"

"Headache, vomiting, diarrhea, dizziness, fatigue. At first, we thought it must be the flu, but that didn't make sense."

"Those symptoms do sound an awful lot like the flu, Tom."

"But five people don't come down with the flu at the same time, do they?"

"That does sound unusual. What are you thinking, Tom?"

"It had to be the coffee. They all drank the coffee. And now they all have symptoms of acute pesticide poisoning. Wait, I forgot one thing. There was just one person who was here who didn't get sick. Josiah's a Mormon, he doesn't drink coffee."

"You're suggesting the coffee was poisoned?"

"Five people drank from the same coffee pot and in less than an hour, all those people had the same symptoms. What else could it be?"

Jovanic could hear hospital announcements over a loudspeaker. "You said Dr. Lashburn didn't show up for the meeting?"

"That's the other thing. He's a stickler for punctuality, and he never misses a staff meeting. Gives him a chance to tell us what morons we are, you know? I thought he would show up any minute, but when I got back from my second trip to the hospital around eleven, he still wasn't there."

"I'm sure you called him."

"That's useless. He never answers the phone, Detective. Ever."

"What makes you think Dr. Lashburn did this?"

"Who else would it be? I shouldn't say this, but he's, well, he's a bit weird. Besides, I can't think of a single other person who might do such a thing."

"Let's take a step backwards, Tom. You said these symptoms are signs of pesticide poisoning. How can you be sure that's what it was, if something was put into the coffee?"

"What the—how can I be *sure*? Holy crap, Detective, I work with pesticides every day. Don't you think I know what the fuck to look for?"

The heated response startled Jovanic and reminded him that on the day they had met, something else he'd said had sparked a similar reaction.

"Slow down, Tom. I understand you're upset, but I need to ask some questions so I can get more of the picture."

"I'm so sorry, Detective Jovanic. I didn't mean to go off on you. I'm just freaked out by all this. What if I hadn't gone to get my teeth cleaned this morning? If I'd gone in to work and drunk the coffee, too. Oh my God, I could have died."

"Has anyone died?"

"Well…" There was a sheepish pause. "Not so far, but the emergency room doctor said two of them are in pretty bad shape. He said he wouldn't know until later how bad it was. What if they do die?"

"Did you take the coffee pot with you to the hospital for testing?"

"No, I thought we could test it ourselves."

"No, Tom, don't touch it. We'll do it at the police lab. Now I need you to keep everyone away from the lab area until I can get there with a CSI tech. Can you do that for me?"

Tom huffed a short laugh. "That should be pretty easy. Everyone who works in my department is here at Antelope Valley Hospital. Well, except Josiah, that is, and he went home. I called you because you came to talk to Dr. Lashburn, and I figured it might be something you should know."

"You did the right thing, Tom. I'm very glad you called me. Now, let me ask you something. If it is a pesticide, is there a possibility the contamination could have come from—I don't know—someone's lab coat? An accident? Maybe someone working with a pesticide and some dust got into the coffee pot, or maybe someone didn't wash their hands properly?"

"No way, Detective Jovanic. First, nobody working here would be that stupid. Second, none of the people in our lab work with actual product. We do the science part, the research. Anyway, the amount you're talking about would be minuscule, not enough to have this much of an effect, for sure."

"Is the coffee pot scrubbed out every day, or could there be cumulative contamination?"

"The night crew cleans it every single night. We have pretty decent coffee here, and the water is always clean and fresh from the water cooler every morning. Fresh filter, clean pot. It's my job to make it most days, but I wasn't here today. When we were on the way to the hospital, Roxanne—she's one of my coworkers—told me the coffee was already brewed this morning when she came in. But nobody knows who brewed it."

That was interesting. Tom said that only he and Dr. Lashburn had been absent. *Someone* had entered the premises early enough to make the coffee and, if Tom was right, poison it. Where was Garret Lashburn now?

"What substance can you think of that would be strong enough to cause this kind of harm, but would also have to be odorless and tasteless?" Jovanic asked. "Seems like something that strong would be bitter enough, or nasty enough to make you spit it out."

"Not necessarily, Detective. Most of our products have an unpleasant odor added to avoid someone accidentally poisoning themselves. You know, like when a gardener sprays your yard and it stinks? But I can think of at least one of our products that doesn't."

"What product is that?"

"It has several commercial names, but the chemical name is diethyl axathion."

The same chemical in the residue from the cherry bomb. Jovanic scribbled the name and underlined it, then punctuated the words with three exclamation points. "I've heard of it," he said. "Isn't it banned in most countries?"

"Yes, but it's approved for use in the US on cotton crops. Since it's not approved for residential uses, we're not required to add the odor."

"What do you think happened here, Tom?"

"You wanna know what I think, Detective Jovanic? What I think is, *somebody* got hold of a decent amount of diethyl axathion and—well, it could have been added to the coffee and nobody's the wiser. Until they got sick. Nothing else makes sense. He must have come in early and brewed it, then left."

"Thanks, Tom. Listen, can you meet me back at Agrichem? I can be there in a couple of hours."

"You got it, Detective. I can go back anytime. I just stayed here until I could confirm everyone was okay—well, as okay as they can be. Just Chellie has been admitted. Everyone else is still in the ER. They all look pretty horrible. Like death warmed over. Oops, I shouldn't have said that."

"No problem. Please make sure I'm on the security list. And Tom—"

"Yes?" Sharp asked expectantly.

"Don't go doing anything on your own. Don't touch anything or even enter the lab before I get there." He considered calling the local cops and sending someone over, but with everyone out of the lab, decided to wait the couple of hours it would take to get there.

Jovanic picked up Cindy Walsh, the crime scene tech on call, and got on the 405 North to the 14 East toward Antelope Valley. As they drove, he brought her up to speed.

In her late forties, Cindy had the kind of no-nonsense approach Jovanic appreciated in the technicians he worked with. Greying hair trimmed as short as his own, she wore a durable grey tactical uniform that did nothing to flatter her stocky body—Jovanic figured she was not out to win any fashion contests. It was more important to wear clothing that would stand up to dirt when she had to roll around on the ground or under cars to collect evidence.

Cindy was a regular Joe Friday—just the facts, little patience for small talk. When Jovanic finished briefing her and she had asked a few on-point questions, she lapsed into silence until they arrived at the Lancaster facility. That was fine with him; his mind was busy with the case.

The rain had disappeared from the L.A. basin, replaced by bright sunshine and warm temperatures. In the high desert, however, the air was brisk, in the high fifties with a stiff breeze.

RJ Scott was on her way to the hospital in Lancaster, where she expected to interview the sick employees and later, the janitorial staff from the night before, and all department heads. Not that Jovanic expected anything to come of those interviews. He would be surprised if they provided anything more than what Tom Sharp had already told them. End result for her report: Nobody had anything new to offer.

True to his word, Sharp had left Jovanic's name at the security station with instructions to allow them straight through. Cindy Walsh followed him in, toting a wheeled case with her equipment and a roll of butcher paper. Inside the case were the biohazard bags, evidence seals, various measuring devices, camera, and other items she would need to collect evidence.

When they arrived on the second floor, Sharp was standing outside the lab door.

"Personally guarding it," he said, "I wanted to make sure no one went inside."

Jovanic found the assistant's eagerness to please grating. He wondered whether the kid was juiced up. Or was it just the thought of involving himself in a police investigation that got him so hyper? The guy might be a cop groupie.

On his earlier visit, the lab had been buzzing with activity, scientists at their stations doing whatever research scientists did. Now it was empty and silent; still as a morgue.

Tom followed them inside. "Any word from Dr. Lashburn yet?" Jovanic asked.

The assistant shook his head, brown eyes owlish behind the round frames of his glasses. "No, nothing. I'm getting worried. Maybe I should contact the lab director. I haven't yet because he'll be mad at me if Dr. L. had called him and there's nothing wrong."

"You can do that if you want to, but I'll be going over to Doctor Lashburn's house and checking on him after we're done here. For right now, where's the coffee pot? You mentioned the conference room?"

"I'll show you where it is. I didn't touch a thing, just like you said."

Tom led them to a glass-walled meeting room near Dr. Lashburn's corner office. An oval walnut conference table and eight chairs took up most of the space. In the corner furthest from the door was a metal coffee station just wide enough to hold the pot and coffee paraphernalia.

Cindy Walsh entered the conference room first and placed her crime scene case on the floor, getting to work without fuss. Jovanic planted himself in the doorway, blocking entry.

"We'll take it from here, Tom. I need you to stay outside the lab until we're done."

The lab assistant's face fell. "Oh, but I thought you might need me to tell you where things are."

"We appreciate that, but I'll text you if we need anything. Thanks for all your help."

Seeing himself dismissed, Tom turned on his heel and stalked off like a boy sent to his room. Jovanic watched until he exited the lab, the door snapping shut behind him a little harder than it needed to.

Cindy hefted her roll of paper onto the table and laid out a long sheet. "What's with the kid?" she asked, taking a pair of sterile gloves from her case and pulling them on.

"Just a helpful citizen wanting to lend a hand," Jovanic's tone fell just short of sarcasm. "Still, I am glad he called me. This could be something." He started taking photos with his phone for his personal notes.

Cindy's digital camera would make a high-quality record. She got it out now and placed it on the conference table along with airtight containers that would hold the evidence. "First, the trash."

She went to the small wastebasket next to the coffee station and photographed each item in situ—as it lay in the receptacle—then moved the item to the paper-covered conference table and photographed it again individually. Lipstick-stained paper coffee cups, stir sticks, creamer packets, napkins, were soon laid out in a neat row.

"Last dive," she said, reaching in. *"Et voila!"*

Jovanic, who had been leaning against the door watching her work, straightened. "You find something?"

"Right on the bottom." She showed him the sandwich bag she had pulled out. "Unless this turns out to be Cremora—which due to the color, I doubt—I would say yes, I found something."

Jovanic could see a few grains of a light tan powdery substance at the bottom of the baggie. He felt a rush. They would not know for sure until the substance was tested, but he had a gut feeling that Tom Sharp's hypothesis—that a toxic substance had been deliberately added to the coffee—was correct.

"And, look at this," said Cindy, breaking into his thoughts. "One more item." She pointed her camera into the trash receptacle again and got a photo. Then, using a pair of long-nosed tweezers, she plucked out a small piece of coffee-stained paper and set it on the table for Jovanic to see: a grocery store receipt that listed a gallon of coffee, nothing more.

"Von's Grocery," Jovanic mused to himself. He noted the time stamp: 5:30 that morning. "Got him." He located the Von's phone number on the receipt and called the store.

During a short conversation with the manager, Jovanic confirmed that a security camera was aimed at the store entry, recording activity at all times. The manager promised to locate and email the segment of the video that covered the ten minutes before and after the coffee purchase.

Few customers would be entering the store so early in the morning. If the images were clear enough, he should be able to identify the person who had purchased the coffee that was used to poison Garret Lashburn's lab staff.

"Criminals are freakin' stupid," said Cindy in disgust. "They look at the big picture and forget about the details that'll hang 'em, like dumping this stuff in the trash and leaving the receipt."

Jovanic agreed. "My fiancée is a handwriting expert. She says people who forge checks pay attention to how the signature looks, but use their regular writing on the other parts of the check. Or they disguise their writing in an anonymous letter, but write in their regular hand on the envelope."

"Enter the fools in the Darwin awards," Cindy said.

"Yeah, they're all winners."

While Cindy continued to label and package evidence, Jovanic texted Tom Sharp to meet him in the hallway at the lab entrance. As fast as Sharp got there, Jovanic knew he'd been hanging around outside the door.

"Tom, I have a question. How do people get into the lab after hours?"

The young man's eyes lit up, presumably at being made part of the investigation. He pointed to the card reader on the lab door. "It's a key card facility. Every entry and exit are recorded in the computer room."

"Does that mean anyone with a key card who works in the building could get in here?"

"Oh, no. It's restricted access. We can all get into the building. People from other sections don't have access to our area, or we theirs."

"Nobody but people in your department can get into this lab?"

"That's right."

"I'll need you to get hold of whoever has access to the computer room."

"I'll call the Security Director. He would have that information."

Less than an hour later, Jovanic was watching over an IT tech's shoulder as he searched the card key entries for the hours after midnight this morning. As the tech scrolled through, he stopped, turning to Jovanic with a frown. "This is very weird," he said.

"Yeah? What's weird?"

"The security cameras were turned off at three AM and back on again at six. Wow, how could that happen?"

"Is that a rhetorical question, or have you got an answer?"

"Oh, the answer's right here, Detective. The cameras were accessed remotely. There are not too many people who have the clearance to do that." He checked his access log. "The password was changed just before the system went down. The commands were sent from a computer at Dr. Lashburn's home."

twenty-five

CLAUDIA LEFT JADE AT the mall and drove around for a while, pondering how to get Jovanic to talk to Dax Odell without arresting him. She knew he considered Dax nothing more than a murdering piece of shit, but Jovanic was a man of integrity. His motto was: *follow the evidence wherever it leads.* Even when the evidence conflicted with his preconceived theory.

When she couldn't come up with a good solution, Claudia made a call to Ann Cunningham. Ann was an old friend and criminal defense attorney known around the courthouse as "The Cunninghammer." She'd earned the nickname by successfully defending more murder charges than most other lawyers in her area.

Claudia explained the situation, ending with the question: "...so, how can Dax avoid going to prison?"

"How did this guy get out of the country to begin with?" Ann wanted to know. "If he was out on bond, a judge would need to review the case and make an order to allow him to travel."

"Dax doesn't live in the US, he's an Irish citizen."

"Then what was he charged with?"

Claudia repeated what Jovanic had told her. "Unlawful assembly and resisting arrest."

"If he'd already left the country, he had to have an attorney appear for him and resolve the case. With a good attorney he might have gotten a dismissal. Otherwise, if there was a warrant out for him, he wouldn't have gotten back into the US."

"He did have a good attorney: Jeffrey House."

"Jeff House is one of the best."

"Joel is trying to build a homicide case against Dax because this poor lady had a heart attack and died when she opened the mailbox and the cherry bomb ignited. The fact that her death was unintended doesn't seem to enter into the equation."

"You said she lost some fingers. That's pretty damn serious, Claudia. Even if she hadn't died, it would be charged as mayhem. The best scenario for Dax would be if the device he placed in the mailbox wasn't ignitable, but the victim herself did something to cause the explosion."

"Like what?"

"Let's say there's this huge spider that keeps making a web on the mailbox and it's pissing her off. She goes out with one of those kitchen torches—you know, like the kind you use when you make crème brûlée?"

"Like I would make my own crème brûlée."

"Use your imagination, Claudia. The victim goes out to the mailbox to get rid of the spider once and for all. She lights the torch and boom, she accidentally ignites the bomb."

"That's cold, Cunninghammer, you are nothing if not diabolical. But I have a feeling Dax isn't gonna be able to sell that one. No kitchen torch found at the scene."

Despite her compassion for the victim, Claudia couldn't help chuckling. Ann laughed, too. Then she got serious. "Do they have any video?"

"One of the neighbor's security video showed *someone* putting *something* in the mailbox during the right time frame. But the person—according to Joel, you can't even tell the gender—is wearing a watch cap pulled down low, and gloves. He was careful to keep his head down, and it was dark outside."

"Sounds to me like he's home free."

"But there's still his handwriting in the geocache logbook."

"Where was the logbook found?"

"In Marina Del Rey, several miles from the victim's house."

"There you go, then. A logbook with his name in it doesn't place him at the scene, does it?"

"I guess not."

"The only way I can see to keep your Dax out of jail is if no one saw him, and as long as he hasn't been in trouble for the same thing before, there's not enough evidence to arrest him."

Claudia brightened. "He's not *my* Dax, but that sounds like good news for him. It's all circumstantial, no fingerprints or any other forensic evidence ties him to the mailbox. At least, not that Joel has told me."

"Convictions can be obtained on circumstantial evidence, but I think he's got a pretty good defense. I'd love to know what happens."

Claudia thanked her and ended the call with a promise to keep Cunningham updated.

She spent a few minutes thinking about why she was making Dax's legal problems her business. The answer was simple: her sympathies lay with the so-called eco-terrorists. She just wished there was a better way for them to communicate their message. Violence was never a good solution.

twenty-six

It had not taken long to obtain the warrant. Like most cops, Jovanic carried a laptop in the trunk of his department vehicle and he used it to make the request to search Garret Lashburn's property. He and Cindy Walsh waited in the employee cafeteria, using the opportunity to grab lunch before leaving the Agrichem campus.

"Just don't drink the coffee," Cindy joked in a low voice as they carried their trays to a table in the corner.

"I'll stick with Coke, thanks. In a bottle."

Before they finished their burgers, which turned out to be better than fast food options in the area, the Judge's electronic signature was waiting in Jovanic's inbox. He phoned Tom Sharp and asked him to print out two copies. Eager to please, Sharp said he would, and ran the document down to the basement cafeteria. From the excitement in his eyes, Jovanic knew the lab assistant had read the warrant before delivering it. Nothing to be done about that.

Back in the Crown Vic he entered Garret Lashburn's address in the GPS.

Lashburn lived on the edge of Lancaster on a wide street where the homes, built in the early 80s, had large yards separating them, not set cheek-to-jowl as in the newer, nicer neighborhoods. No sidewalks edged the cracked asphalt road, just a dirt berm. His was at the end of a short street, an acre of desert stretching beyond it, small hills rising in the distance before the next subdivision. Trees, bare of leaves, stood in most front yards, but not in Lashburn's barren plot of ground. A wood-rail fence surrounded a yard that had not seen a drop of water in many months, maybe longer. A few hardy patches of green struggled to survive in what was left of a lawn that had given up the fight.

"Either he doesn't give a shit how his yard looks, or he went overboard obeying the drought rules," said Walsh dryly as Jovanic drove past the ranch style house and parked twenty feet farther on.

"Yeah, 'gold is the new green,'" he said, quoting the California Water District. "Wait here. I'll check it out."

Jovanic paused on his way up the driveway to peer in the windows of a ten-year-old black Ford F-150 pickup. The doors were locked, the seats empty, as were the floorboards. He got out his phone and dialed Garret Lashburn's home number.

In the still desert air, he heard the sound of the phone ringing inside the house. After four rings it went to voicemail. A woman's pleasant voice asked the caller to please leave a message and promised to call them back very soon. Jovanic assumed the voice had belonged to Lashburn's late wife.

Tom Sharp had said that Lashburn never answered his phone, so the fact that he hadn't picked up might not be significant. But if the scientist was not home, either he owned two vehicles or had left by some other means.

The front blinds were all drawn. Jovanic went up to the heavy screen door and knocked hard. Waited. Knocked again, harder, calling out Lashburn's name.

He went around to the back and found the gate unlocked. The backyard, bounded by the same type of split rail fence as the front, was just as barren. What had once been a flowerbed around rockscaping was now a tangle of knee-high weeds and dead rosebushes. Any interest Garret Lashburn might once have had in the garden had died with the flowers.

Most of the rear windows, like the ones out front, were shielded by closed blinds. The one exception was the kitchen, which faced onto the wreck of a backyard. Jovanic stepped up onto a low brick planter under the window. Through café curtains parted in the middle he could see a rough-hewn wooden table and two chairs, a stove, and a double-door refrigerator.

He jumped down and returned to the front, calling the local sheriff's office for backup in a marked police vehicle. If he had to kick the door in, he would rather not get shot by an alert neighbor assuming he was a burglar. Guns, and those who loved an excuse to fire them, tended to be plentiful in semi-rural neighborhoods like this one.

Where is Garret Lashburn? The thought was still forming when an old man came out of the house across the street and went to pick up a newspaper from his front yard. Jovanic crossed the street and tipped his head in the direction of the Lashburn house. "Have you seen your neighbor today?"

The man eyed him with suspicion. "Who wants t' know?"

Opening his jacket to display his badge, Jovanic introduced himself. "Have you seen him?"

"Nope. I usually see him leave for work early, but not today."

"Do you know whether he has another vehicle? A car, or a motorcycle?"

"Nope. He drives that truck and that's all I've ever seen." The man scratched his stubbly chin. "He had a visitor last night, stayed pretty late."

"Did you happen to notice what time this visitor arrived?"

"Well, I was watching Jimmy Kimmel, which means it was after 11:30 when the guy parked out front there."

"Did you see when he left?"

"Naw, I went to bed around midnight. Car was still there then."

"Just to confirm, you *are* talking about Dr. Lashburn's house?"

The old man shrugged. "The guy who lives across the way there." He jerked his chin at the Lashburn house. "He's an unfriendly cuss. Doesn't talk to anybody around here."

"Would you happen to know how long he's lived there?"

"Long time. His wife was pretty nice, but she's been gone a while. I bet she left him. Wouldn't blame her."

"Why is that?"

"Just, someone who never even says hello, I figure wouldn't be easy to live with."

"Did you ever see him abuse her?"

"Nah, nothing like that. She prob'ly just wanted something better."

"She passed away four years ago. Cancer."

"That so? I'm sorry to hear it. See what I mean about him being un-friendly? If the neighbors had known that, we would've gone over there, brought food or something. We're a pretty decent bunch."

"I'm sure you are," said Jovanic. "Did you notice what his visitor last night looked like?"

"Naw, it was too dark to see, even if I'd been trying to, which I wasn't. We don't have street lights up here."

"How about the car? Could you tell what kind it was? Make? Model? Color?"

The old man shook his head. "Uh uh. It was a car-car, not a truck. And I'd say it was dark. Seems like a lighter color mighta showed up, even at night."

Jovanic thanked him and took down his contact information, though the old man assured him that he knew nothing more. As Jovanic started back across the street, the man called out.

"Hey, it was some kind of sports car, real low to the ground. I don't know what kind, though."

He was still standing in his yard five minutes later, watching Jovanic flag down the black-and-white patrol unit that turned onto the street. The unit parked in the dirt berm in front of the house next to Garret Lashburn's. Two officers got out and identified themselves as Aguilera and Sanders. Jovanic led them around to the rear door and told them what he intended to do. The patrolmen exchanged a glance.

"Want me to do it, sir?" Sanders, the younger one, volunteered.

Punk. "You don't think I can do it? Or you just need the practice?"

"Er, well..."

"Stand back."

Jovanic had already assessed the back door and decided it would not present much of a challenge. He could have broken a window with his asp and unlocked the door. But a bad feeling nagged at him to get inside fast.

He turned away from the door and looked over his shoulder, focusing on the area just below the doorknob. He took a breath and mule-kicked hard. The wood began to splinter at the jamb. He kicked again and the lock mechanism gave way. The door slammed open on its hinges.

Motioning for Aguilera and Sanders to follow suit, Jovanic got out his gun and held it aimed down, next to his thigh. With the two patrolmen backing him up, he entered the kitchen and stood still for a long moment, connecting with the place, listening to the silence.

He called out Lashburn's name, his gaze zipping around the kitchen. Nothing appeared to be out of place, but there was a slight smell of rot from a full trashcan that sat out next to the sink.

On Jovanic's command, Aguilera and Sanders moved farther into the house, weapons drawn. He heard each shout "Clear," twice—three bedrooms, living room.

Then Aguilera: "Man down in the bathroom, Detective."

twenty-seven

THE BODY WAS WEDGED in a fetal position between the toilet and
the shower, making it impossible to open the door more than halfway.
Holding a handkerchief to his nose and mouth, Jovanic leaned around
it and surveyed the scene, careful not to disturb anything. A mild smell
of decay pushed its way through his handkerchief and insinuated itself
into the lining of his nostrils.

Garret Lashburn had died in a noxious pool of vomit. Grey-faced,
eyes half-open and milky, he was clad in a faded blue velour bathrobe
that had seen many turns in the washing machine. There was no noticeable blood except in the vomit, no signs of a struggle.

Jovanic leaned down to touch the body. Stiff. Rigor mortis had set in
and not yet begun to release, which was why he couldn't get the door
open.

The temperature in the house was cold and when he looked, the
thermostat was turned off. Temps had been in the low 40s the previous
night and at mid-afternoon were only about fifteen degrees warmer.
The medical examiner would have to confirm, but considering what
they knew, and factoring in the weather, Jovanic figured Lashburn had
been dead less than fourteen hours. The big question was, had he been
alive when his visitor left?

Sanders, who came up behind him, was enough of a rookie to turn
green at the smell.

"Funny how the flies always know where there's a DB," said Aguilera. He swatted at one as it buzzed past his ear, having entered the house with them. "They must send a message to every frigging buddy in the neighborhood."

"Flitter," Sanders said with a weak grin. "The fly version of Twitter."

Jovanic did not smile. "Go outside and keep the door shut," he ordered the young patrolman. "I don't need you to barf your guts up and contaminate the scene." He turned to Aguilera, "Set a perimeter around the house and make sure nobody gets near the dirt in the front. Neighbor said there was a visitor last night. We might get tire tracks. Then you can both start canvassing the neighbors. Maybe somebody else saw or heard something more than the old guy across the street."

He followed them out front and got started working the phone, called his sergeant, then the Coroner's office. With a green light from Marv Williams, Jovanic and Cindy Walsh would work the crime scene as part of his Venice bomb case. Williams would clear it and the Agrichem lab scene with the local cops.

Jovanic started sketching the scene and making notes, rewinding his conversation with the neighbor. If Lashburn's late night visitor was Dax Odell and he had rented a car in his own name, they would find him. He made a call to Huey Hardcastle and got him on the rental agencies.

Walsh photographed everything, then stretched her roll of paper over the table and started laying out the weeks' worth of microwaveable food packaging that filled the plastic bag-lined kitchen trash container. Stouffer's Four Cheese Lasagna seemed to be a favorite, followed by Trader Joe's Shepherd's Pie, and Swanson's Turkey TV Dinners. An empty 7-Up can. Banana peels and apple cores. It was their rot that added to the rapidly ripening stench of decomp.

No wonder the guy was so skinny. There was hardly enough nutrition here to keep a squirrel healthy, let alone a six-foot male.

On the wooden table in the middle of the country kitchen were two fresh-looking rings. One clean glass stood on the counter next to a bottle of Bushmills Irish Whisky. Jovanic looked inside the dishwasher, which was empty, as was the sink. He checked the bedroom in case Lashburn had carried a drink to bed, but there was no glass on the nightstand.

Moving on to the den, he opened blinds to dispel the gloom. Anemic sunlight filtered through grimy glass, illuminating the million dust motes that sprang up everywhere he walked. He looked down and saw his footprints in the carpet.

The dust was everywhere. Two recliners and a couch had accumulated a thick layer. More on top of the TV, where a picture frame had been placed face down. Jovanic pulled on a pair of nitrile gloves and turned it over, not surprised when he found it as empty as the one in Garret Lashburn's office.

An old-fashioned sewing machine cabinet reminded him of the one where his mother had spent many hours of his childhood, making clothes for him and his sister. They had whined nonstop every time she dragged them to the fabric stores.

On top of a tidy stack of newspapers and circulars on the coffee table was a copy of the *L.A. Times*. Jovanic picked up, coughing at the fine cloud that billowed into his face. The headline read: *10,000 Athletes from 205 Countries.* The opening of the Summer Olympics. July 27, 2012.

Jovanic did not consider himself a fanciful person, but that newspaper left him with the eerie feeling of having stepped into a time warp. He flipped through his notebook, verifying Bridget Lashburn's date of death, which he had scribbled down earlier: July 20, 2012. Lashburn must not have entered this room in years.

The smaller of two guest bedrooms was unremarkable and as untouched as the living room. There was a twin bed covered by a flowered bedspread, matching frilly lampshades on the nightstand lamps. The dresser drawers were all empty. The closet held the detritus of years past: board games, jigsaw puzzles, stacks of well-read books. Most were romances, a few mysteries; a handful about life after death. Bridget, cancer-ridden, thinking about the shadow of her own imminent death? Looking for comfort in those pages, perhaps? Giving comfort that her emotionally stunted husband could not provide, despite his undeniable love for her?

The second bedroom was larger and bore evidence of recent occupation. The bedspread was clean and dust-free; the dresser and nightstand surface were, if not polished, clean. The guest bath fixtures gleamed; the water rust-free.

No clothing or toiletries had been left behind, but Jovanic's gut told him that Dax Odell had stayed here. The motel address he had given the Customs agent was probably intended to throw them off. If the Irishman was involved in the coffee poisoning at Agrichem, or the even more heinous crime of Garret Lashburn's death, Jovanic vowed he would take him down.

Claudia had argued that since she'd met the man face-to-face and spent some time with him, she had an advantage that Jovanic did not. He'd thought about it last night while she slept beside him, asking himself whether what she said had enough merit to outweigh his own judgment. He almost always trusted his fiancée's assessments about people. She was a shrewd judge of character, especially when she had their handwriting to aid her. But where Odell and the protestors was concerned, Jovanic believed her vision was clouded by her compassionate heart and the Irishman's charm.

He took the master bedroom last. The bedside lamp was lit, the bed covers thrown back, as if Lashburn had been disturbed while he slept—possibly by the late-night visitor ringing the doorbell. His clothes had been discarded in a careless heap on a floral damask chair that matched the bedspread. The decorating tastes of Bridget Lashburn, Jovanic guessed, kneeling to look under the bed. Garret was not the type to choose the cabbage roses print. He pulled out the dresser and checked behind it; went through all the drawers.

The fastidiously folded sweaters, socks, and undershirts contradicted the untidiness of the chair. The guy owned not a single T-shirt or pair of jeans. Lashburn's idea of casual was an assortment of plaid, long-sleeved shirts and Dockers-style pants lined up in the closet. Four pair of sturdy shoes sat in a row on the floor.

Jovanic called Cindy into the bedroom and asked her to check the soles of the shoes for any chemical residue that might match the particles she had found in the baggie at Agrichem. While she was performing that task, he entered the garage through a door in the hallway. They had cleared the garage earlier, and he now ran a check and learned that the dusty white 2015 Toyota Camry occupying half the space was registered to Bridget Lashburn.

Jovanic flipped the light switch and stepped inside. A workbench along one wall held a microscope covered by a dust protector, several plastic containers, a notebook filled with mathematical formulas, and several other pieces of equipment one might find in a research lab. Someone had drawn a big red X in Magic Marker on several small containers.

Before prying open the containers with his gloved hands, Jovanic slipped a filter mask over his nose and mouth. Each container held about four ounces of powder in varying shades of tan and gray. One looked like the grains Cindy Walsh had found at Agrichem. The police lab would have to test the substances to determine their chemical makeup, but instinct told him they would find diethyl axathion among them.

In a metal cabinet he found everything Wayne Wyatt from the bomb squad had said was needed to make a cherry bomb: sandpaper, toilet paper, matches, all in a clear plastic container right beside a can of toluene, which could be used as an accelerant. Jovanic photographed it all with his phone.

He heard a large vehicle pull up outside and went to meet the deputy coroner.

Shirley Lorraine was an old friend. They had worked many cases together and trusted each other. Jovanic gave her the rundown and led her to the bathroom where Garret Lashburn's body lay.

Holding her breath, Shirley squeezed through the half-closed doorway, climbing over Lashburn's legs to get inside. Jovanic watched around the door as she crouched in an uncomfortable position next to the body, and began her visual inspection.

"Rigor's starting to release," she told Jovanic after taking the body temperature.

"Time of death?"

"Somewhere between one and five AM, I'd guess." Shirley rolled the body and checked the bathrobe pockets. "Something here." She took out the piece of paper she had found and gave it a quick once-over. "It appears we've got a suicide note."

twenty-eight

"Dr. Garret Lashburn, mad scientist," said Claudia.

Jovanic sat on the bed in the dark beside her, pulling off his shoes and socks. He let them lay where they were, too damn beat to get up and put them in the closet. "Not sure it qualifies him as a mad scientist, but it does mean he was working on something at home. There were notebooks the forensics team took, too."

"Those might be good for me to examine—more exemplars."

"From what I could tell they were mostly mathematical formulas and chemical models."

"There's likely to be some handwriting, too."

"I'll get them for you if you need them. He also had everything the bomb squad guy told me someone would need for cherry bomb-making."

"What about the pesticide on the bomb residue?"

"We took the chemicals to the lab, and I'd be surprised if diethyl axathion wasn't in one of those containers." Jovanic's tie, shirt, and undershirt landed unceremoniously on his dress shoes. "Are you awake enough to look at a suicide note?"

Claudia sat up and switched on the bedside lamp, squinting in the light. "Sure. Are *you*?"

"Babe, I want nothing more than to crawl under those covers, but..."

She pushed back the blankets, pulled on her heavy fleece robe, and went around the bed to sit next to him.

Knowing he was going to ask for her help, Jovanic had hauled his brief-case up to the bedroom with him. He opened it and removed a Mylar folder. "Don't tell anyone you've seen this, but I wanted you to get a look at the original before I booked it into evidence. I can get it back to you later for a formal examination."

Through the plastic Claudia could see a number 10 business envelope addressed to Garret Lashburn with the return address of American Express. The envelope had been opened and, judging by its flatness, the contents removed. She flipped it over. A few handprinted words had been written on the back.

"The ME found it under the body," said Jovanic. "Luckily, his robe protected it from all the fluids. Man, he was leaking from every—"

Claudia put up a hand to stop him. "TMI, Columbo. I don't need that image in my head before I go to sleep."

"Sorry, I always forget you're not one of us."

She knew he was joking and gave him a poke in the ribs before going to the envelope. "It's assumed Lashburn wrote this?"

"Until we know otherwise. You've already seen his handwriting on the nondisclosure agreement. Did he write it?"

"I'll have to make a side-by-side comparison, but my first impression is no, it's not his writing."

Jovanic's brows went up. "You can tell that fast?"

"Not conclusively; that's just from memory." Claudia zipped up her robe and pulled on some thick socks. "Let's go to the office. I'll bring up the nondisclosure on the computer and we can look at them both."

She scanned the envelope into the computer, then did the same with the handwritten notes on the nondisclosure agreement on a second monitor. Apart from the initials "GL" the supposed suicide note was unsigned. The wording was typical of many such notes: *I can't go on.*

"We talked about the known handwriting on the nondisclosure before. It's a small size, a mixture of cursive and upper and lower print with wide spaces between the words. This so-called suicide note is totally printed, and it's a different style of printing from the other."

Claudia tapped a few keys on her keyboard and enlarged the note. She pointed to the g, the h, and the d in the note. "This is block printed—all capital letters. Those are two distinctive styles and people tend to stick to one or the other. Plus, the height of the letters is pretty consistent in the note. In the known writing he mixes upper and lower case with some connections between letters, and the letter heights are uneven." Enlarging the writing again, she tapped the screen on several of the letters that appeared in the note. "There's tremor here, too."

"What does that mean?"

"Tremor has various causes. If the writer is trying to simulate someone else's handwriting it can be caused by nervousness. Besides that, the person has to slow down the writing and remember to change from their own natural style, which can have an effect on the ductus—the actual flow of ink. Illness can cause tremor, too. For example, if someone had a stroke, they might have difficulty controlling the pen. Or Parkinson's can produce tremor. Or even essential tremor."

"Essential to what?"

"Essential tremor is sort of a non-specific nervous system disorder that causes shaking. But all those physiological types of tremor are different from the tremor of simulation in forgery. You said you think your victim was poisoned?"

"That's what it looks like, and after what happened at his lab today, makes sense. I've asked the ME to bump up the autopsy. It's scheduled for 3:00 tomorrow afternoon."

"That's a part of the job I don't envy you," said Claudia. She took a pair of examination gloves from a box in her desk drawer and pulled them on, then slid her hand inside the plastic sleeve. Reaching inside the American Express envelope, she ran her fingers over the back of the handwritten words to feel the degree of pen pressure the writer had exerted on the paper.

"The pressure is relatively heavy," she said, withdrawing her hand. "When you're trying to simulate another person's handwriting you have to slow down and think about what you're doing. Besides causing tremor, that can result in heavier pen pressure. I didn't see the original handwriting on the nondisclosure agreement, but it did *appear* to have a lighter touch."

"You're saying you don't think Lashburn wrote this?"

"That's what I'm saying."

"If that's true, then who did?"

"I know you're thinking of Dax, Joel. You don't have to say it. I can *feel* it. He didn't."

"Good to know I'm marrying a mind reader, babe." He kissed her and stood up. "Go back to bed. I'm gonna hit the shower before I keel over."

Claudia looked at his drooping eyelids, the greyish cast of his skin caused by fatigue. He'd been up since four this morning, driving to Lancaster and back. It was now after midnight. She rubbed his back and gave him a little push. "Go. I'll be warming up your side. Don't fall asleep in the shower."

Ten minutes later he crawled under the covers with a grateful sigh of relief, warm and relaxed. They exchanged a goodnight kiss—he was far too tired for anything more. He was already drifting into sleep as his head touched the pillow.

It was less than a minute later when the sound of a text message jerked him awake.

Claudia groaned. "Can't you check it in the morning?" Even as she said it, she knew it was not possible.

Jovanic rolled onto his elbow and peered at the screen. "It's the Von's manager in Lancaster. He's sent the video he promised."

"At frigging midnight?"

"Says he was in a meeting all afternoon and forgot about it until just now." Jovanic sat up and tapped the attachment to download the video.

Claudia reached over to turn on the bedside light again. She pulled the blanket up and scooted close, she could watch over his shoulder. "It's kind of grainy," she said, praying it was not Dax they were going to see on the video.

Jovanic was silent for several minutes. Then: "*Holy shit.*"

"What is it?"

He turned the screen to let her see it. "It's Evan Lockhart."

"The CEO of Agrichem? Holy shit is right."

"I've got to get hold of Sarge."

"C'mon, Joel, you need some sleep. Nothing is going to change overnight, is it?"

"I've gotta find a judge and get a search warrant going."

"You're going to arrest him for buying coffee?"

"A *search* warrant. There's not enough probable cause yet for an arrest warrant. I'll go talk to him, throw a little chum in the water, and see what I can get before we execute the search."

"An early morning surprise? Can I do anything to help?"

"Yeah, snag a few winks for me."

twenty-nine

Jovanic

At six-thirty AM, fueled by a half-dozen cups of high-octane coffee, Jovanic and Randy Coleman were at the security gate to Evan Lockhart's home. Scott and Hardcastle were waiting for instructions in their vehicle around the corner.

It took a second ring of the doorbell before a response came over the intercom.

"Yes?" A woman's voice, Latina. "Who is it, please? Can I help you?"

Jovanic gave his name and asked for Lockhart. The woman told him to wait.

"They must have hired a new housekeeper already," said Coleman.

"Yeah. It's a long walk to the intercom."

Five minutes went by. Coleman stuck his hands in his pockets as a sharp breeze hit. "Where the hell is he?"

"Keeping the stupid donut-eating cops waiting," said Jovanic, growing impatient. "Making sure we know who the boss is." He raised his hand to press the bell again and was interrupted by Lockhart's peeved voice.

"What the hell are you doing here, Jovanic? Do you know what time it is?"

"We'd like to talk with you, Doctor. Could we have a few minutes?"

"Have you made an arrest?"

"May we come inside, sir?"

Jovanic heard a muttered curse, then a click and the latch popped. Evan Lockhart met them at the back door wearing a Denali fleece jacket and pants with running shoes. "What's going on? I was just leaving for the club. My trainer is expecting me at seven." Red-rimmed eyes and puffy skin told them of a night as sleepless as Jovanic's own. Maybe Lockhart would be ready to confess and save them all the trouble of a search.

Yeah, right.

Without waiting for an invitation Jovanic stepped inside, forcing Lockhart to take a step back. "We'll make this as quick as we can."

Coleman followed, blocking the exit.

"Whatever happened to common courtesy?" Lockhart grumbled. He led them up to the great room, continuing to whine, "You woke my wife. What's the idea of just showing up without calling?"

"Unfortunately, we can't always keep office hours, Dr. Lockhart. We're here because we have some new evidence related to your case and we need to discuss it with you." Jovanic, watching him closely, noticed his eyes shift, as if the irises had contracted slightly.

"What new evidence?"

"I guess you're aware of yesterday's events at your Lancaster facility?"

"Yes, I'm aware of it."

"What do you think happened there?"

Lockhart hesitated as if gathering his thoughts, then launched into an angry diatribe that felt a little forced. "What do I think happened? It's these—these—*eco-terrorists.* They're victimizing us again. Attacking my employees is the worst thing they've done yet. One of the people is still in the hospital. It turns out she had a pre-existing medical condition that made her particularly susceptible to the chemicals that were ingested: an undiagnosed heart problem. And now this—this *misadventure* has affected her in far worse ways than the others."

Despite the way Lockhart kept his distance from the affected employees, referring to them in the abstract, especially the one who remained hospitalized, Jovanic detected what he thought might be a flicker of regret. Maybe he was just now realizing he had not thought through his plan well enough.

"Is the employee's condition life-threatening?"

"According to what I'm told, it could be. Why?"

"Because if any of those employees were to die after being poisoned, we would be talking about murder, wouldn't we?"

The remaining color drained from Lockhart's already pale face. He began pacing the length of the Persian rug, behavior Jovanic viewed as a sign of high anxiety. "Oh. Yes. I, uh—we would, of course. I—I hope you find the people who are responsible."

"You believe there's more than one person directly involved?"

"It's got to be that group—People for Safe Food, or whatever they're calling themselves. Oh God, why would someone do this to me?" He ground his fists into his eyes. The anguish sounded genuine. Jovanic wasn't sure whether he was a great actor or had bought into his own bullshit.

"Why do you think 'someone' is doing 'this' to you, Doctor Lockhart?" Coleman asked.

Lockhart, his arms crossed over his chest as if to protect himself, halted his circuit of the rug and swung around on Coleman. "These people are out to destroy me, can't you see it? It started with the vandalism at the Lancaster facility, then there was the bombing of my house and overseas. Now this. They're obviously escalating."

"Why do you think someone would attack your employees if it's you they are out to get?"

"Well—uh—" Lockhart broke off, reaching for an answer. "It's the best way to hurt me, isn't it—drawing negative attention to Agrichem by going after the employees? I'm the one who is responsible for their safety. You should be looking for someone who wants to ruin me."

"And who do you think that might be, sir? We've asked before, but you haven't come up with anyone."

Lockhart started tugging at the zipper of his jacket as if he was overheated and in need of some air. He opened his mouth to answer, but his gaze suddenly turned to the doorway and he stumbled. Lisa Lockhart was standing there, wearing designer sweats that matched his. Her hair was combed back and held in place by a headband that looked like a braid. Without makeup she looked younger than her years, and vulnerable.

"What's going on?" She moved over to her husband and tucked her arm into his. "This is a very early morning call, gentlemen. May I offer you some coffee?"

"No, thank you, Mrs. Lockhart," Jovanic said. "We apologize for the intrusion, but we're here to clear up some questions that have come up in our investigation."

"Questions?" Lisa Lockhart's eyes darted to her husband then back. "*I* have a question. Have you found the person who killed our house-keeper?"

"We're still working on it, ma'am. We're pursuing a couple of leads."

"But isn't—"

Evan Lockhart broke in, his voice strained. "Darling, why don't you go ahead to the club. I'll catch up with you in a little while."

Jovanic didn't know what message he had telegraphed to his wife, but he caught something passing between them.

Giving his arm a reassuring squeeze, Lisa leaned over and pressed a kiss to Lockhart's cheek. "Don't be too long. You know how testy TJ gets when we're late."

When she had left the room, Jovanic asked Lockhart, "Are you at all concerned about the rest of your staff, Doctor? I mean, another department at your Lancaster campus has been vandalized once already."

"Good lord, Detective, do you think there's a danger to other departments, too? I wonder if we should close the entire facility until this is all settled. Good lord, I—where is it all going to end?"

Jovanic ignored the question. "I've been trying to reach Dr. Lash-burn since yesterday, but he's not answering his phone at the office or home. Is he on vacation?"

Lockhart chose that moment to swing around and walk over to the window. He stood with his back to them, staring out at the ocean view. His expression was hidden, but Jovanic knew it had to be some form of unease.

"On vacation? No. No, Garret isn't on vacation. I would have seen it on the schedule if he were. We may work in different locations, but I review the schedules of the higher-ranking employees in our region. I review them regularly. I want to know who's there, running the show, so to speak." As if realizing he was rambling, Lockhart broke off and pivoted back toward the detectives. His face bore a quizzical expression that Jovanic instantly pegged as phony.

"You know, Detectives, now that you mention it, I haven't spoken with Garret in several days myself. We have a standing arrangement for him to check in with me and let me know what he's working on. Believe it or not, he doesn't own a mobile phone, but he always calls on time from the lab."

"So then, it's unusual that you haven't heard from him."

"Yes, it's quite unusual. We have our scheduled telephone conference once a week. But as I'm thinking of it, he didn't call at all this week and I was too busy to notice. With all this skullduggery going on, I suppose it just slipped my mind."

"When was the last scheduled call? The one he missed?"

"Uh—that would be, uh, yesterday."

"When would have been the last time you spoke with Dr. Lashburn?"

"Let me see." Lockhart tapped the bridge of his nose, considering the question. "I'd say it was—hmm—well, last week, I suppose."

"And what was his attitude at that time, Doctor? Was there anything unusual about your conversation with him?"

"He was always quite curt at the best of times. Our conversations tended to be short."

Bingo. Jovanic caught his wording: *was* always quite curt and *tended* to be. Lockhart was lying through his teeth. He would have used the present tense—'*is* always' and 'tends'—had he not already known Lashburn was dead.

"There was nothing in his mood or behavior that caused you concern?"

"Well, I wouldn't quite say that. And now that I'm thinking about it, Detectives, I remember noticing at the time he sounded rather down at the mouth. In fact, yes, I recall asking if he was all right."

"How did he respond?"

"He, uh, he said he'd been missing Bridget terribly—Bridget was his wife. I believe I mentioned before that she'd passed away a few years back? Cancer. Well, Garret became even more cantankerous after she was gone, more difficult to work with. I had several complaints from upper management in Lancaster. Over the years since then he's gotten worse." Lockhart's voice strengthened as he warmed to his story.

"You know, Detectives, I think Garret's problem is that he's deeply depressed. He refused to go to counseling or a grief group after Bridget died, but maybe it's time I suggested it again. Maybe make it mandatory. In fact, now we're talking about it, I must admit, I *am* worried about him. You say you haven't been able to reach him? I hope he's not—well, to be frank, I'm wondering whether he might be suicidal."

The guy was a pretty good actor after all, Jovanic decided. There was no way a man of Garret Lashburn's temperament would discuss his personal emotional state with his boss, let alone that he was missing his dead wife.

"Would you mind calling the lab to find out where he is?" Jovanic asked, giving him a little more rope.

A bolt of sheer panic shot across Evan's Lockhart's face before he recovered himself. "I'll be glad to." He looked at his watch. "But it's too early now. I'll call after nine when the operations manager comes in." He started walking toward the staircase in a pointed effort to end the interview. "I'll let you know what he says. Meanwhile, I have to get to the club."

The detectives remained standing where they were. "Do you think Dr. Lashburn's department was targeted at this time for any particular reason?" Coleman asked.

Lockhart's hand went up to rub the back of his neck. "No telling, Detective. These people are crazy. These 'People for Safe Food,' they're terrorists. Who knows why they choose their targets?"

Jovanic leveled what he hoped was a deeply concerned look at him. "I think I should tell you, Doctor, we have a concern that whoever poisoned the coffee might come after you next. You did say you believed you are the one being victimized here, didn't you?"

"Well—well—yes, I suppose so."

"So far, you've been the lucky one. Any idea why that might be, Doctor?"

"Why do you keep questioning me this way? I *am* the victim here. Can't you see that? You're acting like *I* did something wrong. Maybe they just want to terrorize me and my family by harming my employees before moving in for the real kill—me."

The man was starting to crumble. Time to tighten the screws. "I'm sure you know that the lab's security cameras were turned off early yesterday morning for about an hour?"

"The operations manager reported it to me. But how did *you* know that?"

"What do you know about where the command to turn them off originated from?"

"What do you mean, where? It was a computer malfunction."

"Not according to your IT manager. I guess you didn't talk to him. Would it surprise you to know that the command was traced to a computer at Doctor Lashburn's home?"

His brows shot up in fake surprise, but a nervous tic at the corner of his eye gave him away. "Surprise me? It would shock me to my core. What earthly reason would Garret have to turn off—oh, no, wait a minute—Detective Jovanic, you can't be suggesting that *Garret* was involved somehow in poisoning the coffee? Why would he do something like that?"

"A good question, Doctor Lockhart. Do you have any answers?"

There was a long silence. "He—the depression—maybe he went over the edge? He always seemed a little paranoid. Do you suppose it could be he was delusional and thought his staff was plotting against him?"

"Do *you* think so?"

"I—I don't know. It's all so—you said he's disappeared?"

Jovanic debated whether it was time to mention the Von's video and let the CEO know he had been spotted buying the coffee that was later poisoned. Ultimately, he decided to save the information as a *coup de grâce* to use once he had what he needed for an arrest warrant.

"Doctor Lockhart, can you tell me where you were between the hours of nine PM on Monday and six AM Tuesday?"

Lockhart started sputtering. "Why would you ask that? What are you suggesting?"

"It's something we will be asking everyone involved so we can rule them out. So—?"

"I was home in bed. I went to bed early that night."

"Can your wife confirm that?"

"Lisa was out of town with our grandchildren in Scottsdale. She got home late last night. No one else was here."

"What about the housekeeper?"

"Lupé just moved in yesterday afternoon."

Isn't that convenient. "You were home alone on Monday evening. Did you happen to talk to anyone on the phone, watch any TV?"

"I told you, I went to bed early. Why would I lie about that?" Evan Lockhart's tone was petulant, but his eyes were as hard as granite. "This 'ruling everyone out' sounds like horseshit to me. What's going on here?"

"What do you know about a guy named Dax?" Jovanic asked, intending for the quick switch of topics to throw the man off-balance.

For the first time during the interview the surprise on Lockhart's face appeared to be genuine. "I don't know who that is."

"I mentioned his name to you when we met in your office—Dax Odell—an uncommon name. Surely you remember. He's Garret Lashburn's godson."

Surprise turned to astonishment. "I do remember the name, now that you've reminded me. But Garret never talked about having a godson. What does this mean?"

"Dax Odell is a suspect in your mailbox bombing."

Light dawned on Lockhart's face. "He had something to do with a note that was found, didn't he? It's coming back to me now."

"Yes, our handwriting expert believes he wrote it."

"Then Garret is connected to the bomb, too, through this Odell character? That's hard to believe."

"That's one angle we're investigating," Jovanic said. "My question is, does Garret Lashburn have something against you, Doctor?"

"Something against me?"

"What would make him enlist the help of an eco-terrorist, as you termed it, to bomb your mailbox, and then, if what you're suggesting is correct, poison the coffee at his laboratory?"

Lockhart didn't say anything for a long thirty seconds while he chewed on his bottom lip. Jovanic waited for him to find a way to use the information about Odell and Lashburn to get himself off the hook.

He went with a big, sad sigh of regret. "I hate to say this, but the ridiculous truth is, Garret blamed Agrichem for his wife's death. He believed her cancer was environmentally caused—by some of our product. But that was years ago. I would have thought he'd be over it by now. I suppose it's been seething in him since then. The man must have been unhinged to do such a thing—to involve himself in a bombing and poison his own staff."

Jovanic felt a wave of disgust at the other man's callous attitude about the death of Lashburn's wife. He said, "So you find this a plausible explanation, that Dr. Lashburn is responsible?"

"I hate to say it, but with him going missing like this..."

"Are you aware of any evidence pointing to him?"

"Well, no, nothing specific, but—" Evan Lockhart broke off with a shrug.

Sensing that he wasn't going to get any further information, Jovanic signaled Coleman to text the other team members to come in. Watching Lockhart's reaction closely, Jovanic said, "Doctor, we're going to need to conduct a search of your premises and I hope to have your cooperation in doing so."

"Search for what? What are you looking for? I've been trying to be honest with you. What do you think you're going to find here?"

Jovanic took note of the way the other man had phrased his statement: *I've been trying to be honest.* Another red flag that meant he was not, indeed, being honest. He said, "Probably nothing, but it's part of our procedure."

"This is outrageous. You didn't tell me this when you asked to come in. I'm calling my lawyer." Lockhart strode over and picked up the desk phone.

No suspect welcomed the police into their home for a search, but a guilty person had stronger reasons to object. Jovanic reached into his inside pocket for the paperwork. "It's your prerogative to call, Doctor, but we have a warrant. That means we are not required to wait for your lawyer to arrive before we begin the search. And a lawyer could lengthen the procedure considerably. With your cooperation we can be done in an hour or so."

"Looks like you've got me over a barrel," Evan Lockhart said bitterly.

"We'll be as quick as possible."

Lockhart threw up his hands. "Fine. Go ahead and search the house, you won't find anything. I have nothing to hide."

Jovanic was sure from the smug expression on the man's face and the way he worded his assent that there would indeed be nothing to find inside the house. But Lockhart had not asked to see the warrant. It covered the garage, too, and any vehicles on the property. Before revealing that information, though, there was something else Jovanic wanted.

Stuffing the warrant back into his pocket unread, he said, "Thank you, sir. And while we're conducting our search, I'd like you to take a few minutes to sit down and write out a statement detailing everything you did from Monday after leaving work to Tuesday noon. For our records."

"You want me to do it *now*? You know my wife is waiting for me, as well as our trainer. Do you have a wife, Detective?"

"You might want to give Mrs. Lockhart a call, sir, and tell her you won't be joining her right away."

While a discomposed Lockhart made the call, Jovanic opened his briefcase and withdrew a yellow legal pad. Claudia would be unhappy he was using lined paper, but it was the best he could do at the moment.

Lockhart made a terse call to his wife. Glaring at Jovanic, he rang off and snatched the pad and a pen with a visibly trembling hand. "I don't like this. I don't like this one bit."

To the envy of his partners, Jovanic elected to conduct the search of Evan Lockhart's vehicles himself. The first thing he observed in the three-car garage was that the bronze colored, low-slung, late model Maserati Gran-Turismo parked there, fit what Garret Lashburn's neighbor had described as a dark sports car.

Once he had his fill of admiring the impressive sedan, which he estimated cost more than he earned in a year, Jovanic got down to business. Taking care not to leave any marks on the fine leather upholstery, he first checked around the front seats, shining a flashlight underneath and all over the carpeting, finding not even a speck of dirt. In its pristine condition, the car might have been driven off the showroom floor yesterday. Jovanic wondered if Lockhart had taken it to be detailed after leaving Lancaster the previous morning. Even if he had, there might still be forensic evidence to be found.

The glovebox held the owner's manual, nothing more. But in the center console was a leather pouch, which he unfolded. Inside was a pipe and a tin of tobacco. And a small glass vial.

thirty

CLAUDIA CHANGED OUT OF her court clothes into sweats and made a fresh pot of coffee. She had driven to the Norwalk Courthouse and waited in the hallway for hours, but in the end, the judge had refused to hear her testimony. The client had put off retaining her too long, refusing to spend the money until the deadline had passed for naming experts. Worse, the case had been an easy one in which she would have loved to testify.

After all the hours she had spent studying the handwritings and preparing her exhibits, Claudia had set the alarm extra-early to drive the fifty miles to Orange County to be in court at 8:30 AM. Court appearances often meant a whole lot of time-wasting, but it was usually worth it. Now it was mid-afternoon and she had nothing productive to show for the day, except a paycheck—which wasn't all bad, but still...

Jovanic had left an envelope on the kitchen table, her name scrawled on the front. She slid into the breakfast nook and read his note: "Need a statement analysis on this, please."

Realizing that he must have dropped it off after the search of the Lockhart home, she took a quick look at the handwritten page, then ran upstairs to make a photocopy to work from. He wanted her comments on the content of the statement, rather than the personality of the writer. She would do as he asked, but as it turned out, there was more she could tell him.

She settled at her desk and started by reading the note through:

"On Monday I was busy the entire day. I had meetings in the confer-
ence room at my Malibu office with the budget committee. Left the office
around six o'clock. Since my wife was out of town with our grandchildren
I stopped at Komodo Venice on Main Street for some dinner. I ordered
Mongolian Stir-fry with tempeh and a Kirin beer. Then to Mo's place,
which is a local bar. Watched the news and sports while drinking a couple
of glasses of wine. Then went home.

By the time I got home it must have been around 8:45. I was tired, so
decided to go to bed early. Then on Tuesday morning, out and on the road
earlier than usual. Showered and got ready to go to the office and back
to work on the budget. No time for breakfast. My secretary had arrived
at the office before me and she brought me a cup of coffee and a bagel.
Stayed in my office alone until one pm, at which time I got ready for a
golf date with a banker friend of mine.

Around 3:00, I was contacted by the operations manager at our Lan-
caster campus with the news that several staff had some kind of food
poisoning. I immediately returned to my office and spoke to our head
attorney to determine whether there was any liability."

Working from the copy she had made, Claudia started by dividing
the statement into the beginning, middle, and end. Next, she used
colored highlighters to diagram the content. She marked all the pro-
nouns in one color, the objective times mentioned in another, and the
connections and any changes in language in additional colors. Soon,
the copy was a rainbow of lies and half-truths.

What she had learned from studying content analysis was that people
do a lot of twisting their words in order to avoid telling a direct lie.

A truthful statement was normally comprised of 25% introduction and
25% conclusion, with about 50% devoted to what actually happened. In
a deceptive statement, the proportions changed. Greater emphasis was
usually placed on the beginning, where the writer focuses on the setup to

the deceptive story. The ending is given short shrift due to the writer's relief at finishing the deception and wanting to get it over with.

She tried calling Jovanic, but the call went straight to voicemail and she realized he must already be attending Garret Lashburn's autopsy. *Damn.* Her important news would have to wait.

Jovanic and Coleman were the last to exit the Lockhart house, leaving Lockhart staring through the den windows, a gloomy portrait of misery and despair.

The homicide team had agreed to meet at Plancha Tacos in Venice for a late breakfast.

Just before he took a bite of his breakfast burrito, Huey Hardcastle said, "Did you see his face? I thought we were gonna have to call the paramedics."

"Yeah, his skin was such a delicate shade of green," RJ Scott added with satisfaction. "Asshole knows we've got him."

Jovanic cut into a mound of pancakes, sopping up butter and syrup. It might not be good for his diet, but right now, he needed the carbs. "If that vial I found in the car has a trace of diethyl axathion we can bust him. I'll get it over to my contact at UCLA this morning for testing and hope she can do it right away."

"Just bat those cool gray eyes at her," Scott said. "She won't be able to resist."

"That's right. No woman can withstand The Eyes." He turned to Gonzales. "Rudy, how about you find us a friendly judge to sign the arrest warrant?"

"Will do," Gonzalez had a mouthful of scrambled eggs. He gulped coffee to wash it down. "I've got just the right guy. You get those test results and I'll call him."

"Let's get to the office," said Coleman, getting up from the table. "Things to do, people to see."

Scott gave him a small wave of her hand. "Oh goodie, Mr. Enthusiasm. See ya."

Jovanic had plenty of work to do, and for about a millisecond he considered going to the office with his partner. But he knew that if he sat at his desk and tried to write reports with the little amount of sleep he'd had the night before—not to mention the several nights before that—he would not be able to keep his eyes open.

He dropped Randy Coleman back at the office and drove up to UCLA. Unlike their previous encounters, White, perhaps sensing his new resistance to her charms, was all business. He handed her the vial in its sealed evidence bag.

She peered into it and shook her head. "There are no guarantees there's enough—or any—material for analysis, Detective. But we will run some tests and I'll let you know the results."

Jovanic held out his hand. "Thanks, Vicki, I'd appreciate if you could make it a high priority. You could help us take a killer off the street."

Her handshake was unenthusiastic. "We'll get to work on it right away. Now, if you'll excuse me."

Jovanic left her office regretfully patting himself on the back. She had been sexy and alluring in a tight knit top and jeans under her open lab coat, and he was proud of himself for resisting the urge to flirt with her. It would have been easy to reignite the interest he had seen in her eyes on his first visit to her office.

He drove home, his head full of Evan Lockhart. They had left their suspect practically pissing himself. Lockhart remained in the den, babysat by Gonzalez throughout the search. No longer smug, the CEO had sat on the sofa in his designer workout clothes, reeking of fear as he waited in silence for them to discover evidence of his wrongdoing. Halfway through the search he had called his attorney, but since there was a warrant, there was nothing for the attorney to do.

It wasn't as though the team had been tearing apart the home or looking for weapons. They had called in a CSI tech to make a mirror image of the hard drive on both his desktop and laptop computers, but in the end, the find with the most potential was the vial Jovanic had discovered in the car.

Arriving home to an empty house, Jovanic remembered that Claudia had a court appearance in Norwalk. He scribbled a note and left it with Lockhart's handwritten statement in a manila envelope on the kitchen table.

The lack of sleep was making him light-headed. Promising himself a thirty-minute nap, he collapsed on the couch. He'd forgotten to set an alarm, and awakened ninety minutes later, groggy and sandy-eyed, with an urgent need to empty his bladder. He stumbled to the bathroom, wondering for a moment where the hell he was.

Then he checked the time.

Shit; one-thirty. Garret Lashburn's autopsy was scheduled for three o'clock and he had to be there. He guzzled caffeine, took a quick shower, and changed into clean clothes. Back on the road, he felt infused with the buzz of energy that came with the feeling that the case was finally starting to get somewhere.

He fought his way on the 405, up through South Central on the 110, switching to the 10 East, when his phone rang.

"Detective Jovanic, this is Tom Sharp? You know, at the Agri—"

"Yeah, Tom. I know. What's up, buddy?"

Sharp spoke in a low tone as if afraid someone might overhear him, but he also sounded pumped. "I thought maybe you'd want to know, our CEO, Dr. Lockhart, was just here and he was acting kind of strange."

Lockhart was in Lancaster? What the hell was he up to?

"Strange, how?"

"Well, he's always kind of a dick, you know? Usually likes letting us know he's a big shot. So, Josiah—that's the Mormon guy who didn't get sick—it's still just him and me in the lab, cause the others are still at home or in the hospital—"

"Tom, focus."

"Oh, yeah, sorry, Detective. Anyway, Dr. Lockhart sort of *burst* into the lab. He was wearing these stinky sweats and he looked like a wild man. I didn't even recognize him at first. Scared the pee out of me when he came rushing through like that. He totally ignored me and Josiah and went to Dr. Lashburn's office. I guess with him being the head honcho and…"

Jovanic wanted to reach through the phone, grab the kid by the throat and shake him. *"Focus,* Tom. He went into the office and—?"

"We were listening outside. It sounded like he was tossing the place. Then a few minutes later he stormed out and took off. Never even looked at us. Acted more like Dr. Lashburn than Dr. Lockhart, you know?"

"Did he take anything with him?"

"Not that I saw. Nothing big enough to be obvious, anyway. By the way, Detective, did you talk to Dr. Lashburn yet? He still hasn't shown up."

"I'm sorry to tell you, Tom, Dr. Lashburn is dead."

"Are you serious?" Sharp's voice went up half an octave. "Oh wow, I can't believe it. I knew something was wrong. Things have been weird as shit around here. What happened to him?"

"Looks like he was poisoned, too. We'll have to wait for the autopsy to be sure."

"Poisoned. Wow. No kidding?" As the news sank in, Sharp's voice rose to near hysteria. "Was it suicide? You mean he poisoned the coffee, then couldn't take the guilt? Is that why Dr. Lashburn—"

Jovanic checked him. "Take it easy, Tom. I'll send someone out there to look things over. Let me know if you see Dr. Lockhart again, or if anything else comes up that seems off. Thanks for the call."

"I will, Detective, for sure. Wow."

Jovanic broke off the call, thoughtful. What was Lockhart up to? He had to have rushed up to Lancaster as soon as the homicide investigators had vacated his house. Was there something in Lashburn's office that needed to be cleaned up? For the rest of the drive Jovanic mused on the question: what had the CEO been looking for, and had he found it?

The L.A. County morgue was a mashup of faux baroque in a three-story, red brick building located on the eastside of downtown on Mission Road. Its square columns, meaningless corbels and Mayan arches kept it from being true baroque style, leaving visitors with the impression of a hallucinogenic-assisted design.

Jovanic dashed inside at 2:50, but it turned out that Garret Lashburn's autopsy had been delayed due to a more urgent case. By the time the deputy coroner got started on Lashburn it was after three-thirty.

The post-mortem confirmed Jovanic's suspicions about the poisoning. The ME explained that poisoning tended to leave little in the way of physical signs. But with what they knew, he was looking for organophosphate poisoning. That meant pesticide. Toxicological testing would be necessary before he could be sure of exactly what they were dealing with.

Dictating as he went through the autopsy protocols, the ME noted dried saliva and tears on Lashburn's face; fluids and froth in the airways, throat, and mouth. The testing would take several days, he said, maybe even two or three weeks or more.

Ninety minutes later, Jovanic was back on the freeway running everything through his head and making a mental checklist for an arrest warrant for Lockhart. He listened to Claudia's voicemail and returned her phone call. "Hey, babe, I'm on the way home. What's up?"

"You mean, besides identifying Lockhart as the writer of the suicide note?"

"You're shittin' me. Talk about a bonus."

"Yeah, I'll charge you extra for that one." It had taken her no time at all to recognize that the block-printed style was consistent with the note, as well as the individual letter forms and spacing.

"That's fantastic. Did you get anything good out of the statement?"

"I can say there are definite indicators of deception in it. First, he spends too much time on the unnecessary details in the opening, plus it shows some missing time."

"What do you mean, 'missing time'?"

"He talks about going to a bar, having some wine and watching TV. The next thing he says is "Then went home." The use of the word 'then' means there's some time unaccounted for. He did something between the bar and going home. He also leaves the personal pronoun 'I,' out in many places, which is a sign of tension."

"That seems kinda thin. What else?"

"It may be thin piece-by-piece, but it all adds up. He says 'I decided I should go to bed early.' That means he didn't *actually* go to bed early, he just thought about it. The next thing he talks about is Tuesday morning. Again, there's the use of the word 'then,' which indicates missing time. The question is, what did he do in the time between Monday night when he left the bar and Tuesday morning when he got to work? There's missing information.

"He follows that by saying he was out and on the road, but it's *after* that when he mentions taking a shower. These items are in the wrong order because he's trying to hide something. We know he was on the road early because he was up all night, killing your scientist guy and then poisoning his employees before he went home to shower."

"Thanks, babe. I doubt we can use this in court, but it's confirming my suspicions. The fact you can identify the handwriting in the note nails it down."

"We can talk about it more after dinner. I called out for Chinese. All your favorites."

"No wonder I love you." A beep sounded in his ear. "Sorry, gotta go."

"Must be your other girlfriend," Claudia teased.

"I've got enough trouble handling just one," he said. "See you in thirty."

When he clicked over it was a woman's voice, but not one he recognized.

"Is this Joel Jovanic?" she asked, mispronouncing his name. He was used to everyone who didn't know him giving it a hard J and a "ck" at the end, rather than "Yovanitch."

"This is Detective Jovanic," he corrected her automatically. "What can I do for you?"

"I'm Tawny Schmitt, LA Homicide. We've got a John Doe and your card was in his pocket. We're hoping you can tell us who he is."

"My card?" he echoed. As he listened to Schmitt, he ran his memory through any witnesses he'd given his card to in the recent past who might have gotten themselves killed.

"No ID and he registered at the front desk as Paul Jones. You any-place close to the North Valley? Maybe you could take a look before we bag and tag him? Coroner's on the way."

Let's see—good food, hot sex, sleep, or go look at a DB? As desperate as he was to get home, there was no choice.

The address Schmitt gave him was a mere fifteen miles from where he was, but at this time of day it could take an hour. Instead of taking the 405 South toward home, he changed direction, calling Claudia back to let her know he would be later than expected. Accustomed to his last-minute changes, she promised to keep the Szechuan chicken warm.

A few raindrops spattered the windshield and he could see from the trees along the roadside that the wind was starting to kick up. The weather report on the radio was promising Stormageddon later that evening. He still hoped to be tucked under the covers with Claudia before it hit.

By the time he got to the two-star motel on Roscoe it was past six-thirty. Two black-and-whites and a CSI van sat behind the yellow tape that blocked off one wing of the building. The coroner had ar-rived, too. Jovanic parked just outside the tape.

"Schmitt called me," he told one of the uniforms, holding his jacket open to show the badge on his belt. "Where can I find her?"

"Lucky number seven, Detective," The patrolman said and yelled out Schmitt's name. A slim redhead in a black pantsuit appeared at the lime green door to number seven. Conveniently, the room was on the ground floor facing the parking lot. *Not such a lucky number for the victim,* Jovanic thought, shaking hands with Schmitt.

"How'd he die?" he asked.

"C'mon in." Schmitt took him into the room and introduced him to her partner, Carl Messing. While Messing noted his information in the crime scene log, Jovanic's gaze swept the guestroom, which was crowded by the three detectives, a deputy coroner, and a crime scene investigator. The investigator was following the deputy coroner around, photographing everything he was doing.

The room smelled better than most cheap motels he'd visited. He put it down to Schmitt's perfume, an aroma he recognized. He didn't know what it was called, but Claudia had recently brought home a sample of the same scent, complaining that it cost more than cocaine and was too expensive for anything but a birthday gift. He'd figured that for a hint.

Two double beds covered in garish orange flowered bedspreads took up most of the space in the small room. On the other side of the narrow expanse at the foot of the beds was a six-drawer dresser which held a flat screen TV, and a small writing desk. A padded chair was turned to face the bed, where a man's body, bent at the knee was sprawled.

"Looks like someone was sitting there having a chat," Schmitt said, pointing to the chair. "Then, BAM."

"Three GSWs," the deputy coroner added over his shoulder. "Two to the chest, one to the face."

"Any defensive wounds?"

"Nope. Looks like he was surprised. Clean entry wound to the chest. The second one's at an angle. GSW entry to the left palm, exit through the back, right into the chest." The coroner picked up the victim's left hand to show him. "Looks like he was sitting on the edge of the bed, put up his hand like you'd do instinctively. Not that it does any good to try to hold off a bullet."

Schmitt said, "Must've been someone he knew. No sign of forced entry. They shot him twice at close range and, when he was down, made sure he was finished with a shot to the head."

"And there's no ID?"

"Like I said, Paul Jones listed in the computer up front in the office. Paid cash. The clerk admitted the guy gave him an extra fifty not to press him for ID." Schmitt's expression showed disgust. "Stupid, these days."

"Yeah, but money talks louder than common sense," Messing said.

"You don't recognize him? Body type, size?"

The man was Anglo and Jovanic judged around five-ten, slim. His blood-speckled hair was black, his skin fair and not old, not young. He wore a white T-shirt that bore two small holes at mid-chest, and Levi's. His feet were bare.

Jovanic gazed down at the ruined face and shook his head. Even his mother couldn't identify him in that condition. "You said he had my card?"

Schmitt showed Jovanic the business card she had retrieved from the victim's pocket. It was indeed his LAPD card. He turned it over, but the back was blank. "What about prints?"

"I'm just about to run them," said the coroner. "He's still warm, no rigor yet. Makes it easier." He manipulated the hands, which were still pliable, and pressed them against the screen of an electronic finger-printing device, then tapped a button and sent the prints to the IAFIS database. Hopefully, the man would be in the system.

"Motel office called it in," Tawny Schmitt told Jovanic. "Asshole on duty who thought it was smart to take money instead of ID, heard the shots a little after five. Couldn't avoid calling that in, right? We show up and knock on doors. No guests present in the adjoining rooms; nobody saw or heard anything." She said this in an ironic tone that Jovanic understood to mean that nobody wanted to get involved.

"What about casings?" He had barely spoken the words when Schmitt's partner gave a triumphant, "Yes!"

Schmitt: "What'd you find?"

Messing, who had been on his knees, sweeping a bright light over the carpeting behind the nightstand, got to his feet and held out his hand. He opened his gloved palm to show the shell casing he had discovered. "Nine-millimeter. Shooter probably picked up the other two and panicked; didn't have time to look for this one. It was lodged between the edge of the carpet and the wall."

"If we ever recover the murder weapon, we'll have a match," said Schmitt, stating the obvious.

Still curious to know how his card had found its way into the victim's pocket, Jovanic stepped outside to speak with the other CSI tech. The property they had taken for forensic testing was stacked outside in bags: a packed suitcase suitable for carry-on luggage, the normal toiletries, and a laptop computer. They chatted for a few minutes, then Schmitt came to the door and called to him.

"Hey, Jovanic, does the name Dax Odell mean anything to you?"

thirty-one

Jovanic

"*Holy fuck.* You've gotta be shitting me."

Tawny Schmitt's eyebrows gave a sardonic lift. "I guess that means you know him?"

The fingerprints had come back with a match to the Irish eco-terrorist.

"He's a suspect in one of my cases. I've been looking for him. He's a person of interest in a homicide."

"Apparently, someone else was looking for him, too, dude," said Messing. "And they got to him first."

"We knew he was back in the country, but I got sidetracked with another homicide in Lancaster, one that's connected. Hadn't got around to pinning him down. Shit."

Jovanic's head was spinning with questions, the first of which was how had Odell gotten his card? An ugly suspicion crept in. Had Claudia given it to him? But when would she have seen him? His exhausted mind stalled on that one. He resisted the thought that she had snuck around behind his back after their argument and met the Irishman on the sly.

"Let me borrow your computer?" he said to the detectives.

"Sure, it's in the van."

Avoiding the puddles in the parking lot, Jovanic climbed into the front seat of the CSI van. The computer monitor lit up when he touched the keyboard. He accessed the weapons database and entered Evan Lockhart's name. If the man had any weapons registered to him, they would show up.

Seconds later he had the result: Lockhart owned a Glock 19 Gen4 9-millimeter. A small semi-automatic weapon that would have done the job on Dax, especially at such close range. Jovanic visualized the scene: Lockhart in the chair, Odell sitting on the end of the bed having a conversation about Garret Lashburn. Lockhart pulls out the gun and shoots. Lights out for Odell.

Schmitt appeared at the van door. "Get what you needed?"

"Yeah. Gotta go. I'll get back to you. Thanks for calling me."

Jovanic went to his car and got out his phone. He tried Evan Lockhart's cell phone number, got voicemail. At the Lockhart number he got the maid.

"No, *señor, el no esta aqui*—he not here," she stammered when he asked for her employer.

"Do you know where I can find him?" He reached for his rudimentary Spanish. "*Sabes donde puedo encontrarlo?*"

"*No, señor. Yo no sé, yo no sé.*"

Jovanic translated her nervous words to "I don't know." He guessed he was scaring her with his urgency, but he was kicking himself in the ass too hard to give a good goddamn. A nasty little voice in his head was arguing that he was partly responsible for the murder of Dax Odell. But how could he have known the consequences of telling Lockhart that Odell was the one who had bombed his mailbox, or that he was Garret Lashburn's godson? He never guessed that Lockhart would go after Odell. Still, he felt sick about it.

"How about Mrs. Lockhart, the señora?"

"*No. No señora. Yo no sé, yo no sé.*"

He rang off and tried the Agrichem headquarters in Malibu, though he did not expect anyone to answer at this time of night. A recording came on, giving the times the offices were open and directions to the campus. The Lancaster lab gave the same result. Tom Sharp had nothing to add when

Jovanic reached him, just his usual morbid enthusiasm at the prospect of helping the police.

Jovanic knew he had to find Lockhart before someone else died. Deep into oh-shit mode, he called Claudia to let her know he would not be home for dinner after all. He did not want to tell her over the phone that Dax was dead. That would require an in-person session.

"Isn't there anyone else who could track him down?" she asked, after he finished telling her about his efforts to find Lockhart.

"Hell, I've called everyone I can think of."

"Do you think he's a flight risk? If he's as desperate as you described, he could be getting ready to run. Hey, you talked to his pilot, didn't you? He has the use of a private plane, doesn't have to buy tickets and leave a paper trail..."

"Claudia Rose, you are friggin' brilliant." Jovanic was already reaching for his notebook to search for the pilot's information.

"Yeah, yeah. Just be careful, Columbo. I want you back in one piece. And breathing."

"I'll call you when I can," he promised and clicked off. Flicking through his notes rapidly, he almost missed the cell phone number for the pilot, Darrell Brown, which had been partially scratched out along with something he'd crossed out above it. Luckily, enough of the number remained that he was able to match it up with a number in the 323 area code in his phone's Recent list. Holding his breath, he tapped it in.

The pilot answered without delay. "Brown. What can I do for you?"

"Captain, this is Joel Jovanic. If Dr. Lockhart is there and can hear you, don't let him know you're talking to me, got it?"

"Got it, but he's not here."

"Do you happen to know where I can find him?"

"Sure. He's en route here."

"Where are you?"

"Santa Monica Airport."

Jovanic's heart, which had at first sunk, rose again with hope. "What are your instructions?"

"I'm not sure I should—"

"Captain, this is a serious matter involving a homicide. I know you wouldn't want to interfere with a police investigation."

"Well, no, but—"

Jovanic cut him off. "This is not about Ms. Vasquez's death, Captain Brown. There's been another murder, and I have to talk to your boss immediately."

"I'm just fueling up and going through pre-flight check for our flight to Arizona tonight. They should be here in about twenty minutes."

"You have to stall him until I get there. And don't tell him I'm coming."

"What am I supposed to say?"

"Blame it on the storm. You have to file a flight plan, check weather at your destination or something. I don't care what you tell him. Just keep him occupied. I'll be there as soon as I can." Before Brown could protest any further, Jovanic tapped End Call and checked the time.

There was one way he could get to Santa Monica Airport in time to stop Evan Lockhart from leaving the area and it made him queasy to think about it. He took a deep breath and reached for his phone.

The dispatcher instructed him to drive to West Valley Police Station in Reseda, six miles from the motel, where a helicopter would pick him up. LAPD Air Support Division was the largest in the world.

On his way there he called Captain Brown back.

"The doc just called," said Brown. "He's in an Uber, but there's a wreck on Venice Boulevard and it's caused a major delay getting onto the 405. He should be here any minute. He sounded pretty tense. You want to tell me what's going on?"

"Your boss is a suspect in the homicide I mentioned earlier. I'm about to arrest him."

"Holy smokes, Detective. You think Dr. Lockhart—"

"Just tell me how I can identify the aircraft you're flying," Jovanic interrupted, dividing his attention between the call and jamming the accelerator as hard as traffic would allow from Roscoe to White Oak.

"It's a Cessna Citation Mustang." Brown recited the registration number on the tail. "Look for Gunnell Properties. You'll see it right near there."

"If he gets there before me, you'll need to be cool until I board."

"Should I vacate the plane?"

"No, I want everything to look normal. I'm not expecting any resistance from him, but once I get on board, you need to remain in the cockpit, out of the way. Repeat, remain in the cockpit."

"Right, Detective, I'll handle it."

Jovanic hung up, glancing at the ominous clouds already gathering overhead. He detested flying at the best of times. The anticipation of being strapped into a tiny metal cabin hurtling through space while bolts of lightning burned holes in the atmosphere did nothing to calm his roiling stomach. A few fat raindrops splattered on the windshield. Stormaggedon was approaching faster than the weatherman had predicted.

On the way to the police station, he called to alert airport police and ask for backup. The smoky-voiced dispatcher told him they were dealing with a situation of their own on the ground and promised to send officers as soon as they were available.

Jovanic swung a right onto Vanowen and turned in at the police station. He hit the call button on the card key box, showed his face and badge to the camera and identified himself. They were expecting him and popped the gate right away.

The Helo Deck was on the parking structure roof, where the blue and white JetRanger was already waiting on the northeast corner. The sharp, fresh smell of ozone hit him as he climbed out of the Crown Vic. No time to gather his guts. He ran to the bird, his suit coat flapping open in a cold, gusty wind.

The pilot, who introduced himself as Buzz, volunteered that they would not be flying at high enough altitude to experience significant turbulence, even with the bad weather. That made Jovanic feel a teensy bit better. He secured his seatbelt and adjusted the headphones he had found in the seat, telling the pilot, "I need to stop a suspect from leaving SMO. He'll be flying a Gulfstream business jet."

"Roger that. I'll radio the tower not to give clearance so the plane can be Ramp Checked." Buzz asked if he was ready. Feeling far from it, Jovanic gave him a thumbs up.

He had heard about the Marine pilots on the force. Unlike other department fliers who took off gently and made a nice, steady flight, the former Marines bolted off the deck and shot across the skies like the crackerjacks they were. From the moment the bird rose in the air, Jovanic had no doubt about this aviator's background.

A few quick seconds later, Los Angeles County, a four-thousand square mile carpet of twinkling lights, spread out thousands of feet below them. Jovanic tried not to look down, concentrating instead on creating a plan of action. Buzz explained that there were two locations at the airport from which commercial jets departed, both adjacent to the runway. He would land close to the air traffic control tower, which would allow Jovanic to run right from the helicopter to the Lockharts' Cessna.

It was with a slight sense of shock when, a mere five minutes after they had lifted off, Jovanic spotted the runway lights of Santa Monica Airport. As they descended, Buzz indicated a Cessna that was nosing out of the Gunnell Properties hangar, pointing toward the runway. They were too high up to read the registration on the tail, but the business jet was right where Captain Brown had said it would be.

They were still descending when Jovanic, watching through the side window, noticed a late model Ford SUV heading for the Cessna. The vehicle stopped and the rear passenger door opened. Lightning ripped open the night sky and illuminated Lockhart's tall frame.

Jovanic was wondering how his suspect, who appeared to be still wearing the sweat suit, had disposed of the Glock after killing Dax Odell. Thunder rolled like the slamming of an immense door and the rain came down in a soaking deluge. Lockhart hunched his shoulders against the downpour and leaned into the backseat to help his wife out of the SUV. Clutching a purse to her chest, she was only marginally better dressed for the weather in a baby blue hoodie. Lockhart put his arm around her shoulders and together they ran to the Cessna, splashing through the puddles that were already collecting on the tarmac.

With a salute of thanks to Buzz, Jovanic jumped out of the helicopter, grateful to be back on terra firma. He lost no time moving away from the rotating blades, whose downwash splashed icy water up his legs and left his trousers soaked.

Fifty feet away, unaware of the helicopter, the Lockharts were hurrying up the air stairs into their plane. It would have been better to collar Lockhart before he entered the relatively cramped quarters of the aircraft, and even better to have backup, but the distance was too great and so was the risk of losing him.

Jovanic jogged after them through the drenching rain, feeling as though a heavenly giant had upended a massive bucket over his head. By the time he reached the Cessna his hair was dripping and his socks were squelching in his shoes.

He took the stairs. Lockhart's urgent voice came through the open door: "...*can't* delay, Darrell, it's an emergency. We have to go *now*. Secure the door."

Feeling as bedraggled as Lockhart and his wife looked, Jovanic stepped inside the aircraft and slid into the aft seat facing them. "Bad night for flying," he said. "I don't think you're going to make it to Phoenix."

Lockhart's eyes bugged. "What the—what are you doing here?"

"Let me lay it on the line for you, Doctor. Here's what I know: You killed Garret Lashburn by poisoning. You then poisoned the coffee at your

Lancaster facility, making it look like Garret did it. And this afternoon, you capped it off by killing Dax Odell." He heard Lisa Lockhart's quick intake of breath.

Evan said, "What are you talking about? I didn't kill him."

"C'mon, Evan. You know you're not going to get away with it."

Lockhart's face crumpled. "I didn't. I swear to you, I didn't kill that man."

"Tell me, why'd you kill Garret? His attitude piss you off? Or was he holding something over you?"

"He was going to ruin me. He—"

Lisa put her hand on his arm. "Evan, *stop talking*. Don't admit anything."

A sob broke from him. "No, darling, I can't live like this. I'm not a killer. I didn't mean for those people to be seriously hurt. I just wanted to make it look like Garret did it." Lockhart turned an imploring gaze on Jovanic. "He—he was threatening to harm our grandchildren. I—"

His wife spoke sharply. "Evan, shut up. Don't say another word until I call Phil Moore." She threw Jovanic a dirty look, and said, "Our attorney."

Jovanic rose and backed up a few steps. "Sorry to break up your trip, ma'am. Your attorney will have to meet us at the station; we've got a lot to talk about. Off the plane, please. You first, Mrs. Lockhart, then you, Doctor."

Lisa Lockhart gave him a look intended to shrivel his manhood. "Leave him alone, you bully. Can't you see how upset he is?"

She was right, her husband was upset, but it didn't matter. He was going to prison for a long time. Lockhart, who seemed to have accepted his fate, fumbled with his seatbelt and pulled himself shakily to his feet. He said, "It's all right, darling. He's just doing what he has to do."

Jovanic waited at the door until the couple had descended the three steps. The cloudburst was over and the night sky was clear. Once they were all on the tarmac Jovanic placed his hand on the other man's shoulder. "Do I need to cuff you, or are we good?"

"I'm not going to run," Lockhart said, his posture deflating like a popped balloon.

Jovanic started to propel him forward, half-turning when Lisa Lockhart shouted, *"Evan."*

A sudden loud crack sounded overhead. For the barest instant, Jovanic thought it was thunder. At the same moment he knew it was a gunshot. Letting go of Evan, he reached for his weapon and spun around.

Lisa Lockhart had a gun in her hand—a Glock 9mm. The first time she had fired into the air. This time she was aiming at Jovanic. "Evan didn't kill Odell," she cried out. "I did."

Jovanic raised his weapon and squeezed the trigger. Evan shoved into him. Jovanic's gun fired with an ear shattering boom.

With a scream of pain, Lisa went down. The Glock dropped from her hand, firing wild, cartwheeling on the tarmac, sliding to a stop under the belly of the plane.

Jovanic pivoted on Lockhart, yelling, "Get on the ground, asshole. Get on the ground! Face down. Now!"

Lockhart clutched at his shoulder, swaying. "I'm shot, I'm shot—Lisa—we need an ambulance."

"I said get down *now*."

Moaning, Lockhart got to his knees and lowered himself to the wet tarmac. In the distance Jovanic could hear a siren getting louder—the airport police. He glanced up and saw Captain Brown, the pilot, watching from the aircraft's doorway. "Keep an eye on him." He gestured at Evan Lockhart. Without a word, Brown came down the steps and stood by while Jovanic, covering both Lockharts with his gun, reached down and rolled Lisa over. The light from the Gunnell building shone on her pale face, pinched with pain. She was lying in a puddle of bloody rainwater, but she was alive.

"Where are you hit?" Jovanic asked her.

Lisa Lockhart glared at him through glittering eyes full of hate, her lips clamped tight. He shrugged and quickly ran his eye over her. She'd taken a bullet to the thigh. Evan's shove had sent his aim awry and probably saved her life. Jovanic had been aiming for her heart.

thirty-two

"Hewett Pflueger was working for Agrichem? You're joking." Claudia stared at Daphne, who grinned back at her from her computer monitor. They were bringing each other up to date via webcam from across the pond.

"There's been a big exposé in the *Times* by your pal, Elliott Field. Besides which, Pflueger's under investigation by New Scotland Yard for interfering with a police investigation. He'll be lucky not to be prosecuted for his rotten lack of skills, not to mention lack of integrity and ethics. And he's been expelled from the BIG for that." Daphne laughed. "I knew you'd be the first to shed tears."

"Boo hoo, I'm getting out my hanky as we speak," Claudia said, pretending to wipe her eyes.

"It turns out that he was the handwriting 'expert'—cough, cough—for the British subsidiary of Agrichem. The manager whose sundial was bombed hired him to analyze the note they found, and then the note in the fairy door. Pflueger, having a reputation for telling the client whatever they want to hear, decided in all his wisdom to pin everything on Dax Odell."

"Poor Dax." Claudia said with a pang of sadness. "All he wanted was to help those people get justice for their families. It all got mixed up with the mailbox bomb here—what a horrible accident that was. When Joel went through Garret Lashburn's papers and emails, he found Garret had, in fact, invented a less toxic formula to replace a killer pesticide the company was selling. But Lockhart refused to use it because it would cost too much to make the change, plus it would be bad PR for the company."

"It's such a shame," Daphne said. "He wasn't a bad sort at all."

"Garret believed his wife's cancer was caused by proximity to pesticides, but he'd signed an agreement years ago that he couldn't be a whistleblower or he would lose his pension and be sued. When he heard about Dax's work with People for Safe Food—Dax was his godson—he enlisted his help to start harassing Lockhart, first by vandalizing several of their locations, and then upping the ante with the explosives."

"Do you suppose they would have done anything worse?"

"I don't know, but Mrs. Lockhart, who confessed to killing Dax, claimed Lashburn had made threats against her grandchildren and she wasn't about to stand for that. Mind you, they haven't found any proof of him making those kinds of threats. But Lockhart went to Garret's office at the lab and found out where Dax was staying. Lisa Lockhart claims she just went to talk to him at the motel without her husband knowing what she was doing. The fact that she took a gun with her puts the lie to that. Anyway, Joel thinks Lockhart told her Garret was threatening the grandchildren to justify him killing Garret and setting it up to look like he'd poisoned the people in his own lab."

"What was poisoning the workers supposed to do?"

"Lockhart wanted to get rid of the threat of exposure. He thought it would make Garret look like the bad guy, especially when he supposedly committed suicide. Meanwhile, here's Dax and company doing their thing. He'd suspected one of the women in the group was a mole for Agrichem, which meant Evan must have known about Dax all along." Claudia gave a half-laugh. "I suppose you could call it an ironic twist of fate that Lockhart ended up wounded by his wife's ricocheting bullet. He was shot in the shoulder."

"Ah, tangled web and all that. Well, luv, it's late here. I'm off to beddy-bye. Give your man a big smooch from me. All right then?"

"I'll be more than happy to do that. Thanks for the news, Daph. Sleep well."

Claudia logged off and tiptoed into the bedroom, where Jovanic was still sound asleep at nearly one PM.

After the incident at the airport, the officer-involved-shooting team had secured the area and talked to him at length, quickly determining it was a righteous shooting. Lisa Lockhart's aiming the gun at him had justified the use of deadly force because Jovanic was acting in self-defense.

The Lockharts had both been taken under arrest by air ambulance to UCLA Medical Center and placed under guard until they could be stabilized and moved to a jail ward.

Jovanic was given a few days off with pay while the shooting team completed their paperwork. He had spent the first day catching up on sleep.

Claudia got out of her T-shirt and leggings and slid into bed beside him, scooting close, but taking care not to wake him. It had been two days since the shooting at the airport, but she still had a need to soak in his warmth, to rest her hand lightly on his chest and feel him breathing. He had downplayed what had happened that night, coming home well after midnight and too exhausted to talk about it. But she had a strong feeling he'd had a close call.

She thought about her own brush with death at Ortiz's hands. It had always seemed like a cliché when people talked about their life flashing before their eyes in a deadly situation. But in those terrifying moments she had visualized her future with Joel being ripped away; had seen his devastation at losing her. And now, here she was, on the other side once again, thanking everything that was good for saving *him.*

How am I going to live like this for the next forty or fifty years? She asked herself. *Never knowing whether he's going to come home, or having to plan his funeral.*

What's the alternative? Her pragmatic side shot back. *Leave him and be safe?*

Jovanic stirred and reached out to her, murmuring something unintelligible before he dropped back to sleep.

thirty-three

EVEN BEFORE DANNY ORTIZ came through the lockup door, Claudia's heart was slamming against her ribs. Studiously ignoring her, the defendant shuffled to the defendant's chair beside his attorney. This time, he was dressed in a jail jumpsuit and his ankles were hobbled by a wooden bar, reserved for the most dangerous defendants. Ortiz would not be attacking anyone today. He leaned back casually in his chair to let everyone know how little he cared about this business.

The bailiff came forward and addressed the gallery. "Remain seated and come to order. The Honorable Patricia Taylor-Gray presiding."

A diminutive redhead entered the courtroom, dwarfed by the bench behind which she would preside. Her black robes, accented by a fern green scarf that matched her eyes, flowed around her small frame as she took the comfortable leather chair.

Judge Gray faced the jury with a welcoming smile. "Do you know why judges wear robes?" Most of the jurors shook their heads. "Let's start with a little court lesson. It supposedly started with the death of Queen Mary II in England, back in 1694, and signified mourning. Before that, robes came in different colors: violet for summer, green for winter, and scarlet for special occasions. Interesting, don't you think?" The smile disappeared and she glared down at the defendant.

Ortiz's public defender had been replaced by a more seasoned-looking African-American attorney, although it was unlikely to make a difference to the outcome. With all the witnesses to the assault, the trial was hardly more than a formality. In an attempted murder charge, the prosecution's job was to prove that the defendant wanted the victim dead, not just injured. The many videos of Danny Ortiz, his hands around Claudia's throat, slamming her head against the floor, made the prosecutor's task an easy one. The real question was the sentence, which was moot anyway. As a third-strike offender, Ortiz had already received a life sentence in the execution of the police officer. Claudia's theory was that the reason he hadn't taken a plea was that taking the jail bus to court for a few days was a diversion from sitting in a cell.

At the thought of spending the rest of one's life in the confines of prison, she could not suppress a shudder. Beside her, mistaking the cause, Jovanic covered her hand with his and pressed reassuringly. Claudia pressed back. As always, he looked strong and confident in his grey pinstriped suit and the hand-painted silk tie she had bought him for Christmas. She snuck a glance at the unruly salt-and-pepper hair, the well-shaped nose, the lean body she loved, and thought back to her musings about the future. She smiled to herself. *We may drive each other crazy, but the love is always there.*

One thing she knew: whatever the future held, she wanted to face it with him.

Would you like to keep reading Claudia's next adventure? Scroll down for the opening of book seven, **Written Off**

December 3

The cabin was the size of a master bedroom; a ramshackle shed whose cedar logs had expanded and contracted until the spaces between them were large enough to admit small vermin. Inside, the musty smell and scat on virtually every surface confirmed that many such creatures had availed themselves of the accommodations over the years while it fell into disrepair.

It had been unused for so long that few in the village of Summerhays remembered that the cabin stood—or more accurately, leaned—in the overgrown clearing in the woods, let alone who had built it. Most folks readily agreed that given the one room, a hunter was more likely than a family to have occupied the place.

No evidence of any dweller endured; no furnishings other than a rough-hewn kitchen chair. No guesses how long the chair had stood in front of the old wood-burning stove, waiting for someone to sit down and warm their hands.

Each summer that passed, the vegetation crept closer to the cabin. What little light that managed to penetrate the sagging windows was murky at best. In winter, even when the trees were stripped of their leaves as they were now, the metallic snow-laden skies darkened the cheerless room to a permanent dusk.

It was through those grimy, sagging windows that searchers spotted the remains of Professor Madeleine Maynard.

Chaos theory—the science of surprises—teaches that one small change to a system can later produce tremendous, and often unintended, consequences. You start the day taking a friend to the doctor and end up making a choice that ends up altering lives. Including your own.

Claudia held open the doctor's office door and followed Zebediah Gold out into the hallway. A week following hip surgery, he was eager to get back to the gym, to walks on the beach, and to driving his car whenever he felt like it. To his chagrin, he was being forced to face the fact that in at seventy, his body was going to take longer to heal than he had expected.

The patience he generously imparted to his psychotherapy clients was less evident when it came to himself, and the unhappy *thump* of his cane on the polished floor shouted his feelings louder than an F-bomb. That he was stewing over something more had been noticeable from the moment Claudia picked him up. The drive to the Beverly Hills medical building had been made in near silence, even when she told a silly joke that on any other day would have made him groan.

"The Buddha said to the hot dog man, 'Make me one with everything.'" Barely a head shake. *"Come on, Zebediah, that was funny. Okay, then: the Buddha hands the hot dog man a twenty. The man puts it in his apron and the Buddha says, 'Where's my change?' The hot dog man says, "Change must come from within."*

Zebediah—ordinarily the most good-humored person you could find—barely responded. He had not flirted with the woman at the reception desk, nor the nurse. Definitely out of character. By the time she pressed the elevator button for the parking garage, Claudia was burning with curiosity and could hold back no longer.

"What did the doctor say? How's your progress?"

"Fine."

Unsatisfied by the noncommittal answers, Claudia stepped inside the elevator, glad to find it empty. In her view, a ride shared with strangers took longer—everyone uncomfortable, avoiding eye contact by watching the floor numbers flash past. Her friend, Kelly Brennan, would have made some ribald quip to break the ice. If she was here now to vamp with Zebediah, she would certainly have found a way to make him laugh.

The doors opened on the parking subterranean garage.

"Would I get an answer if we played twenty questions?" Claudia asked, her voice hollow in the gloomy cave-like underground parking structure. It made her think of earthquakes and being trapped underground. This time, he managed a faint smile. "Twenty questions sounds like fun."

"Is there a problem with your recovery?"

"Not at all, darling, I'll be leaping tall buildings in a single bound by next week."

"Does that mean you got a clean bill of health?"

"All is well. Doctor Rajagopian says I'm right where I should be."

They reached his Lexus and Zebediah handed over the cane, maneuvering into the passenger seat. It was easier for him to negotiate than Claudia's low-slung classic '85 Jaguar.

Before closing the door, she leaned down. "Then what's with all the cane thumping?"

"Too many restrictions. No air travel for the next three months."

"Then, what's the problem? You don't need to fly anywhere in the next three months. Do you?"

"As it happens—" Zebediah started, then broke off. The exit gate arm rose, and Claudia shouldered the Lexus into the endless stream of vehicles on Wilshire Boulevard. L.A. might have dealt the smog a crippling blow, but the traffic monster consumed the Southland with the appetite of King Kong.

"As it happens, what?"

"I do need to fly. To Maine."

"Maine?"

"Yes, darling. It's a large state on the East Coast."

"I know where Maine is, thank you. What's there?"

"Blueberries in the summer. Loads of snow in the winter." Gold shifted his position, wincing as he did so. "Something just came up."

"Something that requires travel to Maine."

"Yes, and now I'm forbidden to go," said Zebediah, then paused. "I have a very large favor to ask. Would you to go in my place?"

Focused on avoiding a collision with a sports car that was drifting into her lane, it took an extra second for Claudia to register what he had said. She shot him a surprised glance. "Wait. What? You want *me* to go for you?"

"That's exactly what I want, sweetie. You would charge your regular fee for out-of-town travel plus all expenses. Money no object."

"To do what? I'm not a licensed psychologist."

"You don't need a Ph.D. to do what's needed in this case. And don't sell yourself short. You know plenty about human behavior. Listen, I've been thinking about the possibility all night, and I know it's a big ask—"

The sudden prospect of an unexpected trip to the East Coast was going to take more than thirty seconds to absorb. "Why don't you tell me what it is you need me to do."

"To interview someone, for one thing."

"Interview someone?"

"I hear an echo."

"Please knock off the mystery. Interview whom?" The question hung in the air between them, the very definition of a pregnant pause.

"A prison inmate. Nothing you haven't done before."

"Getting warmer. Someone in prison in Maine. Who?"

"Does the name Roxanne Becker ring any bells?" Zebediah asked.

"The *serial killer?*"

"One and the same, dearest. Pique your interest?"

Zebediah did not need her answer. He knew her interest to be piqued. He had baited the hook and was dangling the worm in front of her.

It had been at least twenty years ago since Becker was convicted of killing eight men who had hired her for sexual services. Much like Aileen Wuornos who came later, Roxanne had picked up clients from street corners and bars. The ones she selected as victims ended up stabbed to death on country roads and alleys across a wide swath of states. There had been rampant speculation that she killed many more, but it was never proved.

A horn blasted behind them, letting Claudia know the light had turned green while she was dredging up what she remembered about Roxanne Becker. Waving a hand in apology to the impatient driver, she accelerated across the intersection at Merv Griffin Way, puzzling out why Zebediah was asking her this favor. He had been a prison psychologist for many years, working with a long string of hardcore inmates before he could no longer stomach the cruelty of their misdeeds, the often-hideous childhoods that had led them to perform them, and the barbarous conditions of their incarceration.

He had published several articles about serial murder in prestigious journals and textbooks on abnormal behavior. Since semi-retiring, he had taken his practice in as opposite a direction as he could, treating mainly celebrities—an interesting contrapositive, he liked to say. They might be as antisocial in their thinking as the inmates, but in most cases the acting out was less violent.

Titanium hip notwithstanding, an opportunity to interview Roxanne Becker should have attracted him like a heroin addict to a 20 bag. Something was missing; Claudia sensed it as strongly as if it were an empty thought bubble floating between them.

"What's the rush? Why not wait until you can go yourself? Or does Roxanne have a date with the executioner?"

"As it happens, she got the death penalty in Connecticut, where she was originally sentenced. They changed the law while she had an appeal pending. It's no longer a death penalty state."

"Seriously? What happened to all the people on death row?"

"Their sentences were commuted to life without parole. Roxanne was moved to Maine, which doesn't have the death penalty, either."

"All very interesting, but why are you stalling, Zebediah? I'm going to ask you again, what's the rush?"

"Sorry, love. There actually *is* a deadline: a publication deadline."

"You have a new book deal?"

"It's not my deal. The author has been consulting with me on some of the research."

"So, the book is about Roxanne's life?"

Zebediah nodded. "The working title is '*The Road to Serial Murder.*'"

"Who's the author?"

"Her name is Madeleine Maynard."

"I don't recall you ever mentioning her."

"She published a number of textbooks on criminal psych, scads of journal articles. Serial murder is a specialty of hers. She was a professor at a small private university in Maine."

Zebediah fell silent and gazed through the side window of the car. There was nothing more interesting in this section of the Wilshire Corridor than a street full of luxury high rises, and Claudia was quite certain he had no interest in the architecture. She waited, giving him space to get where he needed to go without prompting. When he picked up his story again, his voice was filled with deep sadness.

"I just got a letter from Maddie's attorney that she recently passed away. It was in that bundle of mail you picked up from my P.O. Box yesterday. I've been asked to finish the book and I'm happy to do it. The thing is, the publisher wants it by April 1st. They've already extended the deadline twice. Maddie was out here a few months ago and we worked on the outline, so I know where she wanted to go with it. She had made a lot of progress on the manuscript. That's the other part of your task, if you'll agree to go. I need you to bring it back here."

"She was here in L.A. and yet you never mentioned it."

"There was no reason to."

"Good God, Zebediah, you have a whole secret life that you've kept from me. I'm devastated."

"Very amusing, my sweet. Now, think about the interview you could have with Roxanne Becker. She and Maddie had been corresponding over a number of years and developed a friendship. Maddie visited her at the prison several times. It's only about an hour's drive from her home."

While she listened to him trying to persuade her, Claudia had already started running through her head what it would take to make the trip. Her workload was light over the holiday season. Her fiancé, Homicide Detective Joel Jovanic, would be in San Francisco, where his mother was scheduled for surgery. She had offered to go with him, but he was staying at his sister Jane's small apartment in the City, and she didn't have room for both of them.

Zebediah, beginning to act more like himself now that he had dropped the bomb, gave his most winning smile. "You're a world class handwriting analyst and you're bright, analytical, compassionate. I wouldn't be surprised if you could get Roxanne to supply a handwriting sample. Your analysis would make an excellent added dimension to the book. I have full faith in you to do the best job."

"Flattery will get you everywhere, Dr. Gold."

"I called the attorney, Jim Spencer. According to his office recording, he's out until Christmas, but that doesn't have to stop us from booking your flight. The sooner I get the manuscript in my hands the better. Working on it will give me something to do while I'm recovering. Please say yes."

Claudia hesitated, that uncomfortable hinky sensation still pecking away at her intuition. "There's more, isn't there? What are you not telling me?"

"I would be forever in your debt. You can take the Thursday night red eye and fly to Boston, change planes and arrive in Portland, Maine, on Friday morning. I'll make sure someone is there to pick you up."

"The weekend after Christmas? The whole world will be going home. I'd never get a flight."

"We'll book you in business class. First class if necessary." Zebediah sounded cheered, already knowing her answer. "Maddie lived in an old sea captain's house just outside a place called Summerhays. You'll love it."

"Summerhays? I've never heard of it."

"You wouldn't have. It's not much more than a village. There's a small river near the house; it's quite beautiful in the summer." He made a wry face. "Not so much in December. That's the downside of the job—a taste of Maine winter."

"You've been there?"

"Once or twice."

"Yet, you've never mentioned it." Claudia cast a suspicious glance at him. "What's the big secret about this professor? What did she die of?"

"Mr. Spencer didn't mention the cause of death, but Maddie had severe asthma. I wouldn't be surprised if it was related to that."

Long ago, before Claudia and Zebediah became 'just friends,' they had briefly been lovers. Those days were in the distant past, but the emotional bond between them had stayed strong over the years. She felt the tug at her heart, remembering the many times when Zebediah had been there for her when she had needed him the most—especially last year when she had been suffering from PTSD after a brutal attack. Even Jovanic had not been able to reach her. Zebediah had allowed her to reach out to him in her own time and helped her find her way through the terror. Now it was his turn and she could not find it in her to refuse him.

"You know I'll go. Obviously, this Maddie meant a lot to you. Even if you *didn't* tell me about her." The mild rebuke was meant as a joke, but Zebediah released a long sigh of relief. The silence became so protracted that Claudia took her eyes off the road long enough to steal a glance at him. He was staring straight ahead, his lips pressed tight together. His next words took her breath away.

"Madeleine was my wife."

To continue reading Written Off, get your copy at your favorite bookseller.

Acknowledgments

In addition to my usual critique crew: Bob Joseph, Bruce Cook, Gwen Freeman, Bob Bealmear, Barbara Petty, special acknowledgement and thanks are due to Sgt. Derek Pacifico, Detective Heather Gahry, retired FBI supervisor George Fong, Dr. Doug Lyle, Adam at the Air Support Angels Foundation (LAPD Air Support), and Michael Ferguson at Santa Monica Airport. They all helped me get it right. Grateful thanks, too, to the members of the board of the British Institute of Graphology, who allowed me to use this prestigious organization in the book, including Adam Brand, Elaine Quigley, Tracey Trussell, and Karolina Tolgyesi for their helpful input about London and the Tube. Thanks, too, to Barbara Weaver, whose lovely home in Cambridge, and the fascinating Eagle Pub, made me want to set a scene there. And definitely not least, thank you Janet Williams, my old mate, who has hosted me in Sidcup innumerable times and who let me drag her all over London, along with my cousin Irvine Ford, whose non-stop jokes kept us giggling.

Finally, I attribute whatever success I have had in publishing to the help of Ellen Larson, who has been my editor from the outset.

If I've inadvertently left anyone out, I apologize. It's not that you were less significant, it's me.

Praise for Sheila Lowe

FORENSIC HANDWRITING MYSTERIES

"Dynamite" - Starred review – PUBLISHERS WEEKLY

"Lowe wins readers over with her well-developed heroine and the wealth of fascinating detail on handwriting analysis." - BOOKLIST

"The well-paced plot develops from uneasy suspicions to tightly wound action."

— FRONT STREET REVIEWS

"[A] fast-paced, crisp, and gritty novel that penetrates the world of celebrity and the dark appetites of those who live in that world.

— ARMCHAIR INTERVIEWS

"A perfectly paced mystery with an easy fluidity that propels the reader through the story at breakneck speed."

— BOOKPLEASURES.COM

"Utterly compelling! *"Outside the Lines"* joins the ranks of those rare thrillers that expertly blend nonstop plotting with keen perceptions of the characters—good and bad—who populate this wonderful tale." - Jeffery Deaver, *New York Times* Bestselling Author of "The Bone Collector"

"Sheila Lowe's writing is fast-paced and suspenseful and made believable by her own background as a forensic handwriting expert. Yet another page-turner for Claudia Rose fans." — Rick Reed, Author of the *Jack Murphy Crime* Series

Dead Letters starts at high speed, and it stays there...Lowe presents a clear and compelling story—and thusly a respect for the reader's experience. - PEN WORLD

"*Dead Letters* is an entertaining thriller set in Egypt, Gibraltar, Arizona and London, starring two heroines, an expert handwriting analyst and her intrepid niece. This novel will get your heart racing and also give you a fun education on ancient Egypt history at the same time." — Matt Witten, bestselling author of The Necklace

"Lowe expertly delivers a solid criminal investigation while guiding her readers into a unique culture where tattooing and the murder of a young girl come together on the autopsy table. Hit the lights and siren because this is one fast ride from beginning to end." — Lee Lofland, Author of "Police Procedure and Investigation" and founder and director of the Writers' Police Academy

"This is a good read that's hard to put down. If you have any interest in reading handwriting, there's a lot of good information about that included in the story. You may even have to watch how you write in the future. You don't want anyone to think you're a psychopath..." — LONG AND SHORT REVIEWS

Praise for Sheila Lowe

BEYOND THE VEIL SERIES

The Last Door
"Voicy characters, an intriguing setting, a perplexing situation...the writing is, as always, superb." — Saralyn Richard, author of the Detective Parrott series

"I loved it from the first sentence. Your ability to create wonderful dialogue, and to thread in the story from the previous two books is wonderful." — K. Dickinson

"Great tension, great intrigue, and interesting characters" — Amazon reviewer

Proof of Life
"A delicious glimpse at what happens when the veil between the two worlds unexpectedly parts. I dare you to put this book down!" — Suzanne Giesemann, author of Messages of Hope

"A compassionate heroine bridges the divide between the spirit world and earthly evil in this well-paced thriller. Proof of Life will keep readers flipping pages all night!" — S.W. Hubbard, Author of Another Man's Treasure

"Fiction can sometimes be a powerful and inspirational way to teach us about life and the afterlife. Proof of Life celebrates this truth." — Gary E. Schwartz, PhD, University of Arizona, Author of "The Afterlife Experiments"

"A brain injury, followed by a coma opens a door wide into to the Spirit World. Proof of Life will have you on the edge of your seat, late into the night as you discover we don't die." — Sandra Champlain, author of the international bestseller, We Don't Die - A Skeptic's Discovery of Life After Death, and host of We Don't Die Radio

"A wonderfully human voice, intense emotions, and a deep dive into the Afterlife. Lowe has created a brilliant backdrop in PROOF OF LIFE, allowing readers to explore life-altering questions via the imminently likeable Jessica Mack. " —K.J. Howe, international bestselling author of SKYJACK

"Proof of Life is a heartwrenching and heartwarming story that explores the universe beyond the veil, delving into the universal questions we all contemplate." — Connie di Marco, author of the Zodiac Mysteries

"The voices recovering amnesiac Jessica Mack hears compel her to search for a missing four-year-old boy, a quest that leads her to the doorway between life and the afterlife and challenges her beliefs on every level. This story rocks." — DP Lyle, award-winning author of the Jake Longly and Cain/Harper thriller series

WHAT SHE SAW

About the Author

Sheila Lowe is the author of the award-winning Forensic Handwriting series and the Beyond the Veil paranormal suspense series. She is also a real-life forensic handwriting expert who testifies in court cases. In addition to writing stories of psychological suspense, she writes nonfiction books about handwriting and personality. Her memoir, *Growing From the Ashes*, details her journey from a strict religious cult to spiritual freedom following the murder of her daughter. She lives in Southern California.

To sign up for the newsletter: www.sheilalowebooks.com

Ways to reach Sheila

www.sheilalowebooks.com

https://www.sheilalowe.com

https://www.facebook.com/SheilaLoweBooks

https://www.instagram.com/sheilalowebooks/

https://www.goodreads.com/SheilaLowe

https://www.bookbub.com/authors/sheila-lowe

Dear Reader,

Did you enjoy *Outside the Lines?* If you did, please consider leaving a brief review on your favorite review site. Amazon, Goodreads, and Book-Bub, are always appreciated, or any other. It really helps when you tell others how you feel.

Get the latest info on Claudia Rose and my other books by signing up for my monthly newsletter at sheilalowebooks.com. I promise never to share your information.

Thank you so very much for spending this time with me and my characters.

Be well,

Sheila

Made in the USA
Coppell, TX
01 June 2024

33002481R00164